UNDER HER PROTECTION

PROTECTION

HEATHER PIPER

Under Her Protection

CONTENTS

ACKNOWLEDGEMENTS

It is never easy to thank everyone who has been there when I needed them but I would like to thank my supportive husband Rob for putting up with Hetia over the past few years. I would also like to thank my friend Gavin McTear for his beautiful painting of Hetia and my friends from the Bundaberg Writers Club for their support.

DEDICATION

If there is to be a dedication it should be to the future of our beautiful Earth. May the circumstances that would lead to Hetia's ancestors facing almost annihilation never eventuate and we, who are her guardians in this time do our utmost to prevent such deterioration.

1 PROLOGUE

The quiet little village of Aves nestled into the base of the hills that surrounded the Plains of Parlat and seemed to have been there since ancient times. As there were only a dozen or so houses scattered throughout the village it hadn't warranted anything more than a market place, a blacksmith and a healer. The houses were all fairly small and built of stone or wood, nothing fancy and no one of importance would ever come to the village, so the people led a quiet and peaceful life tending their livestock and crops. Until the day the Horde of Doom struck terror into the lives of those peaceful folk. The morning had begun normally with people coming and going about their tasks and as it was such a beautiful sunny morning the younger children had been all taken into the woods to search for mushrooms by two of the older girls. They wandered far into the woods, so far that they did not hear the thunder of horses and the screams of the women, in fact they were completely unaware that they were the only ones left of their village.

"It's time we returned home," one of the older girls announced, "we have picked plenty of mushrooms for today and we must leave some for the next visit." Taking the youngest in her arms she turned and led them home. As they emerged from the woods they stopped dead as before them the carnage was horrific. Houses were burning and everything was overturned or smashed. Then they saw the bodies lying where they had been hacked down. The two older girls looked at one another and turned the young ones around to head back into the forest. They ran. They ran as fast as the younger ones could manage and they didn't stop running. Breathless with tears running down their cheeks the girls kept the little ones going until they could run no more. Although they had not seen anything of those who had slaughtered their families they knew the danger of being found. Children would not survive an attack and the older girls knew what would happen to them. It was well over an hour before they stopped to listen for any sounds that might mean danger. "We will have to try and make our way to Flessia" one of them said quietly, "but we will stay within the trees as long as we can." They both agreed and began to slowly make their way. The mushrooms had been dropped at the village but these children knew there was food in the forest they could eat and although it would take the rest of the day to reach Flessia they would be alright. The streams would give them water and they could allow the little ones to take their time. The little troupe began their journey in silence. Even the younger ones knew that something was desperately wrong and they said nothing. Not a tear was shed.

2 AVES

Hetia's steps slowed as she climbed toward the crest of the hill. The path had become steeper and the morning warm for early Spring. The acrid smell of burning flesh in the air made her nauseous and the black smoke rising from the other side of the hill told her what she would find when she reached the top.

She wasn't prepared for the carnage below. Stopping, she leaned on a tree beside the track as she felt the blood drain from her face leaving her skin cold and damp. She felt her legs go weak. "Mother, what have they done?" she whispered, "Please help me."

Looking down on the remains of the village of Aves all she could see was the dead bodies and burning buildings. Making her way swiftly down the hill she tried to prepare herself for what was ahead by calling on her training as a Healer. She knew that there would not likely be anyone left alive, she could only hope. At the foot of the hill, amidst the smoke and stench, bodies of animals lay rotting on the ground, the warm weather hastening the process. A cow, heavy with calf had her throat cut in senseless slaughter, dogs with wounds that showed they had been kicked and run over by horses. The sight was bad enough but horrifically, among the dead animals, were the bodies of people strewn across the ground. Her body finally gave in to the stench and sight as she vomited her morning meal among the blood and gore. As she walked on she found the body of the Spirit Leader. He was an ancient man with a beautiful soul. He would have tried to stop the slaughter of his people and he had died doing so. A long gaping slit crossed beneath his chin, the blood mixing with the mystic markings on his neck and chest. He had been slaughtered like the animals that surrounded his body.

Hetia had come to help a young mother give birth to her first child. She had been looking forward to the day with all the joy that usually finished the day of birthing pain. Now with her tears mixed with the dust and smoke grime, she knew the young woman would not have survived this carnage. The baby would also be dead. She felt angry now, so very angry, that she began to think of revenge. Hetia took off the bag slung across her body and searched among the herbs and other healing tools she carried looking for a scarf to tie around her nose and mouth to shut out the stench of the burning, bloated bodies. Taking a deep breath beneath the scarf the air still tasted dirty and acrid. The next human body she came across was covered by flies and had horrific wounds on many parts of his body. His throat had been slashed, one hand was missing and it seemed he had been dragged along the ground by a horse. As Hetia made her way from one body to the next she felt sickened, by what she found.

It was not the first time she had to deal with so much death but it was probably the worst. Her anger grew as she walked among the bodies. This slaughter would have to be stopped. Running away from these men only gave them licence to attack over and over again. On her own she might not be able to bring about the downfall of the Horde of Doom but with help she could. As she made her way among the bodies, looking for any sign of life she prayed for help. Although her training as a Healer prevented her from harming others her other training didn't. She would call upon the secret powers of her early life. The Horde would regret this slaughter of her people.

When Hetia reached the end of the village and the last burnt out shell of a building, once a happy family home, she knew no one was left alive. Hands raised to the sky she pleaded with the Goddess. "Why? Why this carnage, why allow these savage beasts to roam the land."

Anger boiling up inside in desperation she cried out loud. "What can I do, what can I do to put an end to this?" She knew the answer would come in time but how much time did she have before the Horde attacked another village.

Until Hetia could bring some help she rolled up her sleeves and dragged some of the bodies that weren't too heavy into what remained of a large building that had been used as a meeting place, giving them what dignity she could manage on her own. The door was hanging from its hinges but she pulled it shut as far as it would go. The blood and gore would attract the wild dogs that roamed the forest. Perhaps the broken door would keep them out. On her way back through the village, exhausted, she tripped over the pregnant body of her young mother-to-be, her belly slashed through and the babe pulled out then bashed to death. Hetia covered the bodies with some straw she found nearby then made her way back through the village. The pretty little cottages and gardens that had been here on her last visit were now ruined. Stone walls tinged with the black of fire, their roofs gone and the gardens trampled. Such carnage and violence was becoming almost normal on the Plains of Parlat. When Hetia returned to her own village of Flessia she would send some of the men to bury the bodies. She hoped in her heart that there was a chance some had escaped and were in hiding, there was no sign of the children, if any of them were alive but injured, after the marauders had left, they would not have lived long without help. Feeling sick to the stomach and hot with anger Hetia headed back up the trail towards her own village of Flessia, praying to the Goddess they had not also been attacked in her absence.

Considered by many to be the cleverest of the Plains Wise Women healing the sick and helping the Earth become more fertile by working with the Spirits of the Land, she had done her best all of her adult life to do so. For the first time in many years, she felt useless and defeated by the continued onslaught of the Horde of Doom. Heavy in heart but frightened over her Village's fate, she pushed herself hard along the trail. Seeing her village in the distance enabled Hetia to slow down, but she knew this safety would not last. It would be only a matter of time before Flessia would be the target of these thugs.

Hetia was met by one of the Village elders who took her arm and led her to the village square. "We have a group of children who have fled from the village of Aves Hetia. I have given them into the charge of my husband who is feeding them at the moment. Do you know anything of the fate of their village?" "Yes" Hetia replied, "I am afraid that the Horde have attacked them and it could be that all the adults are dead. I didn't find anyone alive but some may have escaped into the forest. Did they tell you anything at all?" "No" replied the grandmother, "it seems the children were far away from the village gathering mushrooms when it was attacked so thankfully they didn't see it happening. The two older girls made sure the little ones didn't stop long enough to see the carnage. I think it would be best if we can move them all to the safety of the big town near the coast where they can be looked after. Once they have been fed a wagon can take them east." "Yes, I agree" said Hetia, "we have to worry about our own children if the Horde find their way here. In fact it wouldn't be a bad idea to move some of our younger ones at the same time. Come, we will call a meeting." The two women called in the village folk. "We should take these children out of danger, along with our little ones." Hetia told the gathered villagers. "Who will bring a wagon and take them to the safety of the East? I believe they would be welcome at the Temple of The Earth Mother. The Priestesses will care for them." Two of the older men came forward. "We will take them Hetia. We can leave in two hours." Just on two hours later a wagon pulled out of the village with the two men on the wagon and four others on horseback to keep guard on the group. It would take a few days to reach the town but they would spend the nights well off the road hidden in the forests in case they met up with the Horde. There would be a few days to safely move about as the Horde seemed to disappear for a week or so after each attack. Once they had reached the town and the Temple the children would be safe.

Later that evening Hetia called a meeting of the Elders. When they were all gathered she spoke. "We have to make some strong plans to keep our village safe." she said. "I have heard stories of the atrocities they carry out and now I have seen it with my own eyes. We are not warriors, we are peaceful people, but we cannot allow our folk to be killed and maimed by these beasts. I am going to contact the other villages on the Plains and perhaps we can come up with some protection. Meanwhile, I can use my own powers to try and keep our village safe but I am limited by my vows not to do harm to any living creature. We need a plan to keep us safe, fighting back is not always an option. I do have a plan however and I would like you to consider it." During the meeting Hetia explained her plan that they could evacuate the village folk and domestic animals into the hills if they knew the Horde was on its way. There were caves up in the hills that were quite well hidden from those who didn't know of their existence. Many, many hundreds of years before the First People of the land had lived in these caves, there were many cave drawings showing their way of life. Only a few hundred years ago some people had used the caves to escape the incredible heat during the Climate Catastrophe as the temperature could be 10 degrees cooler inside. The people of Flessia agreed to Hetia's plan so the next morning the young folk were given the task of taking blankets, cooking pots and dried foodstuff up into the caves. Water was plentiful within the depths of the caves as there was an underground stream running through the hills. It didn't take long for the preparations to be finalised and the people of Flessia went back to their daily lives after posting a lookout a few kilometres down the road in an old abandoned hut. At least the little ones would be safe and Flessia had an escape plan.

3 THE HORDE OF DOOM

The Horde of Doom had been ravaging the land for some time, burning homes, ruining crops, pillaging stores, stealing livestock and killing anyone who was too slow to get out of their way - including children and the elderly who moved too slow. Many houses had been left as stone shells, the roof thatch and all the possessions left inside burned beyond salvage. Crops that were due to be harvested were ridden through and the burnt bodies of cattle too large or too slow to be driven away appeared as strange foul smelling lumps on the ground. Not a village on the plains had been spared over time.

These were wicked, evil men, riding hard over the land with no pity or regret. Each one of these men would kill the others he rode with if they felt endangered and only stayed together to take advantage of their combined strength. They were led by a tall, quiet, dark haired man, dressed in black leather. His hard suntanned face and dark steely vacant eyes seemed to look down on anyone he met with disdain. Tattoos of demons and dragons covered his neck and arms and he gave out an aura of anger and hatred. His horse was an evil thing. A huge jet black beast, savage and strong, with a look that made it seem as if it had been spawned by demons. With frightening screams this savage beast could tear into any flesh within reach of its sharp teeth or, reaching up into the air with its forelegs it would descend to pound its' hooves into any who had the misfortune to get in its way.

With flaming torches the Horde of Doom had attacked villages and farms in their path, burning many homes to the ground in order to flush out anyone hiding within. With screams of fury they had dismounted and taken what they could carry then burned or ruined what they could not. To be found hiding in their path was certain death, to fight back was suicide. Women and girls had been raped then left for dead. These men appeared to have no conscience or pity. The terror the Horde of Doom left behind throughout the land was unequalled in recent memory and the damage they carried out was devastating.

4 THE VILLAGE OF CARLIN

On this day, as the dust cloud came closer it became quite clear that the people of the village of Carlin had left it too late to flee the violence that was to descend upon them. The earth seemed to tremble with a sound like thunder, leaving no doubt that what was coming towards them was about to change their lives forever and many would lose their lives on this day. There had been no time to escape, no forewarning that would assist them in fighting off the terror. They would have to stay and fight as best they could. The men quickly gathered up farm tools and anything that could be used as a weapon. The older children were sent off to find the cattle in the fields and drive them into the hills, while the women ushered the little children and the old people into the strongest building in the village, that of the village Wise Woman. Her house was very old and solid, made of stone with a slate roof and very thick walls. Apart from a few bits of furniture there were shelves lining the walls containing her herbs and potions and bunches of herbs hung from the roof to dry. Down below there was a cellar where the produce the people grew throughout the warmer months was stored, so it could be shared out among the people during the winter months. The smallest children and the oldest folk were led down into the cellar with food and water in case they were there for a long time. There was only one way in and out, through the trapdoor in the floor. It was cold and dark down there so the tiny children wept as their mothers left them behind, but the old folk lit the oil lamps to try and make the place a bit more cheerful, however they would have to extinguish these if there was any danger from above. A small toddler began to cry, the poor little thing could not understand why his mother had abandoned him in this dark, damp room. An ancient grandmother picked him up and took him into a corner where she sat on a wooden crate singing a soft lullaby hoping to lull him off to sleep. It wasn't long before all the babies began to settle as the old folk snuggled them under their arms and onto laps, talking quietly with years of practice with little ones. When the trapdoor leading to the stairs was lowered and sealed a rug and table were placed over to hide it. The older children in the room above were given anything they could hold that might be used to defend themselves if they needed to and were left in the uncertain safety of the house. "Be very, very quiet, lock the door and do not open it unless you know who it is" they were told by the Wise Woman, "we will do what we can but if we cannot defend you then you are on your own. I will try to make the house invisible to the marauders as you have seen me do before, and if you are silent they won't know you are here, but if they find you do not tell anyone that there are people in the cellar. Your bravery will be remembered by the Gods and the little ones will survive. The older children are out in the fields with the animals and when they return they will let you out, if I cannot, because the adults will not be able to open the door. Be brave children, we will do our best to fight off these evil ones but you must do your part by remaining very still and quiet." Before she left the house this brave Wise Woman left a message written in charcoal on the wall that could only be understood by one learned in the ways of the ancients, to say that there were people down below, just in case the children above were discovered and killed and the older ones didn't make it back from the fields. The Wise Woman then left it to the Gods and the older children to protect those hidden in the cellar. Praying to the Goddess for her safe return, the Wise Woman closed the door and turned to face the people. "I will join you in a moment" she said, "I must do what I can to place a protection spell around my house to safeguard the children. I need to do this on my own so please go and man the barricade and I will see you shortly". As she stood watching the others leave her front door it came to her mind that she might not live to undo this incantation. She was now in her 40th year and had spent most of her life as a midwife and healer, however, like Hetia of Flessia she had been well trained in working with the energies of the Earth and if she had the opportunity to use these skills she certainly would. She had taken a vow never to harm any other living being, animal or human, however this was not the time to worry about such things, if she or her folk were threatened then she would try to use anything in her power to save them. Once she had placed her protection around the cottage she turned and ran up to where the others were frantically working to build a barricade.

Those who had armed themselves were waiting behind the barricade at the beginning of the village and were bracing themselves for the onslaught. They had piled up everything that would be some kind of barrier and prayed to the Goddess that it would be enough. At the other end of the village the older children who were almost adults still herding the cattle and horses as far away from the village as they could, with the goats on ropes and using the dogs to chase the horses and cows as fast as they could. They just ran. They were told to keep going until they reached the forest where the animals could be set loose. At least some of them might be missed by the terrible horde that was coming towards the village, but they didn't have much time. The children were told to scatter into the forest to hide once they had freed the livestock. The forest wasn't very big but there was protection amongst the trees. Children could climb and hide in the branches of the tall trees and if the animals were frightened they would run and could be found later on. The children knew that the future of the village could rely on their return and as most of them were in their early teens they also knew what could happen to them if they were caught. Especially the girls. If they survived they would come back and release the babies and old folk from the cellar if no one else was alive. They were facing the worst day of their lives and they were all terrified but knew that only the Gods and their wits would be able to save them if they were caught.

As the teens scattered into the forest they left the animals on their own and, as silently as they could, scattered into the dense forest leaving a lookout up a tall tree near the beginning of the tree line where he could see the village in the distance. The rest found what hiding place they could and they waited, silently, until the lookout would give the all clear.

The Horde of Doom eventually came thundering into the village, yelling and screaming with weapons drawn and nothing but destruction on their minds. "Take what you can and burn the rest" shouted their leader. "If you want the women then wait until we have destroyed their men, then there will be no-one left to fight you for them." He was the first to charge the barricade, his horse a huge black beast jumped over as if it was just a low fence. Some of the men had noticed that he never took part in the carnage himself, it was as if killing was distasteful to him, although he never stopped any of his men. It was if he was being held back by a long forgotten voice. As the others followed their leader over the barricade the people of the village came charging out from the buildings with their farm tools, lumps of wood, old swords and spears. They had no hope of stopping this onslaught. The savages left their horses and started killing and maiming anyone who stood in their path. It was a bloodbath. Screaming to the Gods for help one very brave farmer took on three men, an old sword that had belonged to his ancestors in hand. He slashed and forced his way towards his wife who was being attacked by two men. He was a hero that day, but before long he was dead, lying on the dirt bleeding from many wounds to his chest and head and when they had finished with his wife her throat was cut and she was left to die in a pool of blood. Many others died the same way, defending their little village and their loved ones. But it was all in vain, the attackers were too strong and none of the villagers had any experience fighting men. Once they had finished with killing the men the marauders took the women for their 'pleasure' then slit their throats leaving them to die in the dirt. There seemed to be no one left alive when it was over. It only took an hour or so to kill the people and set the village buildings on fire. Anything worthwhile was taken, everything else was ruined. Only a small puppy, left behind in the confusion, was whimpering and shivering in front of a house. The leader of the gang walked over and picked up the puppy, tucking it into his shirt where it would be safe and then climbed up back on his horse calling the men to leave the village. They rode off as quickly as they had arrived, heading back to their camp up in the mountains on the other side of the Plains. There were bodies all around amongst the spilled water and produce and the barricade was left as just a pile of broken bits and pieces.

The only building left standing that day was the Wise Woman's house. To the eyes of the Horde of Doom it was a pile of dirt and stone. Standing at her front door she had spoken words of protection and the house seemed to change form. The children, babies and Elders were safe and would live to tell the story to those who came along the later. The older children had managed to hide in the fields and the forest and only one or two horses that had wandered back had been caught and taken by the evil ones. During the attack the slaughter was efficient and quick. Bravely fighting their attackers the village folk finally were overpowered. Blood and gore told their tale. These were savage men with no conscience to stop them. Late in the day, when the older children came back into the village they found the carnage left behind. Houses were smouldering or still aflame, there were bodies along the street but as they were still thought of as children by the Gods they could see the Wise Woman's house. Tears streamed down the faces of the young teens as they found the bodies of their parents and friends. Some tried to cover up the torn and bloody bodies with whatever they could find. There were no survivors on the street although it was plain they had fought hard. Only one body from the Horde was found. His body was dragged to the end of the village and left for the wild animals to tear apart. There would be no burial for this savage. The fact that no one was left alive in the street was a sure sign that there had been very little strong resistance from the village folk. However the younger children hiding inside the wise woman's cottage had been so quiet that they had survived. Watching through the window they saw the older ones coming back they ran out to greet them. The realisation hit the children then that their parents and older friends were all dead. Uncovering the trapdoor in the floor the elders and babies in the cellar were released then the grim task of facing the carnage outside became a reality. The Elders called the children together and sent two of the older boys off to get help from Flessia. This was the end of their Village for now until the older children grew into adulthood and reclaimed their homes, and everyone knew it. However, the body of the Wise Woman was not among the dead. Perhaps they had taken her with them or could she have escaped? The children went off to search for her as they knew that if she was alive she would be important to their ongoing survival. There seemed to be no sign of her at all until one of the older children called out that he had found her tied to a tree at the back of the village, unconscious. It seemed the tattoos on her face and arms and the amulets around her neck and hanging in her hair had worried the leader of the Horde. He knew there was magic forces about this woman and ordered his men to leave her alone. There was no good to be had by killing one such as her, it would only bring them undone, so they had knocked her out, leaving her to the elements to deal with thinking that there was no-one left to save her. This was their mistake. Although her incantations had gone out into the Ether too late to save her people, she wasn't finished with the Horde. Holding her jaw where the man had knocked her out she began to think of ways to bring her revenge on these marauding killers and bring about their doom. "We need to gather up blankets and food" she said to the children, "I know you want to feel sad for those who were killed and that is what you should do, but we must survive this ourselves so off you go and gather up what you can and come to my cottage."

As the day wore on those left alive in Carlin returned to the Wise Woman's house where they would be safe for the night. Tomorrow was soon enough to bury the dead and finish cleaning up. After everyone had been fed and the small children settled down for the night, the Wise Woman went outside and waited for the moon to rise in the sky. Closing her eyes she took a deep breath and began her incantations that would help bring an end to the Horde of Doom once and for all.

Following a horrific attack on the village of Aves Hetia had called a meeting of Wise Women, Shamans and other spirit workers. After a very short deliberation they decided to work their magic against the Horde. Any sighting or contact with the Horde would be acted upon by a joint effort of these powerful folk. Now, in the light of the moon the Wise Woman of Carlin sent her message through the Ether to the other magic workers to say that the Horde had attacked Carlin that day. Summoning all her powers, this usually gentle healer once again chanted the words of power, words no untrained ears would ever hear. It was not easy for these women of healing and caring to harm other beings as they had vowed to save lives. However, she knew it had to be done and the sooner the better. Conjuring up images of the faces she recalled in horror, she sent her curses to them. She knew it might take a while but her words would be effective. At least two of the Horde of Doom's faces were imprinted on her mind, the two that had held her down and were about to rape her when their leader stopped them, so she aimed her curse at these two. Images of demons came into her mind, fiery, dangerous creatures that would be sent to enter the minds of the men and slowly drive them insane. She commanded the creatures to enter the dreams of the men, to keep them awake and not allow them to rest. Once the incantations were over she brought her mind and breath back to normal and prepared herself to be calm for her people. She did recall though, that when she thought she was about to die the leader of the gang had stopped the others from what they were doing. Noticing that she had power symbols he had ordered them to tie her to a tree then had one of the men knock her unconscious. He could wait. She would concentrate on the other two first and would continue to send them horrific dreams until she had word of their downfall. The next morning after burying their dead the survivors packed up a few remaining belongings and began their journey to the larger settlement towards the East where there were warriors to guard the town. They would be safe there for a while and it would give their young a chance to grow up before returning to rebuild the village.

She was never to learn if her curses did work, however from that night on there were men in the Horde of Doom who had begun to wonder why they couldn't sleep. Their nightmares were getting worse and one of the men eventually put an end to his nightmares by leaping from a cliff to splatter on the ground so very far below.

5 THE VILLAGE OF RAVAT

Weeks later thundering hoof-beats resounded through a pass coming down from the high mountains as the Horde of Doom galloped into another small village nestled in the foothills. The road into Ravat was through the nearby forest so although there was no way to see who was coming it was quite obvious that danger was on its way. The noise had carried to the ears of everyone in Ravat and it struck terror into their hearts. Birds flew frantically out of the forest as they were disturbed, and the peace and tranquillity that usually reigned was gone. Then there was no natural sound to be heard apart from the noise of the horses. The terrible pounding was coming nearer with each second. In the village the low stone houses seemed to shrink into the earth as the thunder of horses hooves shook the very ground. When the marauders arrived there was no sign of life in the Village. The barn doors were open and there were no animals or humans to be seen. Even the chickens seemed to have scattered into the trees. It was as if all life had been spirited away. Each time they attacked this village the men noticed there seemed to be fewer people and livestock than the time before, but they still came. The villagers who were tired of the continuous onslaught had packed up and left for the safety of the big towns. With the cloud of dust from the horses' hooves the Horde arrived. The men screamed their brutal threats to anyone who may still remain in the village out of sight. Brandishing swords, axes and other weapons of death they came, on savage horses trained to attack anyone or anything that got in their way. This time there was no one to be seen.

The villagers had fled when a message through Spirit had sent a warning and the dust on the horizon along with the thundering sound of hoof beats heralded the coming onslaught. All the people and their livestock had scattered into the forest except for one old man who had refused to leave. This time he would face his fate and try to buy his people some time to get as far away as possible. Too many times the others had helped him to the hiding place where they would watch their homes being burnt and their stores pillaged. The old man was not going to run this time. "Leave me here" he had demanded, "I have lived for more than 95 summers and if my time has come then so be it. Perhaps I can slow them down so the rest of you can find safety."

Reluctantly the people had left him behind sitting on his stool awaiting his fate in front of the old stone house he had lived in for many years. He had come in from the mountains decades ago following years of living with a nomadic tribe. He liked this village. There were no warriors, it was only inhabited by a few folk who looked after travellers on their way across the land and grew a little food to feed themselves and take the rest to market.

Perhaps it would pass the notice of the savage Horde of Doom that this old man was no farmer like most of their victims. Maybe they would hesitate long enough, before sending him to his ancestors to see the amulet of power at his throat, the decorations and symbols of the Earth in his long grey hair along with feathers from the great Eagle hanging from his headband. In his long braids he had woven beads made from the seeds of the tallest tree in the land and dried leaves from the healing plants around his village. There were strange faded blue tattoos on his weathered old face, neck and arms. If they did not notice these things, he thought to himself, then so be it. That was their fate not his. He looked at the leather pouch he held firmly in his gnarled old hand, then undoing the cord that held it together he reached inside for the black stone he knew would always be there. Drawing out the stone he touched it to his lips, then his forehead and his heart. It felt cold but reassuring to the touch. After a moment the rune markings on its' surface began to vibrate gently as it recognised his warm hand. Placing the stone in its' pouch he tucked it into his shirt above his heart where it would be handy should he require it. Calling on the Spirit Energy of the Eagle he had trusted in for so long for protection and power he began to slowly recite the ancient words of connection. Facing the sky he opened his arms and sent out the words of invocation. "Oh great Spirit of Eagle, I ask that you take these words of power and find the ones who are bringing about this evil then fill their souls with fear of the Gods. I ask you to protect my people who have fled this terror and bring me strength to face what I have to do. Please guide my words." Then he summoned up a very powerful curse in a language only used by those trained in the use of very powerful Shamanic magic. Facing the direction of the dust cloud fast approaching his village he sent the words flying into the air to be carried by the Eagle Spirit. Sending a curse was magic that was never used without a lot of thought, and he had not needed to use such power for many, many years. The old man had considered the consequences of such strong magic and had made his decision. After so much misery inflicted by the Horde of Doom on the people of his village the old man found the words came to him easily enough. He had done what he could for his people, so he settled down on his seat to await his fate. He knew that the words of the curse would take hold and begin the work they were sent to achieve. It might take a while, but he was sure that this curse would bring the downfall of these savages and render them helpless.

As the Horde approached the village storm clouds began to form overhead. A sudden rumbling of thunder and flashes of lightning spooked the horses and some of the men stopped in their tracks, looking up at the ominous clouds. Pulling up his horse their leader looked up and sensed that this was no natural storm. However, he called to his men "Are you all cowards afraid of a storm?" None of the men wanted him to think they were cowards so they continued on their way, even though some of them were feeling very nervous. Thundering into the tiny village they began their usual destruction, raiding the few houses and stores that they found and taking the meagre possessions that the people had left behind in the confusion, then they burned anything they could not take with them.

The old man waited sitting quietly until the leader of the Horde of Doom noticed him and strode arrogantly towards where he sat. "What have we here men?" he sneered loudly with his hands on his hips, looking back over his shoulder so his men could hear. Then turning back to the old man he snarled "Are you brave old man or are you stupid, to sit here on your own. Perhaps you are getting ready to meet your ancestors?" The old man looked into the younger one's eyes, "I am neither" he replied quietly "I do not fear you and I have a message for you. There is one who is of the Goddess who, with the help of others like her, will bring you down, and I believe that she will achieve this very soon. There will be nothing you can do to stop her except cease this relentless persecution of our people now. This woman has powers you cannot imagine. If you continue this carnage she will see that you are punished. I give you this warning." Looking away from the old man's eyes for a moment with an uncomfortable feeling creeping into his bones, the leader turned back and retorted "Are you trying to tell me that a woman is going to hurt *me* old man? She must be a powerful warrior indeed." Then pretending to shake with fear he turned to his men who had begun to gather behind him, laughing at the old man's threat. "Perhaps I will have another fate in mind for this warrior woman." he sneered. "No" replied the old man quietly, "she is no warrior, nor will you have your way with her, she has already begun to work on your downfall as have many in this land. Cease this terror soon or you will be punished in a way you cannot fight with weapons and savagery. That is all I have to say. Kill me now if you wish, as I have said, I do not fear you or my death as I will meet my destiny very soon anyway. Know this, your destruction has already begun."

Starreck turned to his men as he thought of what the old man had said, "Leave him alone," he said quietly to his men, " he is braver than all of you put together and he does us no harm. He is just a ranting old man who's mind has gone. Get on with what you were doing." He turned back to the old man, "How do you know about this threat on my life?" he asked quietly. Looking this tall, dark man squarely in the eye the old man replied "The Great Spirit has spoken to me and that is enough. Once more I say, cease this terror or you will be punished." Then he closed his eyes and quietly awaited his fate.

Turning hard on his heel Starreck called his men. "Leave this place now" he shouted, "we have enough, there's nothing left for us here." The men looked furtively at each other as they thought about Starreck's change of heart but after the sudden and unusual storm before they arrived, they obeyed his command. As they left the village Starreck pulled up his horse and glanced back to the old man who still sat on his stool in front of the house with eyes closed. Turning his horse Starreck rode towards the mountains. Before long a shiver went down his spine and he understood that the old man was right. He had noticed the strange markings and decorations and knew that there were powerful energies at work from which he had no weapon to protect himself. He remembered the woman in the last place they had been who was also covered in tattoos and it worried him even more. He thought to himself that the beginning of the end of his reign of terror could have begun and for the first time in many years he felt fear. The men had told him they had been having strange dreams for some while now, some waking up sweating and frightened as demons entered their dreams and turned them to nightmares. Some had left quietly during the night, riding away towards the coast where there was little talk of demons and magic.

Within days of leaving the old man in Ravat these thoughts had begun to come to enter the minds of some of the men during the day as well as in their dreams. They would be caught out by these thoughts while riding along, even thinking they were being followed by demons, seeing shadows out of the corner of their eyes and imagining ambush coming from every dark corner. Because these men were afraid of looking weak to their companions no one spoke of these dreams, every one of them thinking that it was just them alone who were seeing things that weren't there and dreaming of demons, when in fact every one of them were being disturbed by these evil thoughts, day and night. And it was getting worse each day. Within a few weeks several more of the men had gone quietly on their way during the night. Starreck knew he had an enemy he couldn't see. Night sweats disturbed his sleep and he was being visited in his dreams by the old man with the tattoos who said over and over again - "You are doomed, you are to die and there is nothing you can do about it." He would wake startled, looking about in panic then realising it was nothing but a bad dream.

6 THE VILLAGE OF FLESSIA

Many days ride from the mountains and far from the tiny village of the old shaman, nestled in the centre of the broad fertile plains, the farming village of Flessia had survived a vicious attack from the Horde of Doom. The evil horde had ridden in with the intention of raiding, killing and raping but when they arrived there was not a soul or animal in sight. Angry that they had been denied their targets, they had set about burning everything they could. They overturned barrels of water, knocked the wheels off carts and destroyed all but the stone walls. A thick pall of smoke spread out away from the burnt out remains of the houses and barns. Barrels of grain were spilled carelessly on the dirt where they had fallen. When they were done a noticeable difference to raids in other villages was the absence of burnt animal carcasses and dead villagers. After a warning had come through spirit, like the folk of Ravat, the people had driven their livestock into the hills to keep them safe before retreating to a safe haven. They were hiding in the caves deep within the forest until they knew onslaught was over. Strangely the only building left standing in one piece after the raid was the cottage of the local Wise Woman. As with other

buildings of its kind there was no evidence that this
building existed when the Horde of Doom attacked the
village. Made of stone with a steep roof of dark grey slate
the building had been growing slowly for centuries as it
was passed down from one wise and gifted woman to the
next. Originally, many lifetimes ago, it was a tiny one room
building and had been added onto with each new
occupant. Eventually it had grown into the two storey
cottage it was today. Ivy covered the stone walls and an
ancient tree had grown up its' side protecting the walls and
giving the impression the building had grown out of the
ground. The garden was a maze of herbs and vegetables,
each one planted for a special purpose as medicine or just
to feed the current occupant. Some would wonder, as the
tales of burning spread across the land, why some cottages
had been spared and never shown any sign of being
attacked. Nobody asked the question because there were
things you just didn't need to know.

Being forewarned through Spirit that the Horde of
Doom was on its way to the Village, and after alerting her
people of the oncoming menace, the Wise Woman Hetia
had walked around her cottage. With a staff of power in
her hand, she spoke the words of the ancient ones. She
had placed a shield of protection around her home as her

predecessors had done before her. To the eyes of the Horde of Doom and any other beings with evil intentions, this building did not exist but appeared to be a mound of hard rock left there by the villagers for future buildings. Even the garden appeared to be just weeds and stones. The precious stores of herbs and oils inside, some so precious they had been brought from lands far away by travellers, would be saved to help heal the people and animals. The ancient knowledge stored in her mind and heart would be put to use and the healing would begin, once again.

Tall and slender, her dark red hair hanging loosely down to her waist and a hint of early grey touching her temples, Hetia stood a good head taller than most women of the land. In the thin braids that fell down in front of her ears she had woven such things that held the energy of the land. Feathers of owls and ravens to signify wisdom and survival, beads carved from trees with healing energy and dried seeds representing new life. Around her forehead the band she wore was woven from grass, at her throat a black shiny stone with runic markings was held in place with a leather thong. This was the amulet given to her by her old teacher. Hetia's garments, the long shift of cream and the over skirt and waistcoat of brown, were woven from the soft wool taken from the Village goats and her long boots and belt were from the same animals who had given their lives to feed the people. Requiring little of worldly goods, she possessed few personal items. Hetia could be an imposing sight to those meeting her for the first time. However, those who knew the woman saw only the compassionate and caring healer who could hold a wounded bird as lightly as a feather or firmly hold down a thrashing man whilst applying a burning brand to a severed limb.

For many years Hetia had been using her skills as a healer, helping the women bring new life into the world, assuring the dying and guiding them to a place in their hearts where they could let go of life when their time had come. She did her best to heal the wounded and help the ill recover with her herbal potions and sound advice. Children would come to her door with injured and sick animals, where they would be tended as carefully as would the humans who came for her help. This caring healer could also be a fierce enemy if her people or the land around her were threatened. Her knowledge of magic, using the elements of Earth, Fire, Water, Air and Ether could be turned very quickly into weapons of immense power. However, she had also been taught that every living thing has its destiny and to interfere was never to be taken lightly but lately she was becoming quite fed up with this Horde of Doom as they seem to be gaining strength. During her Spirit Walk she had connected to the old Shaman who had begun their downfall with his strong curses in Ravat. She would not let him down because lately the Horde had gone too far in her opinion and had finally made her extremely angry. Now she would act with a more direct approach, she would concentrate her energies and control her work, she would make her magic hurt those who were hurting the land and its' people.

After the Horde of Doom had passed through the village Hetia was the first to return. She had been close by during the raid, watching from on top of a large pile of ancient rocks within earshot of her cottage. Blending into the surroundings was a skill she had learned during her training and this time it was very important to keep very still so she would not be noticed because there was nothing to hide her from being seen. Hetia noticed everything, although she could not see faces clearly from her perch. She watched silently as they rode away leaving the carnage behind and she began to formulate their downfall. However there was much to prepare before she could begin her work so she climbed down from the rocks

and made her way back. The people would gradually
trickle down from the safety of the hills where they had
taken refuge, to silently look over their burnt out homes
and see what they could salvage of their few precious
possessions and Hetia would be there for them. She was
so very angry as she walked through the ruins, and her
anger would be channelled into energy so strong that only
the Spirits could stop her if that was what they deemed
necessary. Standing still for a moment in the street she
took a deep breath then she raised her arms to the
heavens. "Oh Great Spirits of the Universe" she invoked,
"please help me to stop this savagery. I call on the Spirits
of Wind, Rain, Sun, Ether and the Earth to aid me in my
work. These men cannot be allowed to continue. I curse
them and their leader, I ask that you reign terror upon
them and send them far away, weaken their power any way
you wish." She stopped for a moment and gave thought
to her words. To send them away would only allow them
to find other villages to attack. No, she must do this in a
much more subtle way. She called once more on the
energies and begged their forgiveness then sent, calmly this
time, her prayers out once more that the savages would be
stopped by their own folly or the powers of others, but the
leader was hers, she would curse him, bring misery and
sickness to him. He would die slowly and suffer along the

way as he had brought misery and sadness to the people of the land.

Hetia planned her curse carefully to be sure the Horde was disbanded and become leaderless. They would remain unaware of the strong words of power she had sent as a curse. Walking through the Village Hetia surveyed the carnage then sitting in her garden she contacted, through Spirit, the Wise Woman in the next village to let her know they were safe. Over the centuries the teaching of the Mysteries had developed to the stage that with concentration and practice those with the wisdom could send their thoughts to others with the knowledge. It had begun at a time, many centuries ago, when artificial communication had broken down. Once, it was written that people were able to talk to each other over very long distances with long forgotten technology but this knowledge had disappeared with the advent of the Great Climate Calamity. Slowly the world had returned to a simple life. Hetia had been taught this Mystery but had vowed to secrecy because she was told that the knowledge would only be used for evil if it was given to those who intended to control the people. However, folk of magic and spirit had developed this method of thought "talk" and by keeping the secret as one of the Mysteries it would only be used by those sworn to a service of healing or guidance.

Now that Flessia had survived the onslaught, throughout the land the mysterious, ancient words were being sent from village Wise Women and Shaman to others with these silent and secret words as they began the downfall of the wicked, evil beings known as the Horde of Doom.

Standing in front of her door with her back straight and shoulders squared, Hetia took a deep breath and once more circled the ancient building – this time in the opposite direction – thanking The Goddess for keeping her home safe then speaking the ancient words to undo the protection spell. The people of Flessia could once more safely enter her home and seek help. She opened the door and stepped inside. Looking around she saw that everything was in order as she had expected it to be. The jars along the shelves were as she had left them, bunches of aromatic herbs were hanging from the ceiling where they had been placed to dry and the crystals and other pieces collected from the Earth that she used in her work were untouched. It was cool inside, many years of peace and tranquillity, of meditation and healing, had created a haven for Hetia and those she welcomed within the walls. Closing her eyes for a moment she whispered an quiet prayer of thanks and prepared herself for those villagers who needed her help. Collecting her bag of healing herbs and salves Hetia left the house, closing the door gently behind her. She walked towards the tired people coming back to the village with her arms and her heart open. There were not so many who needed her as she had expected. "We are safe for now," she assured them, "come, let us clear this mess and get on with our lives."

The people of the village had fled quickly when Hetia gave them the warning that the attackers were coming and the dust cloud in the far distance announced the misery and violence that was about to descend upon the village. Two years before they had stayed behind to fight back, brandishing their farming tools to try and stave off the savage marauders. The few hunters and warriors living in the village had done their best with what they had at hand but they were no match for the savage and frenzied attack. All they had achieved was losing most of the able bodied adults and a few children too slow to run away. Others who had managed to escape were still trying to block out the screams of their loved ones, the horrors and sounds of death and destruction from that horrific day. Some had only just replaced the personal belongings that had been stolen, ruined or burnt.

This time they were ready when the alarm was raised. Carrying what they could, precious tools, the baby animals and any food they could find in a hurry they had escaped as quietly as possible, herding the few sheep and goats ahead of them to save them from the certainty of death, even leading the milking cows. They fled to the deep underground caverns up in the hills that were kept secret from the outside world. Passing through the dense forest it was necessary to leave the path behind and make their way on an unmarked route. One of the Elders led the way, threading his way between the ancient trees as quietly as possible without disturbing too much of the undergrowth. He was very careful of his steps and urged the people to do as little disturbance as possible to prevent them from being found.

The caves had been used many lifetimes ago by the people who had left the cities behind looking for a better life when the heat of the land became unbearable, and they had lived within the safety of the caves for many years before building their homes in the open.

As the group finally came to a halt the Elder who led the way called upon some of the healthy youngsters to help him move the pile of old dead wood that had been left to cover the entrance, although it looked as though a tree had just fallen down naturally. Once the entrance to the cave was uncovered the people began to file quietly into the cool depth where they knew they would be safe, leading their animals behind them.

Deep within the mountain along passageways that twisted and turned into its' heart, food for the people and the animals along with bedding, firewood and cooking pots had been stored in a huge cave after the attacks on Aves and Carlin. Cool clear water ran from a spring at the back of the cave to fill a pool for drinking and bathing. Fire brands had been pushed into holes in the cave walls ready to be lit and within a very short time the space was filled with light. This was the first time they had needed to use the caverns since they were set up. There were no injuries apart from scrapes and bruises from running through the bushes as they fled the village. Hetia had been warned in plenty of time that the Horde of Doom was on its' way.

A lookout had been posted where he could see the Village below on the Plains so when the all clear was called they gathered their belongings and animals to slowly return to where their homes had been standing just a day before, some now lying in burnt out ruins. There were tears and words of disbelief from those who had lost everything - along with cries of amazement as belongings that were left behind were uncovered amongst the ashes of burnt out homes. Some had buried their valuables beneath the floor and these were retrieved and cleaned up.

As she made her way through the ravaged village Hetia heard the plaintive sound of a child quietly sobbing. She followed the sound, finding a small girl sitting beside the body of a puppy. "He was in a box under my bed" she sobbed "I thought he would be safe, but the house burned down and he couldn't get out". Hetia drew the child to her and held her gently. "Your puppy's spirit has gone to the Goddess" she said quietly, "we can ask Her to look out for his Spirit and send it on its way. Would you like to do that?" "Yyyes please" the little girl sobbed, so they sat together and Hetia sent a prayer to help the puppy's spirit on its way. "Now, how about we see if anything is left here to save?" Hetia asked the child, "Maybe there are some things you can find for your mother and father." Tears drying on her young cheeks the little girl took Hetia's hand. They searched around for a while and came across a few small items, a spoon and a small box with the mother's sewing tools. When they turned over the remains of the child's bed space there was a small carved pig. The girl was content with her finds, although still saddened by the death of her puppy. "Come on" said Hetia, "We will show your mother what we have found." They turned and walked hand in hand across the village where the child's mother was helping an old lady find what remained of her belongings. The little girl offered up her finds to her tired mother then turned and wrapped her arms around Hetia, tears still rolling uncontrolled down her little cheeks.

By the end of the day the people of Flessia had gathered what they could from their burnt out homes, and with a supply of food and blankets brought back from the caves they set up a camp in the centre of the village. Hetia gathered the old men and women and took them back to her cottage for the night. Her warm bed would hold two and the others were placed in chairs by the fire. She brought blankets and coats to keep them warm and served up cups of hot tea. Overnight she had a huge pot of broth cooking slowly so by the morning the welcome brew would warm their old bodies for the day to come. There was a small hut out in the yard so it was also turned over to house a couple of homeless folk. Hetia collected a blanket for herself and left to spend the night in the camp with the younger people. Her needs were simple.

Young men and women were placed around the edge of the camp to keep watch. Those who were feeling guilty about running away to the hills were being counselled by the Spirit Leader, an elderly and gentle old man, to come to terms with the fact that they would have been completely outnumbered had they stayed to fight and protect the village from the Horde of Doom. There was no way they could have made any difference at all. At least they were alive and free to look after their families until the next time a threat came to the village.

The rebuilding of houses would begin the next morning, for on this night the Spirit Leader would lead them in prayer to give thanks to the Goddess for their safe deliverance. The camp fires would keep them warm as they lay beneath the moon to catch what sleep they could.

The sun rose gently the next morning as though it was trying to comfort the people. Its' golden rays crept up over the horizon warming the Earth. However, the people of Flessia had woken early stirring up the cooking fires, filling pots with water and searching through bags and baskets for food to start the day. The children were already running around, finding lost toys, getting under the feet of the adults and acting as if this was a normal day. The adults however, were very quiet as their thoughts turned to what might have happened had they stayed to fight. Many would be dead, many wounded and many would face life alone as had happened the last time they were attacked. At least, this time, they had all survived. After the morning meal the older children were rounded up to help with the clearing as the adults began to find wood and stone for rebuilding the houses. A meeting of the people was held halfway through the morning and a decision made to build shelters for the old people, the sick and injured first, then for those with children. Mothers with tiny babies and children were moved to the big town in the east with the children of Aves. The task of rebuilding began as it had before.

Hetia had begun her day very early, well before sunrise and returned to her cottage. After giving thanks to the Gods and the Goddess she lit her lamp hanging from the beams in the centre of the room and began to prepare mixtures of herbs and special teas to help stave off the

51

tiredness that would take over the people at the end of the day. There were some special herbs to be prepared, one mixture for a pregnant woman who had begun her labour pains far too early when returning to find her home burnt to the ground. Another for an old woman who had tripped whilst hurrying through the trees to the cavern, skinning her shins and causing them to bleed. Hetia realised that at the old woman's advanced age the wounds could fester and become impossible to heal if they were left too long. She prepared a mixture of herbs and oils mixing them into the fat of a slaughtered pig to be applied to the wounds in order to prevent the red, dangerous swelling that so many times would take the elderly before their natural time. The old lady had already seen over 85 summers and she should see quite a few more before leaving this life and preparing for the next. It seemed to Hetia that there were too few people reaching this advanced age these days, too many had given up the will to live with so many attacks on their peaceful life. She was determined to keep as many of her people alive as she could using her healing skills.

However, the young pregnant woman should not give birth for another moon. Fleeing to the hills and the shock when she returned had brought the pains of labour on far too soon. Hetia mixed herbs from different bunches hanging from her rafters, selecting them carefully and blessing the plants that gave them to her. She then ground them into powder and added a few drops of oil from a jar kept on a high shelf out of the reach of young hands who sometimes came to help. Mixing this all together with water she set it into a small pot to heat up on the fire. Hetia would take this to the woman as soon as it was ready. The women of the land knew that a baby born too soon would only die, no amount of care given to the babe would make up for the time it should still be in the womb. The tisane Hetia was brewing had saved many babies from that fate and should work once more on this new mother.

Once the old folk were awake and sipping on the hot broth Hetia gathered her bag of supplies and a clay flask containing the tisane and closing the door she headed off into the village to seek out her patients. Afterwards she would help wherever she could and for as long as she was needed. This was her life as it had been for many healers over many, many years.

Halfway through the day the village elders called a halt to work and gathered the people together for a midday meal. As they sat around the fire eating, one of the elders stood and announced that he would like to speak. Holding in his hand the Staff of Attention, the speaking staff that was used to give a speaker uninterrupted time to say their piece he began. "We need to talk about this tragedy that has happened to us. We need to talk about why we allow this to happen to our village and what we can do to stop it. If we give in and run away each time then the attacks will draw closer together until we are living in constant fear and I am not prepared to do that. I suggest that we find a way to join other villages and fight this Horde of Doom, fight the pestilence that is brought upon us and finish it once and for all. Who is with me?" As he looked around there were many sounds of agreement from those gathered and, as was the way of the people, another elder took the Staff and stood in the centre. "I agree, we need to do something about this Horde of Doom, but where do we start? Where do we find the answers to bringing an end to our suffering? We are not a warring people, we are farmers, peaceful Earth worshippers and we do not have warriors. Our young men and women, strong and brave that they are, are more used to hunting and ploughing. We cannot expect them to fight off these wild and savage creatures that attack us. I believe we should join together with others of the land." For some time many people took up the Staff and gave voice to their ideas. Some only wished to keep going the way they had this time, hiding out in the hills only to rebuild once again, saying that at least they would be alive. Most of the people wanted to fight back, they were not afraid to fight, they just knew they didn't have the skills and knowledge to do so. A decision was made to call a meeting of elders from all the villages of the land to form a stronger force that could fight the Horde. A runner was sent to the next village with the suggestion that they send on runners to the next after that and so on with the elders being asked to meet together where the three rivers of the land meet on the Plains of Parlat in five days time. There a decision could be made on a plan to eradicate the vicious Horde of Doom once and for all.

Before returning to her tasks Hetia walked slowly around the village eyes downcast, searching the ground. She had made up her mind to use knowledge from her time with a Shaman many years ago. After a short search she bent down and picked up a small shiny object, a stud or rivet that was not familiar in the Village. She turned it over in her hand, "I think one of our tormentors must have dropped this" she mused and dropped it into the pouch hanging from her belt. Continuing her search she came across a strip of black leather, the sort of thing used to tie back long hair. She put this in the bag with the metal stud and kept up her quest because she remembered seeing that the leader had long black hair tied back, he also wore all black clothing, he would stand out if she needed to recognise him. By the time Hetia returned to her home she had what she needed so closing the door firmly behind her she crossed to the small table that held sacred amulets and those things she would require for her secret work. Selecting a few items she turned to the hearth and laid them carefully on the floor along with her small collection from the ground in the village.

Aware of the power she could summon, Hetia began by sitting on the floor and quietly centring her mind. Then she began an incantation, calling on powerful Spirits. Slowly at first she spoke the words then built up the power until she could feel the energy around her. Then she asked for their help. "Oh Great Spirits" she called, "I need your help like never before. There is one that must be stopped. He leads a band of marauders who rape, kill and slaughter the people of our land. These are your people Great Spirits, they are under your protection. I ask for this help on their behalf." Then she searched with her mind for the Horde of Doom, especially searching for their leader. His face was elusive as his form came to her mind. Tall, powerful and ruthless, she could feel his energy – this would be enough for her needs. Gathering all her strength Hetia began the second incantation to curse this man. The words she used were ancient, in a strange language and taught to her as a very young woman. She began with a whisper, allowing the strange words to pull in the power from the Spirit world, then louder and louder until she reached a crescendo then slowly returned to the whisper until she was sure enough power had been raised. Finally, she spent some time controlling her breathing and returning back to the present. "You will suffer for what you have done, but I won't let you die" she whispered to the Leader of the gang, "you have to live for a lot longer so you can pay for the savagery you have inflicted on the land. From now on you will begin to feel old and fragile, you will feel as if you are dying – but you are not dying, not yet at least. You will feel agonising pains in your heart and back where you have hurt and killed the folk of the land. May you suffer as those you have left in your wake have suffered. You will live long in pain and suffering until the Great Spirits release you into the next life or they consider you have paid your debt."

Once she had finished her work Hetia felt very weary. She placed the gathered items in a small pouch and dropped them back into the leather scrip she had tied to her belt then she replaced her items of power back to their place on the small table. She knew she should not use her powers to curse another unless her people were harmed. This was one way she could help the people fight back. The curse was sent and would begin to manifest straight away. Hetia did not know if she would ever have proof of her work, however, she did know the power that could emanate from such incantations. Throughout the land she knew that others were also drawing their power to fight this menace for she had received the message from the old man that he had sent his curse to the Horde of Doom so now she had added her strength to his to bring about their downfall.

.

7 HETIA - WISE WOMAN

Many years before the time of the Horde on a high mountain overlooking the caldera below her, a tall young woman stood with her arms wide open and her long dark red hair falling down past her waist. As she warmed her body with the sun's strong rays she greeted the morning sun with the chant she had learned many years before as a child.

"Father Sun I greet thee

Your rays are warm and bright

Mother Earth will accept your love

'till Sister Moon guards the night"

It was mid spring and the sun had risen in a crisp, blue clear sky. Picking up her bag she rummaged inside until her hand felt the hard travelling bread that she had baked several days before. Further poking around produced a package of fruit that had been dried in the sun and a small bag full of nuts and seeds gathered along her journey. The spring that burst forth from the rocks beneath her provided fresh clear water to wash down her morning meal and to rinse the night from her eyes. Filling the gourd she had brought along she plugged it tight then slung the cord it was attached to over her shoulder. This was the start of another beautiful day and she was free. Free of the study her future demanded of her, free of the constraints of the village where she was expected to always be studious and free to allow her thoughts, like her feet, to wander.

The journey so far had been very pleasant. This part of her training depended on the time of year and the food available along the way. As it was spring there were plenty of choices. Berries and nuts were growing on many bushes and trees and there were wild green vegetables and roots that could be eaten raw. She was learning to live off the land, to find food where she could and to seek the herbs and roots that would make healing balms and teas. Under the watchful eye and tutoring of a village Wise Woman, Hetia had spent the past five years discovering the craft of healing. Learning to listen, feel, smell and taste each plant to find out what it could teach her and using the earth to make pastes of different kinds to heal problems of the skin or wounds that would not heal by themselves. She was learning how to extract the oils from flowers and leaves to mix with the fat of animals to make healing balms. There would be many more years before she could confidently work on her own and receive the tattoo that proclaimed her a healer. The Wise Woman had let her know that she would also spend one or two years working with a Shaman so she could learn how to channel the energies of the stones and the earth to hasten healing and make contact with the Spirit realm. A female Shaman had offered her time so Hetia was to live with her in the near future, along with another young girl who was to take the Shaman's place when her life came to an end. Last winter Hetia had aided in a birth, the first of many. This birth was extremely difficult and the mother had passed on to her ancestors, leaving the baby to be nursed by a local woman who was weaning her own child. Following this birth there were two more babies born within a few days and Hetia had helped the Wise Woman each time – each one was different, each one gave her a feeling of elation as she heard the burst of energy with the first lusty cry.

And now Hetia was on her own for a while. She had been sent on this journey twice before. The first time she had managed to get lost and it took her several more days to find her way home. She was unaware that a young warrior had been sent along to follow her at a distance and make sure she did not come to any harm. Remembering her training with the stars when she worked with her Spirit Leader Hetia realised that she could observe the heavens, particularly the large star that was always visible from the back of her house, with this in mind she began travelling at night always walking away from that bright star and eventually arrive home.

This time was different because she was travelling in a part of the country she had been over several times as a child. She had packed her bag with a warm cloak, bread and a gourd for water, some soapwort to clean herself, a pouch for the herbs she would gather and the staff she had fashioned for herself in her first year of training. The staff held the energy of the earth as it was mounted with a beautiful crystal that was said to come from the stars. The stone had "fingers" of blue and it was known as Kyanite. She felt strong when she held the staff and knew that it would be with her for the rest of her life. It was long enough to come up to her shoulder when it was presented to the earth in ritual and it felt good in her hand. In the hills and mountains her staff was also very useful to keep her upright as she slithered down the steep slopes and climbed up among the rocks!

This was the third day of Hetia's journey and it was a beautiful day. Picking up her staff and hoisting her bag over her head and shoulder to hang across her body, she began to slowly descend the side of the mountain, heading for the lush, green growth at its base. It was slower to walk down hill as she had to be careful that she didn't slip. There were no paths and the stony ground could easily give way beneath her feet sending her sliding to the valley below, so using her staff for support she stopped now and then to enjoy the view and to look for the herbs she was to gather. As far as Hetia could see the country was green, the trees were full of berries and flowers and the grass was so many colours of green that it reminded her of the Earth Mother's ability to regrow with the spring rains that had fallen over the past month or so. Taking in a deep breath of the wonderful fresh air Hetia continued on down. This time she had begun her journey in a different direction to the last time and one of her tasks was to look for the herbs that would stop bleeding, especially in cases where the body had been badly injured by wild animals. The herbs would have to stop the hot, searing redness that could develop from the wound and to be able to prevent the yellow ooze that could gather under the skin to burst out at the slightest touch. This was when the injury was at its' worst and people had died from the poison that grew in the blood. She knew what to look for but not where to find it. The old Wise Woman had not told her where the plant would grow or what it looked like when it was still on the plant, until now she had only used the dried leaves gathered by others and kept in jars or hanging from the roof in the old lady's house. To find the plant she would have to rely on her instincts and the knowledge she had gained in her training. This would be a good day to find what she was looking for, so on she went, smiling and enjoying herself.

Finally reaching the base of the mountain Hetia sat down on the soft green grass and rested for a while. Taking a drink of the cool fresh water from her gourd and munching on a handful of berries she had gathered on the way down, she closed her eyes for a moment and "felt" the air. Nothing stirred at first then she felt the earth pounding in rhythm beneath her. It felt like a heartbeat, as if the Earth herself was pulsing, however she soon realised it was a horse approaching the spot where she rested, although Hetia didn't know from which direction. She could feel it coming closer and with her eyes closed she concentrated and could sense – with her spirit mind – that it was one horse and rider. Her senses were developing along with her knowledge and so she used this as a test for herself. Sending out her spirit mind she felt a male presence. The horse was strong and probably very large, so she felt it would be wise to move back into the bushes and watch from a safe distance. Keeping low and moving slowly she stirred the grass back up where she had been sitting then made her way deep into the trees and bushes. They were quite thick and afforded her good shelter.

From her hiding place Hetia saw that the rider appeared to be young. He sat tall on the horse, with his dark hair flying out behind him in the wind. Coal dark eyes scanned the area around him as he rode forward, the horse also alert and watching for danger. The two seemed to be one as the rider rose and fell with the rhythm of the horse. He appeared quite handsome to Hetia, being of the age when young girls noticed these things, and he held himself so proudly that she thought a girl could probably melt in his arms given half a chance, she also was aware that he held his chin high and his shoulders firm. She imagined every taut muscle and sinew of his body and she shivered. Knowing that her training did not allow her to take part in the sexual activities common amongst the young people of her village, she would keep these feelings to herself and enjoy them over and over again. Meanwhile she would watch this handsome man pass by and on to wherever his journey took him and dream of him when she was asleep this night. It would be her fantasy to allow this man to make love to her and take her virginity, all in her dreams.

So busy was Hetia day-dreaming that she didn't hear the horse pull up just a little further along and the rider return to the place where she had left to seek a hiding place. She didn't hear the man as he left his horse behind and followed her tracks into the trees, until his black shiny boots were in front of her. Looking up suddenly she backed away, trying to slither and scramble as fast as she could. But of course it was no use – he just walked towards her, looking down with intense black eyes, trying to fathom what manner of young girl would be alone so far away from a village. He was so intent on the beautiful creature in front of him that he didn't hear the soft footsteps coming up behind until he felt the pin point of a spear blade between his broad shoulder-blades. He turned, and came face to face with a very old woman, she must have been at least ninety summers on the earth but was tall and strong and the force behind the spear was firm and ready to plunge into his flesh. As he turned slowly she placed the spear point directly at his heart and looked him squarely in the eyes. "You might like to reconsider whatever it was that you had planned" the old crone said quietly, "This girl is not for you, or any other man. She is promised as a healer and it would be a very foolish man who would cross the Goddess and take the child's virginity. Perhaps you did not intend for this to happen, if this is so then I beg your pardon and you are free to go."

The stranger turned his head and looked calmly at Hetia then back at the old woman, "You have me at a great disadvantage Grandmother" he replied, "I would not presume to argue with that spear, however, you also mistake my intentions. I found this young woman a very long way from the safety of any village and would have asked her if she needed my help. Others who follow this path may not have the respect that I have for women and she may have come to some terrible harm alone out here in the wilderness. Please forgive me if I have caused fear." He turned to Hetia and offered his hand to help her to rise from the grass where she was still sitting, feeling rather embarrassed at being caught out. She took his hand and allowed him to pull her to her feet, then wiping the grass and dirt from her skirt she turned to the Crone. "I didn't realise you were following me My Lady," she said with a bow of her head, "I believed myself completely alone and was caught out in a time of day dreaming. I know this was wrong and I will try to be much more alert from now on. Would it be alright for me to continue on my journey or do you wish me to return with you?" The Crone considered this for a moment and made her decision. "You will return with me today Hetia" she answered, "We will look for the plants you search for along the way and talk of their use." She turned to the young man and as she spoke her voice seemed to change so that he felt that he could not disobey her, "Please be on your way young man, there is nothing for you here and you have a long way to go. If I have misunderstood your intentions I am sorry and I thank you for your concern, goodbye."

8 STARRECK

The Horde of Doom had been wandering the land for many, many years. Beginning with a small band of thieves and murderers they were joined by escapees from prisons and the armies of the world, banding together until there were over 50 of the worst examples of mankind. They travelled light, able to strike fast and move on, weapons, bedding and some food being their only baggage.

The leader of the Horde seemed quite different to his followers. He stood tall, strong and imposing. Wearing all black, mostly leather, he was almost handsome, his face was lean with high cheekbones, eyes as black as coal and his long black hair flying wild in the wind as he rode. He never smiled, only leering occasionally, and when he did he showed a double row of perfect, white teeth. On his belt hung a vicious looking black whip, its length curled around, to hang near his right hand. Across his back he wore a long shiny sword, available to his left hand by reaching up over his right shoulder. He sat a tall black, shiny stallion, savage and flighty, only obeying his master and the quiet man called Marlick who took care of his needs. No other could get close to this horse and not feel threatened. They were an imposing sight, man and beast together as one. The master's name was Starreck and his horse was Fire and together they were feared. Marlick was honoured and respected among the Horde of Doom for his way with horses, especially with the magnificent stallion, Fire.

Starreck had met Marlick one day several years before when he walked into a blacksmith's forge to have Fire shod for the first time. Marlick was tending to other horses in the stables to earn his keep and Starreck noticed how well he worked with horses. He asked the man if he would look at Fire for him. Others had tried to work with this horse and had failed, usually by being kicked savagely on the first day, or maimed for life and made to leave the Horde of Doom to find other ways to survive. Starreck would find out that Marlick was different. Savage and deadly to other humans with the knives he wore in his boots and strapped to his forearm, but he was gentle and firm with the horses. On that first day in the stables Marlick had walked up to Fire and there was an instant respect between man and beast. He ran his hand over the horse's flank, caressing the shiny coat and talking quietly as he did so. Fire snickered a welcome, nudging Marlick's shoulder and Starreck knew he would need this man to look after Fire. Marlick looked warily at Starreck, sizing up this man who had appeared out of nowhere. "I do not want to work for any man" he snarled, "and I need to keep on the move because there are those who would have my life. One day I might run into these people who have taken a distinct dislike to me and I am getting too old to take them on". Starreck knew that whatever Marlick was running from could be no worse than his own past. "If you come with me I can guarantee that I will look after your back. I need this beast taken care of and you would not need to take part of our – shall I say – activities. You can stay with the camp cook all day if you want, but I need your skill with this horse." Starreck proceeded to tell Marlick about his men and after the horse had been shod Marlick decided to join up with Starreck. Since that time Marlick had only one task, keeping Fire and his own horse healthy and Starreck's gear ready for action. Over the years Starreck trusted him completely with the horse and with his own life, never doubting that Fire would be ready to ride.

Early one morning as the sky lightened and the stars disappeared for the day, Starreck had taken Fire and ridden out from camp to spend some time alone in the hills speaking with the Spirits he believed inhabited the land. On the crest of a hill he dismounted and leaving Fire to savour the fresh dew covered grass, he sat down overlooking the valley below. The sun had just reached the horizon casting its' soft glow across the land and the few clouds above were tinged with pink and grey heralding the rising sun. The valley was glistening with the morning dew and it showed Starreck the beauty that he once saw in all the creations of the Gods. Some months had passed since he had begun to feel the need to be without his men. It had been in the back of his mind quite a lot lately since the nightmares started. He knew that eventually his life of violence and misery would probably see him dead before his hair turned grey, and no doubt he would be left to have his bones picked clean by the carrion birds with no-one to see that he found his way to the land of Spirit. So each morning Starreck made sure that while most of his men were still sleeping, he spoke with his Spirit Guide and "kept in touch". Starreck was tiring of this life, always on the move surrounded by the savages that had attached themselves to him over the years, always looking for another village to attack, one more chance to loot and burn without thinking of the consequences of what he was doing. Deep inside he was feeling sick each time he watched his men killing and looting, and lately he had been feeling physically sick as well. The pains in his chest had been getting stronger and there was a sharp pain at the base of his spine. Perhaps he was getting old and spending too much time in the saddle.

Over the many years he had led the Horde of Doom, Starreck had come to realise that the respect he was given was out of fear not love or companionship, and these days the thought did not make him feel secure. Sooner or later there would be someone younger and stronger who would challenge his position and he would be finished as leader - or dead. He would soon need to make a decision. Should he stay and be challenged or was it time to pass his leadership to another and move on with some form of self respect. This was the question Starreck was putting to his Spirit Guide on such a beautiful morning. Sitting on the hilltop, a peaceful valley before him, Starreck closed his eyes and called on the Spirits. In answer, the Spirits sent his mind back over the years to early days, days of innocence. Back to a time when life was much easier.

Starreck had grown to manhood in a City far away to the south. Crammed with humanity of every race, shape and size, the streets were crowded every day with those going about their business. There were merchants with wagons loaded so high that if two of them collided they would have strewn their goods across one city block. Starreck was called Erik then, named after his grandfather. A skinny little boy with coal black eyes, who would walk along the street holding his mother's hand for protection against the tough street kids. More times than he could remember he would be terrified that his mother would leave him behind in the market place or that he would become lost and have to find his way home alone. This never happened of course, but it was always on his mind. The streets were fascinating to the little boy. Tall men in fancy clothes strode around as if they owned the world, ladies in doorways would smile at him, telling him he would be such a beautiful man one day with those amazing dark eyes. He didn't understand at the time of course, but he loved the attention. Smiling at his reaction, Erik's mother would tug at his hand to continue on their way. Those trips to the market were an adventure, as much as Erik wanted adventure. He had his friends nearer to home and they would do what young boys did, pretend to fight dragons and pirates. But most of all Erik loved to visit his father at work. Erik's father worked hard all day keeping the accounts for a wool storehouse at the docks, where the huge ships with billowing sails would take the local produce far across the world. The docks were a fascinating place for a little boy. He would look out from his father's office window, and dream of one day sailing away in one of those huge ships as they creaked and rocked in the harbour, then at night he would go to sleep dreaming of sailing the high seas, finding new lands and adventure. He had spoken to his father of his dreams and was encouraged to follow this life when he became a man. But it was not to be.

During a particularly dark night, not far past the winter Solstice, a message came that Erik's father had been attacked in the street on his way home from work and was in the infirmary with the healers. They did not expect him to live so Erik's mother left the boy with a neighbour and ran to be with her husband. In the morning Erik was told his father had gone with the Spirits to prepare for his next life, and in the manner of his people, Erik was taken with his mother to live in the house of his grandfather out on the edge of the city. He didn't mind it there because he felt safer. There were no thieves and cut-throats in the streets, the buildings didn't reach towards each other over your head and he could walk around by himself. Although he missed his father very much, he was much happier living with his grandfather, however he also missed the mighty sailing ships, so he made a vow that when he was older he would find work on one of these beautiful vessels and sail off to see the world. Eventually Erik grew up to be a tall strong teenager. But one day Erik's world came tumbling down.

Being born in the City and raised among many different races and spiritual beliefs, Erik had never thought he was any different to the other boys around him. It had never occurred to him that his skin was not pink/white or his eyes were not blue or green. His black hair and almost black eyes didn't stand out in the city. His mother had beautiful waist length black shiny hair held in two thick braids and the silver jewellery she wore with strange symbols went unnoticed among the many different races living in the City. His father was very fair, with red hair and freckles and pale blue eyes. None of this made any difference to Erik He loved his mother and father equally, although he took after his mother in looks – everyone said so. However, none of this mattered in the city.

After a few years in his grandfather's house Erik began to notice that when he and his mother went to the market nearby there were comments made quietly behind lifted hands. There were looks that said something was not quite right – however the people respected Erik's grandfather and said nothing out loud. But Erik noticed. "Grandfather, what do those people mean?" he asked. Grandfather went quiet, he lowered his eyes for a moment then placing his hand on Erik's shoulder he told him. "Your grandmother was brought to this country on one of the huge trading boats. She had fallen in love with a sailor when the ship had moored near the island where she lived so when the ship was ready to leave she begged him to take her along. She was only 15 summers and was from an island nation in the middle of the Great Sea. The people there were free spirits, spending their time fishing, singing, worshipping the spirits of the land and sea. When she was half way on this romantic journey her lover had drowned, washed overboard in a violent storm. The captain had allowed her to continue the journey instead of putting her ashore along the way. Arriving at the docks here she had been the centre of attention, dressed in a flimsy gown with only a woollen cape given to her by the Captain to keep her warm. She wore only sandals on her feet, her meagre possessions wrapped in a bundle.

I was in the crowd waiting for the ship to be unloaded that day when I saw her and I fell in love at that moment. No other woman would ever take my attention.

I took her home where she looked after me and I loved her until she died 30 years later. Your mother was born of this love and she has always reminded me of your grandmother as they shared the same beauty. Since my precious one died there has been no other woman in my life. I will join her in the land of Spirit when my time comes." He finished the tale with tears in his eyes so Erik rose and quietly left him alone.

Over the many years there had been discreet comments about the colour of Erik's mother's skin and that of his grandmother, but most people had accepted the difference and moved on. Until the day a strange visitor arrived. He stood in the town square, wearing a dark cloak over his clothes. He was dressed like a scholar with his arms covered down to the leather gloves that fitted tightly over his hands. His fine black shoes were polished and he wore a wide brimmed hat to keep the sun off his pale skin. Climbing up on a box he had brought with him he began to speak. At first no one took too much notice until he raised his voice to shout. "There are people who look different to you and I" he said loudly "You will know these people have evil and bad spirits within because the colour of their skin and eyes are dark – the colour of the evil ones. They will talk like you, walk like you, but don't be fooled – they are here to cause evil. We have to drive the evil out of these people so they may live in peace like you and I." He continued to shout and call out his evil message as the people gathered around him.

On her way to market Erik's mother walked closer to the crowd to find out what the noise was about, but she caught the stranger's eye and he turned on her. "There is one of them" he shouted pointing "Notice the colour of her eyes, her dark skin and the way she wears her hair hanging down her back, we must drive the evil from her before it spreads into the rest of you. Take her." he screamed, and the crowd turned towards Erik's mother who shrank backwards, tripping over and landing on her back sending her basket flying in the air. The crowd, now in a frenzy built up by the stranger's speech, began shouting and screaming, then they picked up stones, sticks and anything they could get their hands on to beat her with. Finally her body lay in a pool of blood, broken and lifeless. It was all over so quickly that few had realised what they had done. Before anyone arrived to stop them the crowd slunk away to hide in shame, leaving her broken body in the street.

The Speaker, satisfied with the carnage he had caused, simply mounted his horse and with a grim smirk on his face, rode away.

Later that same day, Erik began to worry about his mother as she had not returned from the market. He was a young man now, who had reached his full height, the work he did on the farm had strengthened the muscles on his back and arms. Erik rode well and would take off into the country hunting deer and wild boar for the family. He could move swiftly on foot as well as in the saddle.

Lately Erik's grandfather was getting frail and spent most of his time sitting on the porch waiting to die so he could go to the love of his life in the land of Spirit so Erik had not accompanied his mother to market for some time, preferring to stay with his Grandfather and do the work around the house.

As the sun fell towards the horizon Erik's Mother still had not returned – Erik knew something was wrong so he set out to find her and bring her safely home. As he rode into town the few people in the street backed away from him. There was a hushed silence as they quickly turned and ducked down alley ways and into houses. Erik knew there was something very wrong so he climbed down from his horse and continued towards the town square on foot. When he came towards the place where the mob had attacked his mother everyone had disappeared into the shadows except for an old crone sitting on the common bench with her hands held tightly in her lap and tears in her eyes. "They have killed your mother young man" she cried, "They have done such an evil thing and they should never be allowed to forget what they have done" She stood slowly and raised her hands in the air and cried "By the spirits of the Earth, Fire, Water and Air I curse the people who have done this terrible thing." Turning to Erik she said "By your hand young Erik you should strike down every single one of them and then you should hunt down the stranger who started it all and make him suffer". When she had finished she limped over to Erik who was standing in the street with a look of shock on his face. Placing her hand on his arm she said sadly, "Your mother died here today because she looked different from the others. I say you remind these people that you *are* different, and you are going to make them suffer for what they have done. Your mother's broken body lies in my home young Erik, come with me and I will wrap her so you may take her home". She turned and led the way to her small cottage.

Erik was devastated, from the time he had discovered what had happened he had not said a word. The feelings deep within his heart and belly were churning over and over, his mind was swimming with the knowledge that his beloved mother had been murdered as had his father so many years ago. When the horror turned to anger he vowed silently that he would revenge them both. He would not stop until he found the stranger who had turned the crowd on his mother, and he would seek revenge on the people of this town who had done the evil deed. He would not rest until he had done so.

Erik took his mother's body gently in his arms and cradled her on the saddle in front of him until he reached home. Grandfather came from the house to see what had happened and seeing his daughter's lifeless body he collapsed to the ground. Erik laid his mother gently down on the grass and gathered up his grandfather to carry him to his bed then returned to tend to his mother's body. Under the sky that had now darkened he held his hands in the air with a hopelessness that would not leave him for a very long time and with all his heart and soul he swore to the Goddess. "I will avenge the death of my mother and father. I will never rest until I find the stranger who did this terrible deed and it is my life's quest to carry out this revenge. Then I will return to this town and seek revenge on the people who have beaten my mother to death." With tears in his eyes he turned to the house – to find his grandfather had passed on to Spirit to meet his love. Erik was now alone.

As Erik thought back over his early life he recalled a more pleasant memory. He had been riding the country looking for the man who had killed his mother when he heard some rustling in the undergrowth near the trail. Thinking it might be something worth catching for his next meal he turned his horse and went back a short way. Dismounting quietly he looked about and saw human tracks leading away from the trail so poking about he was very surprised when he discovered a young girl hidden there. He was about to offer her his protection to the next village when he felt a sharp point in the middle of his back. The girl was not alone. She had the protection of an old Crone who was very capable of using the weapon she now held to his body. After assuring her his intentions were quite honourable he had turned to mount his horse. When he looked back there was no sign of the young girl or the Crone, or of the warrior who had stood unseen in the shadows and now disappeared when there was no danger to the women. Could they have gone that quickly or maybe he was charmed by some trick of the Crone to make him believe they were not there when they really were. He considered this for a moment then decided that either way he didn't want to be there any longer and rode away at a fast canter. He would not forget the beautiful young woman, or the Crone, and thought that he would try to find the girl again one day. On this pleasant morning Erik wondered what had happened to that beautiful young woman.

But not that day, for he wished to reach the next town before darkness fell over the land. He had learned that the man he hunted down for the savage killing of his mother was due to talk at a meeting in this town. He had followed the man over the land for many years, always arriving a few days behind. But this time it was different. Erik had talked to a stranger a week ago who knew the movements of this elusive, evil person that he was seeking. And this time he would be there first and await the arrival of the speaker.

The town Erik entered was not so different from many others he had spent time in during his search. There were a few traders, a blacksmith and a tavern. The houses, mostly small with thatched roofs and tiny gardens growing vegetables, were scattered throughout the town and there were small farmsteads on the outskirts supplying the town market. As the sky was beginning to darken Erik looked around for a place to sleep - and wait. It would not be long now and he could avenge his mother's death and put her spirit to rest, then he could get on with his own life. Tying his horse to a rail at the rear of the tavern, Erik made his way around to the front and entered. Lanterns were sending their welcoming light into every corner of the large room where small groups of men sat in quiet conversations. There was a large pot of stew simmering on the hearth and a sign that invited patrons to take what they required and pay at the counter. Filling a bowl and picking up a spoon and chunk of freshly baked bread, he placed it on a table by the window. After paying for his meal he ordered a large tankard of ale, and sat down to wait. Sooner or later Erik would know the speaker was in town. His name was Jorran and he was a follower of what was called the "Light". Although there was little light in what he preached. He usually found a place in the centre of a town to set up a box he brought with him to stand on. From there, he would call to passers by to stop and listen to what he had to say. His speech would be full of fire and brimstone, daring his listeners to follow him with the blessing of the Light, telling them that by following his teachings they could guarantee a place in the afterlife of amazing eternity. He would let them believe that he had a beautiful valley where they could live in peace with riches beyond their imagining. Once he had a large enough crowd he would then pick on someone who looked as though they were different from the others, and then turn the crowd into a frenzy against the person, as he had done to Erik's mother. This was his way of creating followers, for once the people had turned against the good and kind citizens of the town, there was little they could do but follow Jorran as he told them he could help them begin again in a new and better life. He would stay in the town just long enough for the people to give him gifts of money, food and goods in order to take them to the 'promised land', then he would disappear during the night, taking everything with him. Most people would just count their losses, and get on with life vowing not to be caught again. But not Erik He was determined to find Jorran – and he would kill him. This was his vow to his dead mother. To kill Jorran and rid the earth of this menace once and for all, even if it meant that he too would end up being hunted for the rest of his life. And so he ate his stew and waited for the speaker.

It was after darkness had fallen before Erik realised that a crowd was gathering at the end of the street. He left the tavern and made his way slowly towards that crowd. In the centre, standing on a wooden crate was Jorran, the evil man who had been responsible for killing Erik's mother. He felt the bile rising from his stomach as he ventured closer, the blood was heating his cheeks and his hands became covered in sweat. The closer he came, the worse he felt. However, there was a strength gathering between his shoulder-blades, his arms tightened, his hands formed fists and he began to walk lighter on his feet. His whole body was preparing for a fight, he was ready at long last to put his mother to rest.

"You there" called out Jorran in his direction, "You seem to want to hear what I have to say, come closer young man and hear of the beauty of living the life in the Light where you shall be happy for the rest of your days". Erik moved closer, feeling the sweat now running in rivulets down his back as his muscles tightened even more. "I shall come closer to you Jorran" he said to himself in a low and quiet voice, "I shall come so close that you will scream until I send you to your God". Coming into the crowd that had formed around Jorran he gently shoved his way forward until he was facing the speaker, eyes looking directly into the eyes of the killer. Standing firmly only a forearm's length away Erik spoke "Do you remember a town you were in several years ago near the City of Crona where you had a crowd gathered just as this one?" he began quietly, "The people were listening to your speech and you began to pick on a beautiful black haired woman, with eyes as dark as coal and hair plaited down to her waist. You called her evil and told the people she was a bad spirit. You told the people they had to drive her out of the town, when all she had done was to be different in colouring to the rest of you. You made them kill her Jorran, you pushed and shouted at them until they became a mad, frenzied mob - and they killed her. She was my mother, and you made them kill her." He took Jorran by the front of his shirt with both hands and pulled him close. "And now, I am going to kill you." The crowd shrank back and began to frantically look for ways to move away from this young man with murder in his eyes. "Don't do this son," called out one woman, "we will not listen to the speaker any more, just chase him out of town, don't commit such a heinous crime as murder, you will regret it for the rest of your life." But Erik took no notice of the woman and began to punch Jorran hard. As he used all the pent up rage of many years since his mother had died he snarled "You are going to die speaker you are going to pay for all the evil you have created in your life first, then you are going to die".

It was two days later when Erik finally stopped running. He had only paused to water and feed the horse and had kept moving as fast as he could with only a short stop early in the morning to give his horse a break. He remembered squeezing the life out of Jorran after pounding him red and bloody with his fists. As he felt the man's life force slipping away he had passed into the space in his mind where reality no longer mattered to him. He did not remember the final gasp from the man as Jorran went loose in his hands. He did not remember the people taking the slack, dead body from him and pulling him away. He did not remember the kindly man who collected Erik's horse and told him to ride as fast as he could away from the town before the local Peace Keeper sent his men to take him away. Murder would see him executed or imprisoned for life, no matter what the reason. There would be no excuses, murder was murder, no matter what the intention behind it. And so Erik had ridden his horse as hard and as far as he could, not even knowing where he was headed. If he kept going he might be able to rid his mind of the thought that he had killed another human being. But it would be many years before he stopped running. He was now a fugitive.

As Erik returned his thoughts to the present he decided it was time to make his way back to camp. Perhaps it was time to call it quits on this way of life. He really was tired of being always on the road and realised that all he wanted now was somewhere to call home. A house, a farm or even a shack somewhere, but he just wanted to get out of the saddle and away from these desperate men that followed him about. He decided it was time.

He wondered what had happened to that young woman as he rose from the soft grass, stretching his tired body. He returned to his men with a brief thought that he may never get the chance to settle down with a good woman and raise a family. There had been women in his life, usually the kind that he would never consider being the mother of his children, and there had been one or two that had raised his interest enough to regret leaving them behind. How was it that this girl, many years in the past and unobtainable to someone like him, could hold his thoughts at this moment in his life. There were times over the years when he thought he could feel her presence, occasions when he would look around thinking that she may be nearby and then the thought would drift off into the place where dreams and wild thoughts went. When he tried to picture her face now it was difficult, the long hair and the pretty face were blurred and lately the face would be replaced by a strong, older countenance with fierce eyes – just for a blinking of the eye. He hadn't given much thought to it in dreams but today, in reality, the younger pretty face had faded and was replaced by the fiercer, strong face. The thought of it sent shivers down his spine as he rode into camp. For now though, there were plans to be made, men to sort out and places to go.

As Starreck dismounted in the camp the men were grumbling and coughing, as men do when they rise from sleep, the camp fires had been lit and the cook was preparing a meal to break the night fast. At the edge of the camp the horses were being fed and saddled by the early risers ready for the day's ride. The men might be rough and, at times, evil to those they took a dislike to, but they looked after their horses better than they looked after themselves for without a good, healthy horse they could say goodbye to the life on the road and plan to spend many years in the nearest prison or dungeon. A good horse was essential to the life they had chosen, more than any other living creature. Starreck knew that his horse, Fire, was in the very best of hands with Marlick. He would trust no other to keep Fire in top condition so he led him back to his keeper.

9 ENCOUNTER

The Horde of Doom were packing up their camp, putting out fires and stowing their belongings onto their horses when Starreck called Marlick to him. "We need to find some supplies Marlick", he said, "There must be a village or town around here where we can stock up on the food we need for the road. This time I want you to take two of the men, two with some manners, and find a town. We are going to buy what we need, not take it. I have the feeling that it is time we headed into the mountains for a while and I don't want anyone following us because one of the men lost his temper. Buy some flour and beans and some herbs for the healer – ask him what he needs – and get whatever you need for the horses. Maybe some bags of grain to give them some extra strength for the coming winter." Marlick knew better than to ask why so he turned and rounded up two of the men who were known to be a bit more level-headed than the others. He took the money he needed from Starreck's strongbox and with two pack horses headed off in the direction of a town he remembered from many years ago. He wondered to himself, what was the idea behind this retreat to the hills. It was not yet winter, even if it had been, they would not be heading into the mountains, there must be some reason and he was sure that Starreck would eventually let him know. Meanwhile, he would just do as he was asked. They would be back within a few hours. Starreck called to the other men and ordered them to move slowly towards the mountains, Marlick knew he would catch up on his return with the supplies. They hadn't done this for a very long time and, he thought, it would be good to slow down for a while. Like Starreck, he also was getting a bit tired of always being on the move and the violence of the last few years was beginning to get him down. He had been experiencing some very nasty nightmares over the past year, they were getting worse with each day and Marlick was beginning to think the Gods were paying him back for the horrid things he had been doing. He would like to leave this life behind, but didn't want to let Starreck down.

The mountains loomed ahead as the Horde of Doom slowly made their way towards them. Marlick had caught up some time before and rode quietly alongside his leader. Words need not pass between them unless something was amiss, and as the horses walked peacefully uphill the air began to cool and the men of the Horde of Doom began to relax. There was a valley high in the mountains where they would be hidden from view. The path was winding up through the piles of stones and gravel that had fallen down over the years so they threaded their way slowly upwards. The men in the rear had tied tree branches to their saddles and dragged them along behind to make tracking them difficult. Although a good tracker would still find them, the average person following the horses' hoof-prints would be confused. Higher and higher they went until near the end of the day they came across a grassy valley with a clear, cool stream running through it. The horses would have plenty of grass here, and there were ancient caves carved into the side of the mountains. Here they could rest, away from the outside world, allowing their wounded and sick a chance to recover. Men were sent to build crude fences at the ends of the valley so the horses could be left to roam free, and others sent to find a suitable place to set up a camp. They could sleep and shelter in the caves, although many of the men were only sleeping when they were out under the stars. For some time now the demons and nightmares plagued them all. Still, none would talk about it, they thought it would make them seem weaker somehow if they showed signs of fear. Only young Benji and the cook seemed to sleep soundly, neither had taken part in any of the attacks and neither felt they had angered the Gods.

As they settled in to the camp site the healer began to search around for the herbs he needed to deal with the usual problems of men on the move. He found a good supply of the moss he used to stop bleeding and other plants that would treat the dreaded stomach illness that could strike at any time and seemed to be very prevalent in the men lately. Two of the men were sent to hunt meat, others to see if there were fish in the stream that ran through the valley. They were going to stay here for some time so Starreck was able to give the men an opportunity to relax for the first time in months their healer thought this would make the nightmares and headaches go away. Starreck decided to make his camp away from the others and asked Marlick to join him. They would leave the men to themselves for a while.

Again Starreck's mind began to dwell on the fact that he may like to have a son, if not more than one, and leave behind this life that had started so long ago when he was not much more than a boy. Too many years and too much misery was now behind him and at times he felt sorrow and regret after he carried out the violence. It had been some time now since he personally attacked anyone, but he knew he was just as guilty as the men because he stood by and let it happen. The feelings of sadness, guilt and wretchedness kept rising up from somewhere deep in his belly. These feelings had appeared all too often of late, almost every day since they attacked the village of Flessia and the surrounding plains some time ago. It was as if the Gods were trying to tell him something. Perhaps they were wanting him to suffer, to feel remorse or it could just be that he was getting old. The headaches were also getting more frequent, they had begun about a month ago, deep in the front of his head. The Healer had given him a potion that had helped for a while, but they kept coming back and were getting worse each time. Sometimes they would last all day and would not go away until he had slept through the night. The flashing lights in his eyes were also getting worse, they were like little bolts of lightning flashing and shimmering for up to an hour at a time. Sometimes, early in the morning when he would wake before his men, he felt pains going through his bones especially at the base of his spine. Then there were the pains in his heart that were getting worse. "Just your age and living on the back of a horse" the Healer told him, "The warmth of the sun and a good feed should make them go away". It did help for a few hours until the next morning when the pains would come again. He was beginning to feel that he had been set upon by the evil spirits or someone had said the secret words over him to make him age early. Whatever it was he needed to rest, and so he would. They would stay in the mountains for a while, he would rest and he would heal.

Two months passed in the peace and quiet of the mountains. Starreck had begun to relax and some of the pains in his muscles had eased a little now that he wasn't riding every day, the headaches were still there, but not so bad, although the pains in his heart and spine and his stomach were no better and the flashing lights came on every day. The Healer had tried to help but had exhausted his ideas because this was far from injuries and common illness that he had been trained for. There seemed to be no healing plant he knew of that would take away the misery that was beginning to overcome Starreck, and the healer was beginning to think Starreck was right, he had been cursed. When it was obvious that nothing was working the Healer suggested they try to find a Shaman or a Wise Woman to speak to the Spirits and see if they could release Starreck from the constant pains and sickness that was coming over him. He had lost weight and his appetite that was usually healthy was no longer there. His muscles were losing their tightness, his hair was lank and the skin was beginning to sag around his neck and face – he looked old.

Even though these were tough, ruthless men who would kill just for the thrill of it they respected Starreck but more than a few were beginning to think it was time for them to leave and find a stronger leader. Fearful for his master and friend, Marlick sent one of the older members of the Horde of Doom to search the nearby valleys and mountains for a Shaman or Wise Woman. The messenger was told to offer money for their service, not to say who it was for and to hurry. Under no circumstances was he to use force. It was well known that you didn't upset these people, they were to be persuaded not forced, or you would spend the rest of your life in regret for what you had done and it wasn't just Starreck and Marick who were thinking that this was what had caused their leader to become an old man before his time. The messenger was sent on a fast horse with orders not to return until he had fulfilled his task, whether it took one day or many. Starreck seemed to be aging quicker by the day if not the hour. Every day more muscles sagged, he began to limp when he walked and was becoming very bitter and bad tempered. Even Marlick was starting to find things to do elsewhere rather than coming under the glare of his beloved leader. It was better to be doing something useful on the other side of the camp than to see the way Starreck was losing this battle with his body and mind. And it was a battle, a battle that he didn't know how to win. All they could do now was to wait for the messenger to return.

The men were becoming restless. It had been two months of boredom for some of them and many others had drifted away over time. Those who had jobs to do looking after the horses, cooking or repairing saddles and gear were content with the break, the others were beginning to question Starreck's leadership. How could this sick old man lead them now, what about the wealth he had promised them? The restlessness was turning into rebellion and Starreck knew it. He called Marlick to his side one morning to talk about this problem with his men. "Let them go if they want to" Marlick said quietly, "These are fighting men, men who don't know how to be at peace, if they need to fight then let them go", he looked Starreck in the eyes and said quietly, "I will stay by your side and so will some of the others, we would not leave you as you are and we understand that you are not well. Just leave it to me and I will get rid of those who are restless." Starreck nodded, "Tell them that they are free to leave, I owe nobody and they owe me nothing, let them find their own way. But tell them from me, if they tell anyone, even their women, where we are and I find out, they will regret the day they were born. Tell them I will then hunt them down and skin them alive." He sank back into the sheep skins he used to soften his bed and closed his eyes. "It is the beginning of the end," he thought to himself, "the days of raiding and fighting have left me."

Twenty men rode out that day, with their belongings tied to their saddlebags, another 15 left quietly in the night taking their horses higher up into the mountains, heading into the far distance hoping to find their way home back to the coast and Dagrel, the man who ruled the gangs roaming the land. The rest stayed behind. Some of these men had no where else to go, and some of them had become tired of life on the road and, like Starreck, had begun to think of settling down for a while since they were also suffering from headaches and bad dreams thought to be sent by the Gods because of the killing and evil deeds they had carried out. The youngest of these was Benji, only 18 summers, he had only begun to shave his face of hair and had only been with a woman when the men paid for him to spend a few hours with one of the whores in a town they passed through, for his birthday. He looked up to Starreck as his father, his own father had deserted his mother when he was born and she had died of the coughing sickness when he was only 14. Starreck had found him one day walking along the side of the road looking very lost. He thought of the time that Dagrel had taken him under his wing and took the lad along. Benji would stay with Starreck to the end if he could but he had never been a part of the raiding. He told Starreck that he couldn't hurt another human being and was afraid that the men would think him a coward. But Starreck had defended the lad and given him the job of helping the cook, they would stay in camp when the others went out to attack and slaughter, so although Benji knew what was going on he stayed quietly behind and did what he was told.

When the messenger sent to find a healer returned he came over to where Starreck was curled up in his sheep skins. "I know of a healer Starreck, she lives three days' ride from here across the plains and into the hills past the last village we sacked, I think it was called Flessia. This healer lives by herself and has great powers of healing. I came back to let you know that I would be away for a while and that I hadn't deserted you" he said, "I will rest tonight and go tomorrow to fetch her". Starreck thanked the messenger and sank back into his skins. Six more days of pain and misery and he would know what this was that had struck him down. Now all he could do was rest.

10 DAGREL

In the heart of the coastal town of Ban, Dagrel was rising from his bed, hawking and coughing as he crossed to the window. The sun had risen some hours before and he realised that he was hungry. The young girl who had shared his bed for the night was huddled in the far corner wrapped in a sheet crying and nursing her bruises. She gathered her clothes and silently slipped from the room and slunk off into the street to disappear into the crowd. She vowed to get as far away from Dagrel as possible and stay away. He was a cruel monster of a man and he frightened the life out of her.

Dagrel dressed and shouted to his lackey waiting in the outer room. "Bring me food and send a message to Starreck and the others that I want them here tomorrow morning." He would be obeyed, to disobey was not worth the effort. Turning back to the window he looked out to sea not even aware that the girl had left the room. He needed to build up his coffers once again and Starreck owed him big time.

When Erik had killed Jorran and fled before he could be captured, he had stayed on the move for several days. Eventually reaching the town of Ban, he stopped off in a Tavern near the waterfront where Dagrel ran his business. Young Erik looked frightened, dirty and lost, just the sort of person Dagrel would take advantage of. Watching Erik enter the tavern he called the young man over to him and offered him a meal and a pint of ale. It wasn't long before Erik was drunk and the next morning he found himself tucked up in a small bed high above the street overlooking the sea. With constant grooming it was only a matter of time before he had changed into the kind of lad Dagrel needed to lure people down dark alleys and into quiet places where they could be robbed. This had led to bigger and worse crimes as Dagrel raised the boy into manhood. Erik changed his name to Starreck and eventually became the leader of one of Dagrel's marauder gangs. They called themselves the Horde of Doom. Dagrel had several of these gangs working throughout the land, each one independent but answering in the long run to Dagrel. Any loot they couldn't eat or use on the road came back to him to sell on and he would be fairly generous with what he gave in return. Although they mostly hated the man they were also afraid of him. Dagrel ruled with an iron fist.

11 THE SUMMONS

In the village of Flessia Hetia packed her soft brown leather shoulder bag with dried fruit, nuts and the hard bread she made into small loaves for travelling. She added a pouch of healing herbs as was her habit and her crystals then hefted the bag over her shoulder. The crystals were known to strengthen the energy of leaves and roots enabling them to work more powerfully. Wrapping herself in her warmest cloak to ward off the early morning chills, Hetia collected a water gourd and walked out through the door, closing it firmly behind her. The day was yet to begin and the sky was showing the early signs that the sun would rise in an hour or so. Slowly she walked the circle of protection around her house, quietly chanting the ancient words that would deter the curious from entering the house while she was away, for this could be a long journey, then turning she left the village behind her. A plant grew in the hills many days' walk away that was reputed to heal the mind after an incident so traumatic the person's memory disappeared. She had experienced this kind of illness after the first time her village was attacked by the Horde of Doom. One of the women had been brought to Hetia by her distraught husband who was clearly disturbed because his wife could not remember him or their children after she had seen her mother attacked and killed. The wife was saved from the same fate when her husband returned home, but her memory was gone. For over a year her memory had not come back, so her husband could not leave her alone unless there was someone to look after the children. Hetia had heard of a plant that could help the memory return within a few days, and she meant to find it. To find the plant and learn its use she would have to talk to another Healer or Shaman who knew how to use it, as preparing the herb incorrectly could kill instead of heal.

Heading north into the hills, Hetia felt light hearted. Many years had passed since she had enjoyed her own company. There was always someone seeking her out for advice, for healing or just for a chat about something that was troubling them. Many times she had wished to be able to feel nothing more than the pleasures of the earth and sky, the wind in her face and the gentle rain that would clear all heaviness from her. This morning was perfect. The sun had not yet arisen, there was a very light cool breeze, and the birds were just waking up, making their little chortling sounds that would turn to warbling as the sky lightened to day. As Hetia walked, small night animals scuttled under bushes and out of her way, returning to their burrows for the day. "It's alright little ones" she said quietly "I won't hurt you, just go about your business and live in peace." She continued her journey with a smile on her face, and as she walked the trees and bushes around seemed to welcome her. Looking up into an old gnarled tree the branches appeared as strong powerful arms reaching up towards the sky. Leaves were thick at this time of year and created a canopy that appeared to safeguard the walker below. As the breeze pushed the leaves gently aside it touched Hetia's face, cooling and refreshing her skin that had grown warm with walking.

The sun rose and as the day warmed Hetia took the cloak from her shoulders and sat down on a fallen tree, taking a sip of water from her gourd. The fallen tree had left a clearing in the centre of the forest she was walking through and the sun filled the clearing with its early morning light. Yellow wild flowers were growing all over the clearing, as if to soak up as much sun as they could in their short life. Bees had begun their day's work and the gentle hum filled the air. So peaceful was this place that Hetia had half a mind to stay longer. However, after a few moments she stood, stretching and looked around, she was ready to be on her way again. The day felt right, it would be a quiet journey and she was making good time with the path untrodden by others in recent times, she knew the path ahead was clear – "Good, I would prefer not to meet up with anyone today." she said to herself. Walking alone allowed her to reconnect with the Earth, feeling each footfall as a touch of love and peace from the Earth Mother. Thoughts cleared from her mind as she walked and, continuing the journey this way the sounds of the forest faded away allowing her mind to turn inward, stepping forward, trusting the Goddess to keep her on the path and slowly, reconnecting her spirit to the Earth. She lifted her mind from the present, and felt the fresh breeze on her face and hands, she felt the air entering her body as she breathed and absorbed the goodness from the air. Her body was strengthening as she walked and her heart was beating steadily allowing her mind to drift back to a time that seemed so very long

ago.

HETIA

In a clearing deep within the forest behind Flessia the young woman placed objects on the ground to form a circle. She used pine cones, wild fruit, a large shell found a few years back on the edge of the lake beyond the Plains and completed the circle with stones, feathers and twigs. In the centre she stood, very still with eyes closed as she absorbed the sounds of the forest. When her breath calmed the young woman removed her garments slowly, placing them neatly in a pile beside her. Listening once more to the birdsong and the rustling of the trees she began to sway, gently at first then with eyes closed she began to dance. Her arms were moving in slow rhythm, circling, reaching out, up then down to the earth, her movements becoming faster and faster as she felt the power rising within her body and mind. The energy she was building was very strong. Her lessons under the guidance of the Wise Woman were finally at an end and her tattoos, tribal and those of a healer and worker of magic were completed. She was ready to work on her own, ready to find her own way and this was her Ritual, her Rite of Passage, as she danced wildly in the clearing deep within the forest.

As the energy and power built up and reached its peak a shimmer appeared around Hetia. The colours of blue, purple and yellow emanating from her as her bare feet lifted gently from the

Earth raising her bodily into the air. With eyes closed she felt the power, allowing it to hold her, every hair on her body standing on end, nothing holding her above the earth except the power she was generating within. As she felt the power reach it's apex she slowly released it to the Universe and began to float to the Earth once more. Her feet lightly touched the soft cool grass and she dropped slowly to the ground to lie on her belly, arms outstretched, face down. Hetia embraced the Earth, the cool, damp Earth. It was like the touch of a mother. "I give myself to you Earth Mother" she whispered, "I will never give myself to any man, I will nurture you and the plants that grow from your belly. I will use your plants to heal the people and the beasts of this land. I will do this until I pass from this body to rest before rebirth. On your life Earth Mother, I do swear this".

It was several hours later when Hetia returned to the village of Flessia, quietly returning to the house that was now hers by right. The old Wise Woman had passed silently to Spirit while Hetia had been in the forest, so when the young woman entered the house she began to prepare the old woman's body for the Rite of Passing, then to the funeral pyre that was the tradition – no Wise Woman's body was allowed to rot in the ground. Her ashes would be gathered and scattered through the forest. To return to her Mother.

And so Hetia remembered as she walked:

Continuing her journey to visit her friend the Shaman, Hetia walked in a trance-like state for half a day, almost unaware of the distance she had covered, until her body asked for water and food. So it was with pleasure that she found a stream to replenish her water supply and cool her feet. Sitting on a moss covered cool rock, she laid her cloak on the grass beside her and placed her bag on top. She had made good time and it was a beautiful day so she could give herself a rest. After eating some of her rations Hetia lay back on the grass closing her eyes and feeling the warmth of the sun on her face and body while the cool earth beneath moulded to embrace her, like a comfortable feather bed. Sleep came for a short while until a rather noisy bird woke her from her reverie. Rising thoroughly rested she used the sun and her surroundings to work out where she was, realising that she would reach her destination within a few more hours. Hetia was heading for the cottage of a friend who was a Healer and a Shaman with knowledge of the mysterious plant she was searching for. Lifting her hands to the sky, Hetia gave thanks to the Goddess for her safe journey so far and sent out a spirit message to her friend Mariat to let her know she was on her way. It wasn't often that she used this power of thought messages, however, the energy of the forest was powerful and Hetia knew Mariat would enjoy receiving the message.

Mariat was a similar age to Hetia, they had known each other for many years and usually met up at the large gatherings when the villagers from the surrounding hills came together to sell livestock and the goods they made or grew throughout the year. Mariat and Hetia shared a love of the natural flow of life and a peaceful feeling passed between them when they were together. Mariat had the gift of foresight and was able to receive Hetia's spirit messages, so Hetia knew that by the time she arrived at the cottage a hot meal and a warm hearth would be waiting. So when she set off after her rest she headed north at a pleasant pace keeping her mind open and enjoying her surroundings. The trees were now shading her from the warm sun, allowing the breeze to cool her down. The pathway began to widen as if this part of the forest saw travellers more often. Then the dense forest seemed to part, forming a clearing and in the centre of the clearing was a small cottage with a wisp of smoke coming from the chimney. Ivy covered the walls and the roof was thatch which gave the impression that the cottage seemed to grow from the forest into the clearing. The windows were small and homely with lace curtains to filter out the sun. In front of the door hung a wind chime made of hollowed out animal bones, clunking in the breeze. In the garden food was growing, for the occupant liked to keep to herself most of the time. A few chickens wandered about, and a large orange cat was curled up on the door step. He lifted his head to see who the intruder was that had dared to waken him from his afternoon nap and seeing a friend he stretched lazily and curled around Hetia's legs in greeting. "Hello old friend" Hetia said softly, "Is your human friend at home?" The cat purred and led her up the path. The cottage looked homely, welcoming the traveller as she left the forest behind. Before she reached the door Hetia was wrapped in a warm embrace from Mariat who had been baking in anticipation of her visitor. Her apron was covered in flour and pieces of unbaked bread stuck to her fingers. Mariat was the picture of domesticity, so different from Hetia whose efforts in the kitchen revolved around necessity. Mariat's round figure gave the impression that she would be at ease with a flock of children, although she had devoted her life to her work and never married. Fair wavy hair fell out of the cap she wore whilst baking and her round cheeks were rosy from having the oven on to cook the batch of buns and cakes that Hetia looked forward to enjoying with some of the home made jam she knew would be brought from the pantry. Hetia was always comfortable with her friend, it was as if they were meant to be close friends from the start. The two women hugged each other for moments then entered the cottage. This would be a pleasure, an opportunity to drop defences for a while, Hetia could relax.

The inside of the cottage was warm and cosy. Bunches of herbs were hung from the ceiling, drying in the warm air. The smell of freshly baked bread and other delicious odours emanated from the hearth and the sound of a stew bubbling away over the fire created a feeling that made Hetia completely give in to her friend's hospitality. The cat was rubbing himself around Hetia's legs, vying with Mariat for the attention of their visitor. Taking a chair near the fire Hetia took off her travelling shoes and raised her feet to a small stool placed there for such a purpose. The women, comfortable within each other's company, told of the events of the past few months. Day faded into evening as they shared a meal then talked well into the night. Sleep came over Hetia quickly in the soft feather bed she was given. The best sleep she had experienced for a very long time. No dreams disturbed her this night, she didn't wake until the morning sun peeked through the window. It was with pleasure that she joined Mariat out in the garden for a morning meal of bread and honey.

Hetia was pleased that her friend would help her in her quest to find the herbs she sought. There was a place in the mountains, two day's walk away, where the herb could be found. The walk would give them time to talk of the way to prepare and use the herb, so they packed what they needed for the journey into a couple of large bags, slung them over their shoulders and, setting guarding spells around the cottage, made their way to the mountains. Once more the forest seemed to welcome Hetia and her friend. The trees took on a protective feel allowing the women to walk peacefully enjoying the journey. On the second day, sitting by a running stream, Mariat asked Hetia to join her in contacting her Spirit Guide, the only way to find the herb they were seeking. As they sat quietly, a picture formed in Hetia's mind of a beautiful valley, high up in the mountains. There was a very green glade near the base of a cliff where a cave had formed. As she allowed herself to be taken by Spirit she found she was walking along a path that lead through a grassy plain then to the forest and back to where they were sitting. The Spirit Guide had shown them the direction they were to take, so gathering their belongings the two women headed off on what they thought was the last day of their search. The day was peaceful and the path an easy walk. As was shown to them the path led over a grassy plain and in the morning sun the two women had shed their cloaks and donned the wide brimmed straw hats they had both worn at their backs. Reaching the higher ground they searched for the pathway that would lead them up into the mountains. This path was steeper but wide and safe, so with the help of stout branches they made their way slowly upwards.

High in the mountains, following the pathway shown by Spirit, Hetia and Mariat at last came to the place where the herbs were to be found. The sun had reached the horizon and was disappearing for the night, so in the evening light they set up a little camp. Mariat explained to Hetia how the plant grew. "It really is a clever plant," Mariat explained, "During the cold winter months when the snow falls, the plant allows the top to die off, leaving only the roots to feed on the earth. Then when Spring melts the snow the herb grows back again, remembering exactly where it lay on the ground before Winter. We will gather only the old leaves, leaving the young ones to feed and grow. Once we have gathered the leaves we will dry them and I will explain the incantations you will need to learn in order to use the herb properly. If you use it without the incantations then whoever takes the herb could die, quickly." In the morning they gathered the leaves together, Mariat showing Hetia the correct way to take them in order not to hurt the plant. The gathering took many hours as they wandered along the valley, they would need a fair supply as it was not easy to do this journey often. Tying the bunches of leaves together they hung them from a low growing tree to dry out. Over the next two days they practised the incantations, making sure that Hetia knew them by heart, for no incantations were ever to be written down. It was a peaceful place in the valley high above the forests, perfect for the learning of lore.

During their absence a rider had arrived at Mariat's cottage. The man leapt down from his horse and was making his way up the path when he was stopped dead in his tracks by an invisible force. Knowing that this was the cottage of a Shaman he stepped back, calling out. The only answer he received was a hissing sound from the large orange cat curled up on the pathway. Turning to the cat he said "I don't suppose you can tell me where she has gone, I shall have to find out for myself" he walked around outside the garden until he found footprints leading off into the forest, two sets of footprints. Noting their size and other signs, he figured out they were both women and began to follow their trail.

As the morning sun crept over the edge of the mountains turning the dull colours of morning into the bright hues of day, Hetia and Mariat began their return journey with bags full of the dried herb to be used to restore the memory of those who were the victims of The Horde of Doom's attacks. Used incorrectly though this herb could strip the mind of its memory leaving the person like a child with no knowledge of the years in between. Care was always taken with these remedies. The path down from the mountains was fairly steep, rubble had gathered on the unused ground, forcing the two women to walk slowly and continue their discussion of other healing herbs that required a Shaman's knowledge. Hetia respected Mariat's knowledge and showed deference to her when they spoke of such things. As they reached the lower slopes they were so engrossed in their conversation that they failed to hear the approach of a rider who pulled up in front of them. Startled, the two women stepped back to see who this person was who had rudely approached without a hail or comment. About to let loose a tirade to the man, Hetia was cut off before the first word left her. "Are you Mariat the Shaman?" the man shouted down from his horse, "If you are then I need you to come with me straight away, my master is dying and we don't know what else to do. Ask your price, I am instructed to pay you what you ask."

Hetia, taken aback at this sudden and loud request, turned to Mariat and allowed a silent thought to pass between them. '*Do you know this man?*' the thought emerged in Mariat's mind, '*No, but I am sure we are about to find out who he is.*' Turning to the man Hetia spoke, "Who is your master and why do you speak to us so?" The messenger climbed down from his horse, took a breath and softened his face as he spoke more quietly. "I apologise, my master lies ill in the mountains, he has some kind of wasting illness and although our healer has tried it is obvious that his skills are not enough. He seems to be aging before our eyes and we don't want to lose him. He is our leader and teacher. "Does your leader and teacher have a name?" Hetia asked, "Of course" answered the messenger, "His name is Starreck and we live in the mountains. Can you please come, I don't know who else to turn to". Hetia looked at Mariat and the silent words that passed between them spoke of an agreement to help if they could. "First of all, I am not Mariat, this beautiful friend of mine is, and secondly you do not need to offer us riches to come and help, but we do want your word that we will not be harmed in any way and that you will return us to our home when we have done all we can".

"Agreed," said the messenger, "my master has promised this and I pass on his words. But hurry as each day he grows much worse."

They began the trek back to Mariat's cottage where she could gather together her healing "tools" then they made their way towards the mountains where Starreck and his men were camped. The journey was no longer pleasant for the two women as it had been on the way to gather herbs. The cool forest trees seemed to be warning Hetia of danger, of an energy she would meet. She couldn't put her finger on it but something told her that she should be very, very careful. The messenger was not the danger, he was courteous, friendly and did what he could to make the journey easier, even though he looked rough and just a little edgy. Hetia sensed more. Alert now, she began to attune herself to the Earth, grounding her energy for what may come. Mariat was doing the same. The messenger walked beside his horse in order to stay at the pace of the two women and an easy companionship developed over the miles. Talk of the seasons, the beauty of the mountains and the bountiful gifts the Goddess bestowed on her followers. It seemed that the messenger was relieved to spend time talking of ordinary things in the company of women, for it appeared that he spent most of his life with men. He didn't once talk of what his people did, he became elusive any time the women broached the subject so they decided to leave it and find out for themselves. They knew they had the powers to overcome any normal attack or danger for simple use of Hedge Magic was the easiest to use. Four days later they walked up through the pass, the sides of the mountains like walls of a fortress on either side, guiding them to the camp where Starreck lay. As they came to a point where the trail lost sight of the camp for a moment four men leapt out from behind the rocks grabbing Hetia and Mariat from behind. The messenger tried to stop this but he was overcome by another man who had waited for this moment. "Let us have these two" they said to the messenger, "we reckon they are responsible for Starreck's illness and if they get a chance up there at the camp they will probably finish him off." The messenger struggled free and very angrily said, "I promised them there would be no harm to them and I'll bet Starreck doesn't know you are doing this." The other men sneered at him and one spat out the word "coward". "I am no coward but I also know that these two were given Starreck's word they wouldn't be harmed." At that one of the men came from behind and hit the messenger over the head, knocking him unconscious. "Take these two and tie them up" the one who seemed to be in charge sneered, "we will deal with them tonight. They are women aren't they? I haven't seen a woman for months cooped up here in the mountains and I'm not afraid of this pair." Laughing he left the tying up to the others and made his way back to the camp. The one who had been knocked out was also tied up and the three of them were left far enough away from the camp so that if they called out no one would hear them. As the day darkened Hetia had worked herself loose of her bindings and was freeing Mariat. "I think I have worked out who these lot are" she said quietly, "but I want to see the man we were brought here to heal before I do anything about it. Are you alright Mariat?" "Yes I am fine" she answered, "but our friend here seems to have taken a nasty blow. Let me see what I can do for him, you keep an eye out for those others, we don't want them to come back and find us free. No, he is alright, just still out of it. I am sure they will come back for him but we should untie him first." Letting the messenger go the two women used the dark shadows and some basic magic to blend in with the rocks and make their way towards the camp. The camp-

123

fire made it hard for anyone in the camp to see out into the dark so they were able to get quite close. They could see that on the edge of the fire there was a man lying on a bed of skins and he was being attended by another man who was helping him to eat. Passing silent words between them Hetia and Mariat had decided to use the ignorance of magic to work to their advantage and suddenly 'appeared' beside Starreck's bed. This caused such a fright that the men all dropped their plates of food and backed away. "They are witches" one yelled out, "I told you so. We should have killed them not tied them up." At this Marlick turned on the men demanding to know what was going on. He took hold of the weakest of the men and threatened to cut his throat if he didn't tell him what had happened. After only moments the whole story came out. They begged forgiveness as cowards do when they are caught out, and said they were only trying to protect Starreck. Furious with the men Marlick turned to Hetia and Mariat. "I am so very sorry for this ladies, I told them you were not to be harmed and now I find out they had no intention to leave you alone. Please, know that this was not Starreck's idea." He turned on the men once again - "Get out of here you lot. Go now, get your horses and gear and leave. You are not to turn around, you are to go and do not come back. The last thing Starreck needs now is idiots like you making things worse. Go now."

Starreck had grown even more thin and fragile than he had been before the messenger left. Seeing his distress Mariat immediately went to his side with Hetia behind her. Hetia looked deeply into Starreck's fading eyes, a sense of recognition passed through her mind, however, she decided to keep this to herself for the moment, not quite sure why, but knowing that it was important. Mariat passed her hands over his fragile body, feeling his energy to see if she could find where his illness was centred. As she came to his heart she felt a strong darkness. Moving on, keeping this thought between her and Hetia she found also that the energy of his lower belly was also dark, almost clammy. The energy she was feeling was not that of a just and fair person, it reeked of violence, regret and sadness. Feeling that she needed to talk quietly to Hetia of her findings she left Starreck's side telling him that she needed to contact the Spirits for advice. The women moved off to the area they were shown to set up their camp and began to bring the energy of Spirit into the small area. They quietly raised a protective barrier around their little encampment so they would be safe within its boundaries. There would be time to gather their thoughts before they needed to begin any healing and this gave them leave to observe the camp and its inhabitants. The men, knowing this as work of Shamans, left them alone to their chanting and incantations.

In the safety of their own small camp, Hetia spoke to Mariat that she knew this man, Starreck. "I was a maiden, in training with a wise woman, and I met a young man whose name I did not hear, he was handsome and I was young, but it was never to be and we went our separate ways. I am sure that this is that young man, but his energy is so different now. In that brief encounter I met a young man who had felt a great sadness, but there was no violence in him. Some great tragedy must have befallen him over the years. However, I believe that I have read his thoughts and those of some of his men. I think we have managed to fall into the hands of The Horde of Doom and its leader." With this knowledge Mariat quietly answered her friend, "Then we must be very careful that we don't let him die, at least not while we are here". Hetia nodded and added, "And I know why he is so ill. After the sacking of Flessia I spent some time gathering knowledge of The Horde of Doom and its leader who I now know is Starreck. I collected some small items that had been left behind by them along the way and spoke the ancient words to bring them down, especially the leader. I devised this illness Mariat, and I am probably the only one to take it away, although I know there were other curses sent his way by a few more of my kind. We must keep this to ourselves for a while as we think over what can be done to stop this violence". "Agreed" answered Mariat "at least now I know why he is ill, we can use this but we must be very careful. If anyone has any idea who did this then we are in deep trouble".

The women had been together for quite some time, making movements that seemed strange to the men in the camp. None of them understood the way of the Shaman, not even their healer who was learned in the use of plants and mending broken bodies. With a bowl of water, some herbs and Hetia's crystals the women walked slowly to Starreck, sitting down beside the pile of sheepskins that had been placed around him to ease the pains. "We will do our best" said Mariat, "It will depend on the depth of the curse that has been placed upon you, for a curse is what you are suffering from. I will try, for it is my way that I try to heal anyone who comes to me for help. No matter who they might be." Starreck looked up to her and saw in her eyes that she had knowledge of him that she was not speaking of. A shiver went through his bones as he realised that he was entirely at her mercy, because no matter what she did to him, right then he was as helpless as a new born babe. He found he could not move or talk, he could only breathe, his heart was fluttering very fast and the blood seemed to be draining from his veins. Whatever was happening at this moment, he could not call for help nor fight back. This feeling was not coming from the woman Mariat but from the other woman who's name he did not hear, but she seemed familiar somehow. She had him pinned down, as if he was tied down to the ground and struck dumb, although there were no bindings that he could perceive. Panic began to rise within him as he gave himself in to these two women who would either save him or slay him.

Smoke drifted up from the incense being burnt around the still form of Starreck, a pot put to heat on a small fire held herbs taken from Mariat's bag. The two women had silently 'spoken' in their thoughts and had come to realise that if they let Starreck die they might be in trouble with the other men in the camp. Silently the women decided to wait a few days and allow him to seem to recover a little. The herbs they had gathered to use on those whose minds had turned could also be used to change a person's way of thinking. With a little help from incantations, they would try to change Starreck's thoughts back to a time when he was young, before he turned to the life of violence. There would be a peaceful soul in there somewhere, and the herbs would help that soul to come back to the fore. It would be necessary to give him some of the herbal tea then silently say the incantations over him. Turning to Marlick who was sitting a short distance away Mariat said, "We will give him a drink to allow him to sleep until tomorrow. He should then be able to tell us a little to help us to remove this energy that is binding him. Please make sure he is not disturbed until he wakes naturally and then let us be the only ones to speak with him". Marlick agreed and went to tell the men they were to stay back out of the way. A small amount of the tea was dribbled into Starreck's mouth, which he swallowed, and as he drifted off into a dreamless sleep the women went to their little camp to rest.

Being left alone for the night Hetia and Mariat were rested and refreshed when they awoke the next morning. They had been in deep conversation well into the night, making plans for the next day before falling asleep. One of the men brought them a meal of porridge and honey in the morning which they ate slowly to gain time. They were ready for the next step in their plan to free the countryside of The Horde of Doom. It wasn't long before Starreck began to stir and Marlick, who had spent the night by his side, called the women to him. "He has awakened and his eyes are much brighter" he said, "I will leave you to do what you must" then he walked away to see to his horses and to look after his own food, leaving them in peace.

Mariat began by offering Starreck the herbal tea, telling him it was a pain relieving drink. As he was sipping the hot tea Hetia and Mariat silently spoke the incantations that would make the memory herb work in the way they required. After a few minutes they looked down on him, "Well Starreck," said Hetia, "I believe you have been giving everyone a very bad time lately. Your biggest mistake was to keep attacking Flessia because I became very angry with you over that. It is my village and they are my people and you were like a plague that had to be removed. Your second biggest mistake was the old man with the tattoos that began to gather the magic of the land and those who could wield it, he was the enemy you would never even think of. Would you have anything you would like to say about that before we take our remedy further?" Starreck looked into the eyes of the woman who had held him prisoner the day before. "I suppose I am at your mercy." he said weakly, realising what was happening to him "Maybe it is time I passed from this world before I become a person that even I would despise." "Oh no you don't" hissed Hetia, "I would like to know a bit more about the man who changed from a beautiful innocent youth to what I see before me today. What have you to say for yourself?" Suddenly recognition hit Starreck, "I know who you are." he whispered "You are the girl who has haunted my dreams for many years. I am so sorry I could not stay longer that day in the hills, it was a day that changed my life forever." Then as the memory herb began its' work, he told her in a broken voice the reason he was on the road so many years ago. He told her of catching his mother's killer and the years of carnage that followed. He also told her of his recent regrets then emotion rose within him and tears rolled uncontrollably down his cheeks as he told her that he would give anything to make up to the people he had wronged, but he thought that death and an eternity of being withheld from the protection and peace of the Gods, was his just reward.

As Hetia and Mariat listened to Starreck's words they sent silent words to one another. 'I really believe that he means it' Mariat sent to Hetia's mind, 'Perhaps we should give him the opportunity to atone in some way.' 'I understand your reasoning' sent Hetia 'however, it is not our decision to allow forgiveness, it is the decision of the people who have been devastated by so many years of violence' She turned to Starreck, "You say you would give anything. We can lift this sickness from you, however, if you wish to regain full strength we will not do this until you have faced the people that you and your men have terrorised all these years. It will be difficult, they will probably want to take your life. However, the choice is yours. We can heal you sufficiently to ride to a meeting of the elders, where you can state your case. It is their way to listen to what you say as they believe it is your right to speak up for yourself, then they will decide if you live or die. They will probably seek retribution in some way as you have caused much pain to their people. If you agree to this we will begin to remove some of the bindings, then you can come with us, alone, to face your fate. Otherwise, we will leave you to die. If any of your men think they can make us heal you completely tell them to think twice before attacking a Shaman and Wise Woman. Our powers are very deep indeed as you can attest".

Starreck looked into Hetia's eyes and realised that these words were true. There was a very deep mystery there in her eyes, something ancient and strong. "I will give instructions as you say and you will be left alone. I will go with you before your elders. I have never faced death in this way before, I can face a sword, beasts and any other danger, but this wasting away is the worst danger I have ever faced. Please, I beg of you, do as you will and I will stand before your Elders." He called Marlick to him and quietly told his man what was happening to him. Marlick, in his quiet way, understood and nodded, he touched Starreck on the arm gently and went over to the men. There was quite a fuss as the men raised their voices in protest at the thought of their leader being taken away so quietly to his fate. They did not want him to face it alone and began to look menacingly at the two Wise Women. Marlick calmed them down and gave them orders to break up camp. The Horde of Doom had finally been disbanded and they were to all go their own way. A few who had been with Starreck from the start held back, not wanting to leave the man they followed, but Marlick assured them that he would not let Starreck face his fate on his own, that he would go as far as he could with him. This seemed to satisfy the men and they began the task of packing up several months of camp, distributing the gear they had gathered and riding off in twos and threes. The loyalties of men such as these were not strong, most would find a new leader or take to the road on their own. Most headed towards the coast to meet up with Dagrel.

Marlick came back to where Starreck was lying, with Hetia and Mariat sitting on the ground at his side. "The men have agreed and are leaving to go their own way. However," and he faced the women with his calm countenance, "I will go with you to face the Elders. Please don't protest, it won't do you any good. First of all, Starreck, you are in no fit state to get about without help, and there are things that I can do for you that the women can't. I will also stand by you through to the end as I have done all these years and nothing any of you can say or do will stop me. I am coming." He sat down at the end of Starreck's bed waiting for someone to speak. "Well I suppose that's decided then" said Hetia, "I will admit that the thought of hitching Starreck's weight up onto a horse didn't appeal to me and as you say there are things you can do for a man that we might find a bit distasteful. However, you are under the same fate as Starreck. You will face the Elders and take their decision. Otherwise, you will also succumb to the same mysteries as your leader here and you know I can do this". It was agreed, so the women began the incantations to remove some of the "spell" that was binding Starreck. Leaving just enough to keep him weak but able to ride and walk, they bid him rise from his bed. For the first time in weeks he was able to stand without aid but with no strength in his body to do more than walk slowly. They began to pack up the camp, they would make the journey back down out of the mountains.

They didn't notice Benji in the shadows silently watching, his mind made up that he would follow Starreck, intent on guarding his hero. Moving quietly to his horse that he had tied away from the camp, he wrapped rags around the metal on his reins and saddle to silence them and packed his gear. Waiting among the trees until Starreck was taken away, he began his lonely vigil following just a short distance behind.

12 THE SEER AND THE WARRIOR

On the broad Plains of Parlat some distance from Flessia, a camp was being set up. In the centre of the camp a circle of logs was formed to act as seating for the Elders on their way from villages as far away as the mountains, many days walk from this new camp. Men began arriving herding animals they would slay, these would be prepared for cooking and mounted on mighty spits then turned slowly over the fire by a succession of boys too young to be hunters or warriors. The exercise was considered excellent for developing muscles they would need to be strong in their growth to manhood. Other provisions began to arrive on wagons along with those who would prepare and serve the huge amount of food required, for there would be many folk arriving to take part in the gathering. The people were to come to a decision as to what could be done to rid the country of the Horde of Doom once and for all. Too many lives had been lost and too many homes had been burned, it was time to put a stop to the carnage. By night time the camp was filling up with people, horses, dogs and shelters. Even though the reason they were at the meeting was life threatening, it gave the people a chance to catch up with old acquaintances. The camp fires burned brightly as stories were told, tales of bravery and fear, of lost friends and kin. It was late into the night before silence fell.

Early the next morning, before the sun appeared over the mountains, the Elders came forward to take their places in the circle. With the village Shamans and Spirit Leaders sitting in place behind each Elder the circle was complete. The Elder of Flessia, the eldest of all the Elders of the land, strode into the centre of the circle holding in his hand the Staff of Attention. The circle ceased their chatter and turned their eyes to the Elder of Flessia. Holding the Staff high he asked his Spirit Leader to beg the indulgence and blessings of the goddess on the meeting. Once this was performed the Staff was passed around as each Elder had their say about the problem at hand. There were angry words interlaced with calm advice as the stories were told. Many villages were in ruins and many were ready to gather strength and go forth to find their enemy rather than wait until the next attack. As the Staff reached the tall aged Shaman with feathers in his hair and many tattoos upon his face he stood, and gathering together his thoughts he looked up into the sky and begged the blessings of Father Sun. He then looked around the circle with his many, many years showing upon his lined old face and spoke loud and clear to the awaiting group. "The Horde entered my village some time ago, they were led by a man, tall, dark haired riding a very strong stallion. This man who seemed to be the leader in all ways would not let his men attack me for he saw about me that air of mystery that seems to frighten people who do not understand that we are by nature a peaceful people. They seemed to take into account my tattoos, my look and my stature and (laughing quietly) they didn't seem to want to mess with me. Before they came my people had left the village and they took with them their valuables, their cattle and other livestock and went into hiding. I was the only one there and I can tell you now that these raiders do not want to argue with magic. They do not want to argue or have anything to do with the things they don't understand. I do believe that the best thing that we can do to rid ourselves of this menace once and for all is to utilise what power that we do have. Perhaps we could enlist the aid, at this stage, of other Shamans like myself and our Wise Women and perhaps between us we can show you how you can use the powers that nature provides to bring down these people once and for all. I am a gentle man, I have spent my many years trying to heal and look after people who are less able to look after themselves and I do know that there are many others like myself. One such person is Hetia from the village of Flessia and I am sure that many of you are aware of this powerful woman. I suggest right now that we put our energy into bringing together those who can use their powers to 'gently' persuade these evil people to change their ways. Perhaps we can teach them to be peaceful, although I believe most of them are beyond this solution." At this last comment a few people around the circle smiled and were amused at the words of this very elderly man. "No, I do believe that we have to stop them altogether." he added " I do not condone killing them even though they have killed many of our people. This would only succeed in bringing our peaceful ways down to their level of thinking. There are many ways to put an end to violence and I am sure that this peaceful country we live in would lend its energies to our work. We must find a permanent solution though, although we may be just delaying the return of evil at a later time."

When the old Shaman took his seat once again another in the circle took the staff, standing and nodding his head in agreement with the old man. "I think this is a very good idea," he said "we should use the talent that we have but first of all perhaps we could find someone who can pull us all together into a useful group. We all have different ways of using our natural born gifts and perhaps we can find someone who can help us teach some basic protections to our people. So I agree and think it is a very good idea to use the talents of the Shamans, Wise Women and natural magic to finally rid ourselves of this menace." From this moment there was much agreement and quite a lot of suggestions from others standing behind the elders. It was well past dusk before a decision was made as to the action they needed to take.

"I know of a warrior with knowledge of magic drawn from the Earth, Wind, Water and Air," offered one of the Elders. "he was called upon to help the land past the northern mountains when they were going through a terrible drought. I have heard stories of his prowess. Tribes and leaders have called upon him to help fight against evil and it is said that he has amazing powers to overcome the mightiest enemy. Evil beings are known to tremble at the very presence of the man. However, in order to find this warrior, whose name is Artiane, we will need the help of a strong Seer, for he can only be sought through the spirit world as he spends his life in the deep forests." "Thank you" replied Flessia's Elder, "please send word throughout the camp until such a Seer is found."

The next morning, tall and stately, dark robes flowing behind her, an elegant young woman strode through the camp to face the Elders. She wore tattoos in the style of a Seer and had an amulet of clear crystal around her neck. "You need my help" the Seer, Satiane stated, "I will do what I can for you. Tell me who or what it is that you seek." "We seek the warrior Artiane" replied one of the Elders. "We need his skills to show us how to fight the evil that has beset us. Can you help?" The Seer smiled to herself at their request and made her way to the centre of the circle. There she sat upon the log placed for her and closed her eyes. Those in the circle sat in silence for some length of time whilst the seer went into what seemed like a deep trance, then suddenly she opened her eyes, stood up and announced, "The one you seek is far to the south, in a sacred grove. He seeks to further his knowledge of the forest so he will stay there for some time. If you wish I will travel to the Sacred Grove and speak with him. Let me know what you require of me." then she turned on her heel and as suddenly as she had appeared in the circle, she strode back to her tent to await the Elders' instructions.

"Well, what are we waiting for" called out one of the Elders, "I suggest we send one warrior from each village with the seer, this will ensure that she will be safe on her journey. We should ask her to start first thing tomorrow morning." All agreed and the meeting was disbanded for the day, the Elder of Flessia making his way to the Seer to give her their decision. Exhausted from the long meeting the night before, the Elders went to rest in the camp before returning to their villages the following day. Now the people felt that at last they might have a fighting chance against the Horde of Doom that had terrorised them for so many years.

There was a feeling of hope in the air that next day as the camp on the Plains turned to more everyday tasks. The people who had accompanied the Elders had brought along goods in the hope of trading and set out their wares on the grass. To many folk this was an opportunity to make up for those things that had been lost in the last raid. Personal items of jewellery and clothing were sought out. There were well made hunting knives and bows for sale, leather boots and belts. Although there was still so much to achieve before peace could be found in the land, the daily necessities had to be dealt with if life was to be anything close to normal. Some of the older people had memories of peaceful times, most of the young did not. There were children running happily through the grass who had never known what it was like not to live under the threat of constant danger.

Meanwhile the group who, along with Satiane, had left at first light that next morning to find the warrior Artiane. They were well on their way as the sun began it's descent behind the mountains at the end of that first day. The Seer was an excellent rider as were most of the people of the area, so they were able to make good time. On the first night they camped beneath a huge oak tree, its broad spreading branches sheltering them from the dew fall. Satiane felt the presence of the huge tree and the many travellers who had made camp beneath her shelter. The ground was cool and soft and covered with moss where Satiane chose her sleeping place. The warriors set to the task of feeding and rubbing down the horses so Satiane offered to make the evening meal. She had always enjoyed cooking, it gave her pleasure to smell the aroma as the food bubbled within the pot placed over a low fire. They had brought with them all they would need, dried meat and a few root vegetables mixed with a handful of grains, so Satiane had walked about the little camp and found some wild herbs to add to the meal. With the horses settled for the night the warriors wandered over as the night air carried the delicious smell. However as they were still within the reach of the Horde of Doom guards were posted. Halfway through the night the guards were relieved so that everyone was refreshed in the morning. It would be a long journey travelling at full speed but the warriors were in agreement that Satiane's cooking definitely made the journey more pleasant.

Each morning the Seer spent the first waking moments in trance tracing Artiane's journey. On the second day she felt his presence as he in turn sensed her probing thoughts. 'Why are you following me?' the thought came back to her from Artiane, 'I was trying to contact my Spirit Guide and I felt instead your presence in my mind. Can you tell me who you are, and why you are searching for me?' Satiane smiled to herself, this was not the first time she had felt this particular presence. 'We need your help' she sent the thought through the morning air, 'my people are in great difficulties and we are coming to ask for your assistance. If we keep up the pace of the past two days when can we expect to catch up with you?' The thoughts that came back to her were familiar and the words that came back were simple. 'You will probably find me in two days' and I will try to come towards you as well. I look forward to catching up with you again my love.' The Seer smiled at this for she knew who the Artiane was.

Many years had passed since their last meeting. There was no wonder she was able to contact his mind for Artiane was her brother.

As they left their camp on this day the leader of the warriors who rode with Satiane the Seer scanned the horizon for any signs of danger. He noted the wisps of dust rising in the distance and vowed to keep a sharp lookout. As he knew of the prevalence of 'dust devils' in the Plains, he was not too concerned, but it was not wise to be complacent when they were so far from home. The long grass swayed in the breeze, and it was long enough for someone to be able to lie flat and hide, but not high enough to hide a horse. Just before he turned his eyes to search in a different direction the warrior noted a small herd of deer taking off from their feeding place, the dust had been of their making so the warrior relaxed a little, but he knew the deer may have been spooked by something else in the long grass so he watched carefully to see if there was any other movement. Scanning the bowl of the Plains he saw no other danger, only an eagle soaring high above, seeking its prey. They mounted and went on their way.

As Satiane and her warriors travelled on they found themselves in unknown territory. The familiar

Plains were left behind and the ground became uneven. The trail began twisting and turning to avoid gullies and dry stream beds. There were tales passed down around campfires of a time when water flowed freely in this place. The skeletons of old trees hinted at a time of lush growth and it was believed that these dry plains were once productive farmland. Every child was told of the Climate Catastrophe centuries ago and how the air became hotter until everything dried out. Eventually the Earth had changed, the air settled back to a reasonable temperature and people adapted. Satiane remembered her mother's stories, handed down through the ages, it was said that the only way to prevent it from happening again was to tell the story to each generation. She could see, in this place, how the land had been so different to what it was today.

The party rode fast for the next two days, only stopping when the light faded as it was not wise to put the horses at risk of stepping into a hole or tripping over tree roots. The road they travelled was narrow as it made its' way towards the forest. The warriors watched the ground as they went, to make sure no rider had gone before in recent times. The only signs were from the feet of the deer as they made their way into the hills. At the end of the second day the group entered a dark and dense forest.

The pathways were narrow with overhanging branches that could knock a rider from his horse, so they dismounted and led the horses carefully into the forest. As they went deeper there was a strange eeriness in the air as the long thick branches of the trees met above them to shut out what light was left of the day. It would be difficult to go very far in the failing light, so as the day was nearly ended they decided to set up camp. Coming to a small clearing with a stream bubbling gently as it made its' way from the hills above, they began their preparations for the night. There was plenty of water and grass for the horses, so they were hobbled and let loose for the night. Satiane felt that perhaps it would not be long before Artiane arrived, so she settled down to build a small fire and prepare a simple meal. It was well into the evening and the fire was banked for the night, when a shadow appeared at the edge of the clearing.

Cloaked and hooded in darkest green he stood silently, blending into the darkness of the trees as if he was part of the forest. Many years of discipline had enabled Artiane to walk without even breaking a fallen twig. No stone would be disturbed and small creatures had nothing to fear from this man so they did not feel threatened. The earth beneath his feet welcomed the steps as he gently made his way, his feet shod in the soft skin of a deer he had found dead of old age. His boots encased his feet and were tied to his shins with the same leather, protecting him from sharp nettles and twigs. Across his shoulder, sitting on his hip was a bag made from the same deer skin. He had thanked the spirit of the dead deer for providing him with these objects necessary for a man walking the earth. Within the bag were the dried fruit and nuts that sustained him during his quest for knowledge in the forest along with herbs and small flasks of oils that he would use if he came across an animal that needed his skills as a healer. Hanging from his long hair were the symbols of his gathered power. There was a long eagle feather for strength and a softer one from an owl for wisdom. Tattoos of strange symbols on his face and arms signified to any who met Artiane that this was a man of the forests who was schooled in the Shamanic ways. He was part of the forest.

No sentry had seen or heard Artiane approach the camp. Satiane was facing the opposite direction when her face broke into a smile. She rose gracefully from the log she was sitting on and turned to embrace her brother. The sentries, startled at his arrival with not a sound to break the silence of the night, drew weapons and closed in on the stranger. Satiane waved them back as she walked towards the newcomer, "It has been a very long time" she said smiling, "I thought you were across the sea or had travelled to some other faraway place as I have not sensed your energy for many years". "Yes" Artiane replied "Sometimes I forget the passing of time and many moons can come and go as I become involved in some new challenge. This time I was visiting with the People of the Forest, some call them the Elves, to learn of their uncanny connection with the trees. I learned many things from them and from the Dryads who inhabit this Forest. Trees can be elusive some times." Satiane laughed at this comment for when they were children her mother was forever calling Artiane down from the huge oak tree that grew behind their cottage.

Arm in arm, matching each other in height and build, Artiane and Satiane came to sit by the fire. The Seer introduced her brother to the others in the group, happy that she didn't need to probe a stranger's mind to discover whether or not he would be easy to work with. She knew this man so well as they were inseparable as children. The discussion turned to the reason for their summoning of Artiane, each warrior telling the tale of their own village's encounter with the Horde of Doom. Sadness showed in their eyes as they remembered loved ones now lost forever, and the fear and destruction of their people over many years. Reliving these events was very hard, for every one of them had lost at least one family member or friend. Even Satiane as she had lost her lover three years back and the memory brought tears to her eyes and sadness to her heart. His final words of love were remembered from when she found him dying of vicious wounds following an attack by the Horde of Doom. The sky was becoming light above the treetops by the time they bedded down for a few hours rest, for that day they would need to head back towards home, the first part of their journey completed.

In the morning Artiane rose from his sleep early and let out a long whistle. From the forest a beautiful grey mare trotted into the clearing. She was bare of saddle or reins and came straight up to Artiane nudging him with her soft muzzle and murmuring gentle sounds of greeting. "I would like some breakfast before we travel" he said softly into her ear "You may have been munching on fresh green grass but that is not enough for this warrior." He smiled and walked to where the others were sharing food and helped himself. "I am ready when you are" he told the others, "The sooner we move the better." Returning to the mare he wrapped his arm around her neck, holding her gently for a moment then spoke quietly to her. He turned and as he walked back to Satiane the mare followed behind. Satiane waved her hand to the warriors to show they were ready to leave and they all headed back out of the forest to begin the journey home. The first few hours were slow as they led their horses through the denser part of the forest then reaching the open grass they mounted, Artiane's fingers intertwined in the mare's long mane, then the lead warrior once again scanned the horizon. This time the way seemed clear, so they gave the horses their heads and sped across the plains. The day was warm, with a bright blue sky enabling the travellers to enjoy the ride and by the end of the first day on the Plains they had covered many miles which gave them plenty of time to have a good night's rest. Not so many stories were told this night as they curled up in their blankets, they were glad to be returning home where they could protect their people.

Artiane lay looking up at the sky, the stars twinkling in the clear night. He gave thanks to the Spirits and the Goddess for his safe journey and glanced at his sister who had dropped into a gentle slumber. Lying in the quiet of the night he allowed his mind to wander back to their childhood. As her older brother Artiane had wanted to guard his little sister, but she would have none of it. Her gift of sight had developed very young so if danger was present she would usually sense it before he did, grabbing him by the hand and pulling him towards home. He thought back to the moments when they would use their thoughts to 'talk' to one another to the bewilderment of their parents. It made him smile, thinking of how they would suddenly leap up and take off, calling back to their mother or father that they would return safely. Most of their plans were made silently around the mealtimes or in the early morning so the sudden exit at the end of the meal or as they rose from sleep came unexpectedly to their patient parents. He dearly loved Satiane, although they didn't see so much of each other these days, he knew she would let him know if ever she needed her big brother.

The attack came in the early hours of the morning. The guards that had been set didn't hear it coming, neither did Artiane or Satiane for the attack was not what they had expected. There was no sound of horses or men, only the sudden onslaught as the guards were attacked from the gloom of the night. Woken suddenly the rest of the travellers grabbed weapons and launched themselves at the attackers. There were only three of them so it wasn't long before the warriors were able to capture the attackers and bring them to their knees. These were desperate men, on the run by the way of them. "You will tell me who you are and where you are from" demanded the warrior leader, "if you do not then you will not be put to death – yet – you will be made to talk sooner or later." Satiane laid a hand on the warrior's arm. "Wait a moment," she said quietly, "there are other ways to find out what they are up to. Please let me have a moment". The warrior, knowing her to be a Seer, stepped back but with his knife held closely to the man's neck. "Now" said Satiane to the attacker, "I am going to find out what is going on."After a few moments she stood back and looked at the warriors. "These three men are on their way to meet up with the Horde of Doom. It seems that they lost their horses in the forest because they are too stupid to hobble them overnight so they thought to take three of ours. However, they are to meet with a man called Dagrel who has taken over the Horde since their other leader became ill and disappeared, so now we know who we are dealing with. They are very scared of this Dagrel so I take it he is a nasty piece of work. However, they only know that Dagrel is leading his gang to a place on the other side of the mountains to our Plains with the intention of reforming and starting up all the misery once again. It seems that they know very little more as they

have been travelling some time to reach their destination."
Turning to the warrior leader she said, "You can do what
you like with these three, there isn't much more they can
tell us." Tying the three by the hands it was decided to
take them along and allow the Elders to decide what
should be done, so it was a slow journey back from then
on but with some knowledge of where the Horde was
gathering.

By the time the group finally reached the place
where the meeting had been held several days ago, most of
the villagers had left for their homes. Crops needed to be
tended and work had to be done. The only ones left were
the warriors, Elders and their attendants, with the warriors
taking over the task of running the camp. The riders
handed their three prisoners to the Elders gathered there
and the horses over to one of the younger warriors,
although Artiane's mare, having no reins, remained with
him, following him around like a quiet shadow. Turning to
the mare Artiane whispered a few quiet words to her and
she turned to follow the other horses. He would see to her
needs as soon as he was able, but he smiled, as he knew
from old that she would probably persuade someone else
with nudges and blubbery kisses to feed her while they
tended the other horses. They had been together for a long

time and he knew the mare was very independent when it came to her appetite. As Artiane and Satiane walked to where the elders had formed a circle, the Elders greeted the warrior and thanked him for coming to their aid. "We are glad to see you here and we will deal with the three prisoners in time. Now that we have some idea of our enemy we can plan our defence. We need your help to fight this scourge" the Elder of Flessia explained. "We are not strong enough to fight them on our own. Our warriors are few and only when all the villages join together are we strong enough to fight. The problem is that the Horde of Doom usually attacks a single village and they don't have time to get help from the warriors from other villages. Most of our warriors are also our hunters, so they are often away finding meat for the village. How can we fight an enemy that appears out of nowhere and is gone by the time we send for help?" Artiane listened to this and other pleas from the Elders and once they had all had their say he walked slowly into the centre of the circle. "I will teach you how to use the weapons that are available to everyone." he explained "These are the earth you walk on, the air you breathe, the water you drink and bathe in and the fire you warm yourselves with and cook your food. This enemy can be defeated, but not just by physical strength. You can defeat them by understanding the Spirits

155

of those elements that I have mentioned. I will need to
teach the Spirit Leaders and your Seers, your Wise Women
and Shamans how to work with those Spirits in defence
and they will help you. These are people who already know
the Spirit World, they already work with their own Guides
and can summon the power that is required. With this
knowledge your people can defeat this enemy. Instead of
waiting for them to attack, we can call on the powers of
the Gods and Goddess and banish the Horde of Doom
from this land once and for all. We begin tomorrow as we
cannot waste any time. Please, speak to those that I need
to train and ask them to be here after breaking fast
tomorrow morning. We will then begin at once."

As the Elders rose and left the circle they talked
quietly among themselves for a while and agreed that
although the warrior's ways sounded a bit strange, they had
nothing to lose and until now all else had failed. They
would trust this warrior, whose reputation was strong, but
would only give him a limited time to prove he could do as
he said. Meanwhile, tired and hungry they made their way
to their own camp fires where their Warriors were waiting
with food.

The next morning was grey and damp as the Elders sent their Spirit Leaders, Seers, Wise Women and Shamans to hear Artiane. The only one not available was Hetia, who had not yet returned from her journey. The Elders knew that she would return soon and had sent a youngster to wait at her cottage for her return. The others gathered around, wondering what this warrior knew that they did not. They all had much knowledge of the elements, however, they had no experience at summoning those elements to be used in warfare. Once all were assembled Artiane spoke, "You need to set up a camp closer to the mountains so I can teach you how to use the elements as they manifest near your villages, not out here on the plains. We will meet at the base of those mountains over there" and he pointed north towards a particularly craggy peak they all knew as Scraggy Top, "Meet me at that place as soon as you can gather your possessions. We will be there for two weeks so you need shelter, food, water and any other comforts you would like to bring. It would be wise to bring any talisman or charm you use to practice your ways as this may help you to channel your powers. But please be quick. I will see you there tonight. You will have no trouble finding me , I will leave you a sign." He turned and taking his sister by the arm led her away towards her tent. "We will travel together" he said quietly, "I need to catch up on your life." Sitting next to a small fire they spoke of their lives since their last meeting many years ago, leaving the others talking among themselves of this strange young man. He had seemed to have an aura of power, some had noticed a faint glow that appeared around him. Then with determination that they would finally be able to contribute something to the warriors that had been trying to protect the people, the group dispersed to do as was asked, to retrieve their belongings and head for the hills.

During the two weeks of training Artiane taught his pupils well. They stood out on dry ground with not a cloud in the sky, then combining their power with strong incantations they learned how to summon storm clouds and a heavy down-pouring of rain, enough to quell fires that may be started by the Horde of Doom and to disrupt their attacks. They stood on a hillside and with words as ancient as time itself they called in howling winds, strong enough to unseat the strongest of riders and send tree branches hurtling through the air. They climbed to the top of the nearest ancient crater and learned how to summon fire from the earth and lightning from the sky, then finally they stood on solid ground and raising energy together they found they could open fissures in the ground to swallow whole men and horses. Every day brought new power, combined with amazement, as new skills were taught and tested. The air prickled with power and the ground seemed to be constantly trembling. They were already students of the elements so Artiane was able to push them hard and in a very short time they were able to work with summoning and incantation by themselves. It was very tiresome work. They stopped only for food and drink and worked well into the nights learning how to use the darkness to confuse the enemy into believing the stars had disappeared. Sleep was welcome each night and once they laid down to rest it was only moments before that sleep took over. Practice was constant and by the end of the two weeks Artiane was confident that he could rely on his pupils to give a very good account of themselves if the need arose. So in the end they finally packed up their camp and returned to their villages, full of hope and confidence that at least they had some knowledge that could be useful. They had also decided on a plan to contact each other by thought, should their village come under attack, a skill taught to and used by most Shamans and Wise Women from a very early age. Signal fires would also be prepared on hilltops near each village that could be set alight in relay, this way anyone spotting the enemy could warn the whole valley and the Plains that the Horde of Doom was on its way.

13 HEALING

By the time the Spirit Leader of Flessia returned to his village Hetia had arrived home from her journey. She had with her Mariat, her friend who many in the village already knew and liked, and a stranger who looked very pale, sick and weary. He was taken to a small hut behind Hetia's cottage where he was ordered to only come out to use the privy or to wash in a basin set outside his door. People who saw him noticed that he walked with a stick and was bent over like an ancient one. Food and a herbal drink was brought to him by either Hetia or Mariat during the day and all the people had been told was that she was trying to heal this stranger of an illness that was in his mind and that he should be left alone. There was talk among the people that the stranger was mad, because he could only speak very quietly to Hetia or Mariat, and even then did not have much to say at all. He did not smile and only nodded if anyone called out to him. Most of the time the stranger stayed in the hut and kept to himself, and after a while he began to look a bit better but he did not smile. As Hetia was their healer and wise woman they did not ask her who he was, only accepting her silence as they respected her judgement. Within the walls of the hut Hetia and Erik spent many hours alone together and Hetia used

161

her healing knowledge to rid Starreck's heart and mind of the hatred built up since the death of his mother and grandfather. Using herbal concoctions she slowly built his body back to that of a healthy man and with meditation and smudging she slowly altered his thoughts to those of peace and tranquillity. Hetia had knowledge of an ancient race who used this method in their daily lives and practised love and compassion as a way of dealing with difficult situations. As a Shaman and Healer meditation was part of her daily life, however this was the first time she had used it as a healing tool on someone else. It took some time but she could see a marked change in the man after only a few weeks. There developed an understanding between them, a respect that would eventually last until they parted through death, and Erik began to see that there was a chance for him to release the evil being he had become.

One morning Hetia was summoned to the Elder's presence. "I would not normally ask you your business Hetia" he said, "but I must know something of the stranger you brought with you. We know who Mariat is and she is always welcome here, but some of the people are worried about the stranger in the hut behind your house. Can you tell me anything at all?" Hetia closed her eyes for a moment, thinking of what she could say that would not insult the Elder's kindness. "We were summoned to attend to this man by his people who were very worried that he seemed to have some kind of wasting sickness. When we arrived we realised that his mind was very confused. He seemed to be very unsure of himself, not knowing what was happening to him. He seemed to be losing his memory, growing old very fast and in fact, he seemed to be dying. We did what we could for him there, but it seemed best to bring him here where we could apply our own herbs and treatments. We are using a special herb that I found in the mountains. I learned that it could help our people who lose their minds when they have faced terrible danger, and I thought this herb would also help the stranger. His name is Erik and he comes from a city many, many days' ride from here. We hope that when he is better he will return to his City where he can take up his life once again. I cannot tell you any more than that at the moment, but he is no danger to anyone. He has said that once he is a little better he wishes to speak with the Elders, I believe he has something very important to say to you all." The Elder smiled and touched Hetia's arm, "Thank you my daughter" he said softly "I know you will do your best to heal this Erik and we will wait for the day when he speaks with us. Go now, your stranger must need you." She turned and walked away, not having lied to the Elder she didn't feel too bad about not telling him everything. However, the Elder had been told by the Spirit Leader that this man could be the leader of the Horde. If that was so the two men knew that Hetia would have a very good reason to keep his identity a secret and had made the decision to keep this knowledge between themselves for the time being.

Marlick had ridden most of the way with Hetia, Starreck and Mariat, however at Starreck's request he had made his way to one of the other villages nearby. There he asked for work amongst the people until Starreck became well enough to speak to the Elders. He was not recognised as one of the Horde of Doom, no-one had seen his face before as he hadn't taken part in the raids, staying back in camp to take care of the spare horses. The first village he came across was very pleased to have a healthy man to do some work as they had lost many strong men fighting the Horde of Doom. His touch with the horses and cattle found him working with these creatures as a healer, and at other times working as the blacksmith, for their Smith had been injured fighting the Horde and could not tend his forge as he should. This life gave Marlick a chance to see the people he had wronged, and although he took food and shelter for his work, he would not take their coin. He would bide his time then eventually face the people with Starreck – for he too had become very tired of the life they were living.

Benji had found the caves in the hills behind Flessia. Well stocked with food and blankets, it was an ideal place to watch over the village where his hero was recovering. He let his horse wander freely and began his lonely vigil. The following weeks went by very slowly for Benji. He was becoming lonely and a strong sadness began to take over as he curled into his blankets at night. There were many restless nights as bad dreams of people screaming and wailing disturbed his sleep. One rainy, cold morning he left the cave, walking away with only a small amount of food and a water flask. After wandering for several days, cold and hungry, he came across the village where Marlick had settled. Seeking out the quiet older man, Benji begged him to take pity and share his meagre dwelling. Not minding the lad, Marlick gave him work to do and they settled into a routine life of work and friendship. There was little left in either man of their former selves. It was as if they had a rebirth, and only they knew of the deeds that had led both of them to this place of peace.

Two moon cycles after Hetia had spoken with the Elders, Satiane walked out to the field behind her yard, a bundle of arrows in her arms and her bow struck across her shoulders. Glancing around she noticed others were making their way into the field. The row of "targets" had been rehung since yesterday, bags of hay with a big black cross in charcoal to represent the head of the 'victim'. As she reached the place where the bowmen practised Satiane dropped the bundle of arrows on the ground then reached for her bow. It was a large bow for a woman, but years of practice had strengthened her arms. She placed an arrow against the bow and string then, drawing it slowly back against her ear she let it fly towards the target. The sound of the cord as it released the arrow made her heart flutter as it brought back the power she felt with a bow in her hand and a spear tied to her saddle. As a child she was taken by her father on hunting trips, he believed it was important for his daughter to be as proficient as his son with a bow and spear. To be able to shoot from a moving horse was a way to guarantee a full belly. So the brother and sister were both taught in the same way. When they both were able to sense the presence of prey or danger it was a bonus. Both children showing very early in life the signs of their special talent of foresight. Today Satiane was eager to brush up on her skills.

Flessia, and the other villages of the land had settled down to a new routine. The people carried out their normal lives in the morning then after a mid-day meal the men, older boys and girls and the strong women would join Artiane the Shaman and Spirit Leaders along with those from other villages, and they learned to defend their homes and their lands. Some of the men who had trained as warriors were teaching the others how to use the long, strong bows that had been used in the land for many generations. They required a strong arm to load an arrow into the bow so the boys and girls were given a smaller version that would still be deadly should their aim be true. Teenage boys were sent to the forest to cut down young saplings to become the straight, deadly spears that would be used to bring down an enemy or his horse, and it came about that the women were very good at throwing and thrusting spears. In close combat a woman had a lot more to lose than her life, so using the spears became very important to them. The blacksmith was hard at work with his apprentice making spear and arrow heads. All the villages were alive with activity as they prepared for their future defence against the Horde of Doom. Even the young children were given the task of making sure there were plenty of arrows at the feet of those practising on the target range, and the old people had learned the art of fletching, the arrows they made were very true. Goose feathers were trimmed to shape and size, then following the instructions of the craftsmen, were bound to the arrow shafts with care. The elderly became very good at their new trade and enjoyed sitting in the company of others with a common task. The herd of horses available were also used by the better riders to charge in close, throw a spear or shoot an arrow and retreat just as quickly. This tactic could be used rather than hand to hand fighting, where loss of life against a more aggressive foe was inevitable. So over the long months of winter every one in the villages of the Plains, including the old and the very young, were in some way involved in becoming ready for any onslaught that may arise.

Meanwhile, in the village of Flessia, Hetia and Mariat were slowly working their healing on Starreck, now known as Erik once again. The herb for the mind was working well. Erik had spent many weeks in solitude coming to terms with his past life, Hetia was his only human contact. No herb or potion could remove the guilt he had begun to feel as the enormity of his actions became apparent to him.

Hetia entered the small hut where Erik was recovering, pausing for a moment to allow her eyes to adjust to the dim light. Erik was sitting up, propped by cushions. His eyes were closed and, for a moment, Hetia thought he was asleep. She placed the beaker of tea she was carrying on the floor by his bed and for a moment she stood quietly, with her hands suspended over his chest. She knew that the heart was a powerful energy centre and had spent some time asking the Great Spirit to heal the heart of this man in her care. "I am not asleep" Erik's said quietly, "and I can feel the power you are sending to me. I cannot understand why, but it fills me with a peace I have not felt since I was a child. Please continue." Hetia stopped what she was doing and gave thanks to the Great Spirit. "I do not need your permission to continue" she said curtly, "it is best if you are sleeping when I do this. You should not be aware of it, that is not how I work." She turned to leave, then turned back. "The Spirit Leader has let me know that he is available to you if you wish to talk to him about anything" then turned back and left the hut.

Erik looked around as she left. The hut was small and dark with only a bed in one corner and a low stool and table to share the space. No windows had brought light in when he arrived and it had the smell of chickens and dirt. The floor had been swept clean to show the stones and the straw that filled the bed was clean. Having been used to house the garden tools and a shelter for the chickens on rainy nights, there had never been any need to make it more comfortable.

Over time Erik had made it bearable once he had been able to get around. He knew he was here for some time so might as well do what he could. There was a deer skin rolled up in the corner that had been cured some years before and he shook this out to see if it could be used as a mat on the floor. The curing wasn't bad and there was no smell, so Erik took it outside to air in the sunshine while he went back to see what else could be done. Within a week Erik had built a shelf on one wall and hammered some stakes under it to hang up his cloak. Hetia had given him a cup and bowl which he proudly placed on the shelf. He wondered at how much he enjoyed being able to do these simple things and it was a very long time since his life had been anywhere near normal. "Can I make a window in one wall?" he asked Hetia one day, "it would be nice to have some light and I can make a shutter to close over it at night." "You can do what you like with the place" she answered "you might be here for a very long time". As she turned to walk away she smiled to herself, knowing that her healing was working much better than she had thought possible.

After a few months of solitude within his hut, Erik had taken a short walk from Flessia. Climbing a hillside he found a quiet place where he could look over the valley and contemplate his past life. This became a place of healing for Erik, of coming to terms with his deeds, and he found himself alone with his thoughts. Watching the activities of the villagers from this place one morning, he decided it was time to be honest with the Elders. There were many years of his life when he had no thought for anyone but himself. The only person he had any respect for had been Marlick, his trusted and loyal friend. They had shared many hours talking of a time when they may be able to live a peaceful life, perhaps with a good woman and children. Marlick would talk of a farm of his own, some stock to look after and perhaps a small blacksmith shop. But they had always been dreams, shared at night by a fire while the other men slept. In the light of day his anger with the world would take over once again, the man he had become rose with each dawn and once more he would goad his men into bloodshed and violence against the world that had taken his family. It was in sleep that the demons would rise to create the restlessness that had become a regular way of life. The terrors had become worse with every strike on helpless villages, he knew that a life such as this could not go on forever.

Now, Erik could begin a new life, but he would have to deal with his past. If the village elders decided he was to be sent to the Gods for his past deeds then so be it, but he didn't want to go on in that old life any more. He would ask for a meeting of the Elders as soon as he could and perhaps the whole village if the Elders thought that necessary, and he would face his demons once and for all.

The Spirit Leader had not needed to be told of Erik's past, he knew through his own Spirit Guide the truth of the man in Hetia's care. Understanding that Hetia had her reasons for not telling anyone of the man's past, he had held his tongue.

That night, after the evening meal, Erik approached Hetia. "It is time I spoke the truth" he said with a heavy heart, "I cannot live in your village any longer without telling the people who I am. I have been responsible for the killings, pillaging and ruin of this and many other villages over the land, and I must face my victims. I would like you to call a meeting of the Elders and I would like you and Mariat to be there. I need the people to understand that you kept my identity a secret until I was able to face my punishment. Before you brought me here I would probably have died very quickly at the end of a spear or arrow and they would never have known who their tormentor was. Please, call the meeting tonight." Hetia nodded quietly, stood and went to find the Elder.

The villagers gathered into a circle. At the centre a log had been placed on its end and there sat Erik. His shoulders and his back were straight as he prepared himself to face the people. No one took much notice as two men walked quietly into the village, one was young, the other much older. Erik had discovered they were living nearby when he overheard a conversation about the new blacksmith and his apprentice. They went straight to the place where Erik waited, greeting him silently and stood at his back. Erik no longer felt alone as he had before, and he realised there was no point in story telling, he needed to speak straight to these people. And so he began. Telling them who he was as a boy, the reasons he had hunted down the man who would start him on his evil journey and finally to his regrets that would lead to this night. "I do not tell you this for forgiveness," he said when he had finished, "I tell you this so you may judge me and know who had been leading the terror upon you all this time. I sit before you now and you must do as you see fit. The two men who stand at my back are also at your mercy, this is Marlick and this is Benji and they rode with me for many years although neither took part in the raids." He rose, turned and left the circle with Marlick and Benji at his side, heading back to the hut to await judgement.

After a few moments of silence the Elder stood and faced his people. "We have heard from the man we call Erik and acknowledge his two men" he said, "now we must decide how we will act towards them. As you all know, it is our way to talk about this with the Staff of Attention, and I ask one of the young people to go to my house and fetch it now." A young girl sitting near the front rose to her feet, bowed her head in respect to the Elder and went to bring the Staff of Attention to the meeting. "In the meantime" the Elder added, "I ask you to think of your own personal feelings. There will be plenty of time for discussion, so I ask that you sit in silence for a few moments to consider your own thoughts." He sat down until the Staff was brought to him then stood once more to face the people. "It is your right that you speak your piece before the elders bring judgement. Who would like to begin?" Hetia stood and took the Staff, she told of her part in placing a curse on the leader of the Horde of Doom. She told also, of meeting the young man Erik many years ago. Then told of her recent journey into the mountains with Mariat where they had used the herbs to subdue the man who now lived in their village and the course of action she had decided upon to heal his mind in order that he could now face their judgement. When she had finished another of the elders took the Staff and spoke. It was well into the depth of the night before everyone who had something to say had spoken. The children had been taken away and bedded down for the night and many of the elderly folk had begged the indulgence of the people and gone to their beds. Those left behind had begun to put forth ideas on how to deal with the problem.

The sky was beginning to lighten to dawn when the Elder stood, placing the Staff of Attention on his seat, for he no longer needed it. They had come to a decision. "Hetia, please call Erik to us, we would like him to hear of his fate before we call an end to this meeting". Hetia walked slowly back to the hut to fetch Erik. She had agreed to the request of the elders. It was a fitting way to deal with not only Erik's past but with their current situation. For over the past couple of weeks there was word that the Horde of Doom was back, terrorising the people of another valley some three days ride away. As Erik, Marlick and Benji could not possibly be involved in the terror, it was appropriate that they now be given a chance to redeem themselves. Erik could live with the people of Flessia, becoming a servant to whoever needed his help. His food would be his only reward and he would be asked to use his knowledge to help those who were going to fight back. The other two would return to the village they had called home these many months and word would be carried to the Elders of that village for the same treatment. These villagers were not killers, they could not put these men to death, and it was certain that they would need their knowledge. Hetia brought him to face the people once more.

As Erik, Marlick and Benji made their way to the centre of the circle the Elder rose. "Please stand together where you can be seen by all those present" the Elder said, "we have come to a decision. If you do not abide by this decision you will be given the opportunity to talk of your reasons for this". He then went on to explain what the people had agreed to during the night. When he was finished the three men were asked to leave and consider the people's decision. They did not need to consider as they looked one to the other and nodded their heads in agreement. "We agree to your decision" Erik stated, "It is much fairer than any of us deserve. We had expected to be leaving this life behind after today, and we do assure you that we will abide by your decisions and do our best to do what is required of us. I cannot say sorry for lives lost, only that we can do what we can to help those left in need." The Elder dismissed the circle and walked away with the three men. "There will be many who cannot forgive you, and you must understand this, however, if you do decide to try and leave without fulfilling your duties you will be hunted down by our warrior-hunters, and they will be allowed to do what they will with you. However, I believe you will stay and do as we have asked". He turned and left the men alone. Marlick and Benji said their goodbyes and made their way back to the village where they were to stay and Erik returned to the little hut behind Hetia's house.

After leaving Hetia, Mariat had begun her journey home with a spring in her step. Although she enjoyed spending time with Hetia the life in Flessia was much different to the one she led in her quiet little cottage with

the large orange cat. Hetia had offered her the use of a
pony who was trained to return home once his journey
was ended, but Mariat decided to use the opportunity to
gather up some herbs for herself so decided to walk.
There were also many mushrooms and other fungi to be
found along the way, especially in the dark forest she
needed to go through. She had never been afraid to do
this journey alone, The training she had undertaken had
taught her to just melt into the shadows if she found it
necessary to avoid danger, and it was this forest that she
was heading into as she thought of the past few weeks
with Hetia. Within a couple of hours Mariat had made
good time and was halfway through the forest when a
raven in the trees above her called out. It was the sound
they made when there was danger to their kind and Mariat
took note. At the same time there was a strange energy
emitted from the trees around her and she decided that
some care was to be taken. Leaving the trail Mariat silently
made her way into the thickness of the undergrowth and
stayed very still. She had just managed to hide when the
sound of horses, walking, came to her ears. It was faint at
first which gave her a chance to make sure she was well
hidden, then in front of her were three riders. One tall,
dark and ugly who seemed to be in charge and two others
who sent a chill down her spine. They were taking their

time and talking quietly among themselves as they rode so she was able to catch part of their conversation. "It seems that there are some very easy picking around here," said the leader, "perhaps Starreck was just too lazy and headed for the hills rather than do what I told him to do. We have to take charge of this lot before someone else finds out that there are some easy pickings. Now I noticed that there doesn't seem to be many warriors around here, they are just farmers and towns folk. I just want to have a better look around before we go charging about. That last town, what was it called, Flessia, yes that was it, from what I heard it seems like they have a witch there who can call on the Gods. Now that's a woman I don't want to get on the wrong side of but I tell you this, she would be worth something to her people so maybe we can use her somehow."

Mariat went very still and when she heard this it made her feel quite sick. She would need to warn Hetia that these men were after her. When the three men had disappeared along the trail Mariat began to breath properly again. She had used an old trick of 'blending' in to the forest which also required her breath to slow down to almost nothing. Now that she felt the danger had passed she relaxed, sat down on a tree stump and prepared to send her psychic message to Hetia. After a few moments of trying she realised that there was no response from Hetia. She didn't know that at that moment Hetia was in deep mind conversation with Solcaan, leader of the magicians. She tried again, still no luck, so with the intention of trying later Mariat returned to the trail and the journey home. She was sure that there was no hurry, she would contact Hetia when she arrived home.

Darkness overtook Mariat as she left the safety of the forest, there was a full moon so she decided to keep walking and sleep in her own bed that night. The large bag she had over her shoulder held some travel food and a water flask so it was with pleasure that she kept going. After a little while she sat down for a rest and closed her eyes for a moment. Suddenly there was a huge rough hand over her mouth and another around her waist. Struggling with all her energy Mariat twisted and turned and lashed out with her fists. It was no good. The man holding her was huge and strong. Mariat tried to bite his hand but that only got her a punch to the head. Lying still, trying to think quickly, Mariat pretended to be knocked out but she was very aware of the danger she was in. Savagely the man began to tear off her clothes. "I'll have a piece of you my darlin'," he mumbled, "just what I need before the boss gets back. Now just you be good and you won't get hurt. After all, there's just you and I here anyway and no one can hear you if you shout." Mariat realised that right then it wasn't her life that was in danger but she wasn't going to give in to this brute. Using all her strength she brought up her knee and kicked the man in his groin then pushing herself off the ground she began to run. Her legs felt like lead but she kept going. "Oh no you don't" he snarled, "you aren't going anywhere and you are going to pay for that kick." He caught Mariat by the back of her shift and threw her once more to the ground. He had a knife in his hand and she knew he would use it so groping around for something hard she grabbed a rock and banged it against his head. He yelled and dropped the knife but he was still strong and with a shriek of anger he picked up the knife and plunged it into Mariat's heart. She didn't have time to do anything else. She just stared at him and with her dying breath she cursed the man for all time. The curse of the dying was feared by all, especially those who had no respect for the Gods, and it was no wonder to this man, in the near future, when he began to slowly lose his strength and would die in misery and pain by himself out on the Plains before he could return to the camp where the Horde were waiting for Dagrel. No one would miss him because these men often went off by themselves and didn't return, but Mariat would be missed. She would be missed by all the people she had helped in her lifetime, she would be missed especially by Hetia but it would be quite a long time before her friends would know she was gone and before anyone would find her body. Only an hour's walk away a large orange cat sat up and howled a long mournful howl and began to prowl around the house. His friend had died and he would miss her more than anything else in his life.

Erik had become more content with his new life in Flessia. His spirit guide came to him more often than before as he found regular quiet moments sitting on the hill overlooking the village. In his heart he knew he could never atone for the misery he had brought to so many, but he was given the chance to try. The kindness that was shown him by these peaceful souls often brought tears of shame to his eyes. He had begun to look upon them with respect, to see the strength they had as they went about their daily lives. He had deep admiration for them, from the smallest child to the eldest adult. And he had fallen deeply in love with Hetia.

Spending so much time in her presence was like drinking the nectar of the Gods to Erik. He would do anything for her, and he did. She had not asked very much of him, only that he kept her woodpile full, tend to her kitchen garden and keep the grass short around her house and, most of all, she had requested that he would go to his little hut each night after sharing the evening meal together and not leave the village. This was his 'prison'. It was a prison he gladly returned to each night. He knew that he would never marry, have children and leave Hetia. Although he felt that he would eventually be allowed to, with the leave of the Elders, he had no desire to do so. Hetia had his heart and he was content to live in his little hut behind her house.

Erik did not know that Hetia felt the same. No spell or incantation was in place. The mutual love, never spoken of, would keep them together for this lifetime. It was accepted that Wise Women may not marry, it was said that they could not perform their healing arts as well if they lived as others did. Hetia would watch Erik each night as he walked the little pathway back to his hut, and she would smile wistfully at the possibility that she might one day relent and ask him to stay with her – but she never did. Occasionally, in peaceful moments, Hetia thought that perhaps they would meet again in their next lives on a more intimate level, she would like that, but in this lifetime it was not to be.

During the delights of Springtime and the long warm days of Summer the people of Flessia turned out into the fields, tending the crops that would feed them through winter. There had been more than two years since the Horde of Doom had been sent on their way. As Autumn crept towards Winter and the days became chilly towards evening, the harvest began. Celebrations were held at this time of year and the songs of harvest were heard throughout the land. The Spirit Leader was brought out to bless the crops before the harvest began and Hetia was asked to select what she needed to dry and keep for her medicines. It was a yearly ritual and although everyone took it very seriously, it was a time for pleasure. Music, dancing to the sound of drums and feasting would take place before the winter days drove the people indoors to their fires. This time Hetia took Erik by the arm and brought him to the place of celebration. It was the first year he had been allowed to join in the festivities as it had been felt that his presence would upset those who had lost family and friends to the Horde of Doom. Smiling and gently pulling him along, Hetia enjoyed the pleasure it gave her to be able to share the occasion with him. Reaching the place of blessings she released him and went to stand with the Spirit Leader. Handing her a long curved knife the Spirit Leader invited Hetia to select the best of the plants that she would take and dry out. Although it was only a ritual and tradition, she would select only that which could be used. The first cut would make powerful medicine, so she asked for the blessings of the Goddess as she sliced through the stems. Holding her selection high for the people to see she smiled and went back to Erik. "This will be used as a poultice should someone be pierced by one of the poisonous spikes of the Dreaming Bush. The bush can kill within four days if the wound is not tended. Only this plant will calm the poison. So I will also take more of it to be dried. Thankfully I have not had to use it for many years as the Dreaming Bush only grows in one place, many days from here, but we need a supply – just in case." Erik understood that she had just shared something very important with him and felt honoured. They put the ritual knife and the cut plant on a table that held the sacred objects of the ritual and went to join in the celebrations. It was well into the night before the people returned to their homes, falling asleep to dream before they would have to waken early the next morning to finish off the harvest.   The small group of Shaman and Spirit Leaders who had brought about the retreat of the

Horde of Doom continued their work. Artiane had taught them well. He had returned to the forest where they had found him in order to finish the study he had begun there. Bidding his sister a fond farewell he called his horse to him and they rode quietly away.

The others, who now called themselves magicians, were strengthened by his teachings. They met once each full moon to work with each other and the Energies. This work was powerful, so as they gathered their knowledge and practised, trees could be persuaded to fall to the ground, clouds cover the sun or moon and fire begun by thought alone. They found their own individual strengths and it was not long before they built a tall tower of stone where they could work and keep their 'tools' of power. Crystals, feather wands and other artefacts were gathered to be kept there away from prying eyes. The tower was forbidden to those not involved in their work and besides, no-one wanted to enter this place anyway. Their work became very secret, their ways seemed strange to most. The power was becoming intense. The magicians in the tower were all men, led by a kindly old man called Solcaan who believed that magic should only be used for the greater good, but most of the men who had moved in to live there permanently like the priests of olden times, had become very elusive indeed. They began to wear long robes with hoods that could cover not only their head but their faces too. Over a time they had developed secret ceremonies and it wasn't long, despite Solcaan's protestations, until they were conjuring up magic that had been looked on as dangerous in the past.

From her cottage in Flessia Hetia knew of this work. It disturbed her a little as she knew the dangers of moving this way, too much power was always dangerous and the use of magic for anything but the common good had been forbidden for centuries. One morning before the villagers rose from their beds for the day, Hetia borrowed a horse and set off towards the Tower. As the horse travelled at a gentle pace on the grass, wet from the early morning dew, Hetia allowed her thoughts to wander. The village had been peaceful for some time now. Babies had been born, the crops were growing well and food was being stored once again for the winter time. Hetia's thoughts drifted to Erik. He was part of her life now and she smiled to herself at the thought. It suited her to have him around looking after the jobs that it was best for a man to do. Chopping wood, mending things and the heavy digging of her garden when it was time to put in the seasons vegetables and herbs. She felt quite content with him there in her back yard in the little cottage. "What a journey this had been." she thought, remembering the time as clearly as if it was yesterday. She had been taken by one of the Horde with her friend Mariat to tend Erik in the mountains, sick with an unknown wasting disease. Turning her eyes up to the sky she called aloud, "Such are the challenges you throw to me my Goddess. Always interesting and for that I give you my thanks".

Hetia continued on her way, the sun had now risen over the mountains and warmed her face. Each step the horse took on the grass allowed the tiny bells tied at Hetia's ankles to tinkle. The tune they played sounded like the little birds called Bellbirds who darted among the trees. The insects were now swarming about as the day warmed, the click of the grasshoppers and the gentle hum of the bees played a sweet melody as Hetia allowed her mind and body to relax into the rhythm of the horse's gait. It was a couple of years now since the Horde of Doom had been seen so she felt safe in her journey.

Arriving at the tower door Hetia dismounted, left the horse to graze on the lush grass then held up her walking staff and knocked loudly on the door. No ordinary staff was this with its rune markings and inset precious stones. The staff's markings had been added to over the years as she grew into her role as healer and Wise Woman. Hetia knew that if there was an occasion where a bit more 'energy' was required she could call upon it's strength to draw power from the Earth.

There was no answer so she knocked again this time louder. After a few moments she heard the sound of a latch opening, the door swung ajar and she was confronted with a young man who was a stranger to her. "I would like to speak with one of your elders young man" she demanded, "fetch me someone in authority now please". Taken aback by Hetia's demand the young man reversed into the Tower shutting the great door in Hetia's face, and fled up the stairs to his Elders who occupied the top floor. Still waking from sleep, the Elders went to a window and looked down at the woman who was demanding an audience. "It is Hetia" one said with a smile, "why, I feel like we are about to be chastised like naughty children. Go bring her in" he ordered the young man "Show her in to the kitchen and make her a hot, calming drink and offer her something to eat. She will have risen early to be here by now. And don't upset her or I assure you that you will regret it. Although I suspect that shutting the door in her face didn't do you any good. Tell

her I'll be down in a minute or two when I am dressed".
He turned to the other Elders with a smile "I think we may
have overstepped ourselves my friends. Our actions have
reached one who is much more powerful than people give
her credit and certainly quite capable of giving us a bit of a
hiding. Leave this to me, I shall go down and face the lady
with the respect she should always be given." He turned
and walked down the stairs with a spring in his step. He
was looking forward to seeing his visitor.

Her cup of tea held between her palms with the
steam rising to her nostrils, had a calming effect on Hetia.
She assumed that the nature of the tea was a deliberate
attempt to allay any fire she was about to unleash on the
community of magicians. Inwardly she smiled, "Good,
they are worried about me" she thought "I didn't know I
was held in such regard. I shall take advantage of that."
Placing the teacup on the table she nibbled on an apple
while she waited calmly hearing the residents of the Tower
bustling about upstairs. She knew they were dressing
deliberately in robes that would assume power, before
descending the stairs to meet her. The senior member was
not so particular, throwing on his everyday robe he had
left them to their preparations and scuttled down the stairs
with a smile on his face.

Solcaan, Elder and senior member of the community, had known Hetia all her life. He had been asked to officiate at her naming ceremony when she was born and it was he who had recommended Hetia to be trained in the traditions of Wise Woman. He smiled as he entered the kitchen, his arms wide open for the embrace they usually shared. This was not to be this time. Hetia rose from her chair, feet firmly planted on the floor and looked him squarely in the eye. "You are over-stepping the line in your work here Solcaan" she said firmly, "I can feel the energy you are creating all the way from Flessia. There was a strange shift in the curtain between the worlds the other day and we both know how dangerous that can be. What you do here is usually none of my business, but this is the business of anyone who uses power to heal and protect. What are you up to?" Solcaan dropped his empty arms and came to sit at the table. "You are right in coming to me Hetia" he said "we are gathering strength, but we are exploring ways of protecting the people and we think we may have discovered a way to send our enemy from here to another time or place. We have been combining our skills and we are at the door of something incredible. If you could feel it from Flessia then it must be powerful indeed."

191

He paused and searched Hetia's face to gauge her reaction. All he saw was anger. "Solcaan, you know this is forbidden. Many years ago there were workers in magic who went beyond what they were supposed to do. People were disappearing never to be seen again and the landscape was changed forever leaving so much drought and misery to the farms. Then it was nearly the end of life as we know it as they tampered with the forces of time. It was even believed that they caused the Earth to warm up to a level that made life impossible in some places. They were stopped but they did cause chaos throughout the land. This work is forbidden and now it looks like you and your cronies are at it again. You were very young and not yet schooled in Shamanic ways when the law came down on those who caused the chaos, I was not yet born in this life, but we both know the tales told by the fireside. Learning the ways of the Elements is one thing, tampering with this business of time and space is not the same. We don't need to open those doors again."

Finally Hetia sat back down on her chair then leaning forward with her arms on the table she said quietly, "Please, put an end to this work. You don't want to unleash that power. I trust you Solcaan, but it only takes one member of your community to want total power and we will have a much bigger problem than the Horde of Doom to deal with." She sat back in her chair and waited for an answer.

"Hetia, you are dear to me and you know how much I respect you. I will consider your words and discuss this with the community. Perhaps you are right." Solcaan's eyes dropped to his hands for a moment, considering the position he was in. "As you say, someone here could use this power for evil ways. For now though, will you share food with us?" Hetia smiled at last. They had often shared food over long talks on their respective works, and she enjoyed his company. "With pleasure Solcaan" she replied, "I am sure your food store is well stocked." Solcaan called the young man, who had been waiting behind the kitchen door, to bring food and drink and to invite the rest of the community to join them. Feeling a little nervous in Hetia's presence the rest of the residents joined them, they knew, magicians they may be, but you don't upset a Wise Woman, especially this one.

After the morning meal Hetia rose to leave, "Please remember my words Solcaan" she said on parting, "you move in dangerous ways. The people of this land would not be able to withstand the terror that could be unleashed should you find your way back through that curtain. We are meant to stay in our own world, not cross over into others we do not understand, nor do you or any other in our world have the power to withstand the terror you could unleash." With that she turned and left the tower, to ride swiftly back to her village.

14 CAPTURED

Hetia had her mind on the conversation with
Solcaan as she rode along. She made up her mind that she
would have to keep an eye on those magicians. If they
ever found a way to the other world it would be nothing
short of the end of the life they lived, because it would
open the doors to unspeakable changes. Within her own
mind and allowing the horse to find its own way home
Hetia didn't notice that she was being followed from the
shadows of the nearby forest. She also didn't notice the
two men who were catching up to her and it wasn't until
they came alongside that she realised that allowing her
mind to wander had brought her into danger. "Hold up
lady" one of them called gruffly, "we need to talk to you."
Hetia, realising that these men were not looking for a
friendly conversation dug her heels into the horses flanks
and took off. However, galloping with all its might her
pony was not as big and strong as those of the two men
and it wasn't long before they caught up with her. She
tried to dodge off to the side but got only a few paces
when she was herded back towards the trail. "Oh no you
don't lady" the other one snarled, "you are coming with
us. We have someone who would like your company."
He grabbed the reins of Hetia's horse from her hands and

turned off into the forest. She tried to turn the pony with her knees but the man holding her reins was too strong. The pony began to buck and kick but this only made the men angry and one gave the pony a nasty punch to the side of its head. Hetia spoke quiet words to the pony and it settled down. Hanging on to the saddle with all her strength Hetia began to think of ways she could free herself and the pony when she was pulled up suddenly just short of the trees. Dismounting from his horse the one who had taken the reins roughly pulled Hetia down off her pony. "We're not going to give you the chance to use any of that magic stuff lady so just for now you are going to be a bit incapacitated." Then taking a rope from his saddle he pushed Hetia's hands roughly behind her back and tied them together, then he took the scarf from around his neck and gagged her. Realising that she couldn't do much with her hands tied Hetia decided to wait and see what they had in mind so she deliberately relaxed her body to stop her from being hurt and pretended to go along with them. Throwing her back up on her pony the man grabbed the reins once more and they all entered the forest. It was a long ride for Hetia, bound and gagged, because she had to hold on with her knees, but she used the time to centre her mind. Unknown to the men riding silently along in front and behind her Hetia was already working on her rescue. Concentrating with all her energy she began to search for the mind of Solcaan in the magicians tower. It didn't take her long to find him for the connection of the morning was still powerful in her mind. 'Solcaan,' she silently called, 'can you hear me?' 'Yes my dear' replied Solcaan silently, 'what's the matter?' 'I have been captured on the way home by two thugs Solcaan," she replied, "I believe they might belong to the Horde of Doom and they are taking me somewhere in the forest, probably to meet with their leader. I want you to contact Erik in Flessia and let him know that the Horde seem to be returned and that is a terrible thought. I shall keep in touch with you and let you know where I am. Tell Erik not to worry, these people usually don't touch anyone they think might be involved in magic so I think they just want to know what our defences are I am not frightened so please make sure Erik understands that. Meanwhile I will watch and wait and find out what they want." "Alright Hetia" Solcaan answered, "I understand. I will have two of my young magicians ride to Flessia and tell Erik what you have told me. Don't worry, we will save you once we know where you are. These men have to be stopped, the sooner the better, and maybe they don't realise that they have just given us another weapon to use against them. Stay safe."

After this silent conversation with Solcaan Hetia began to notice her surroundings. They had ridden for quite a long time before they stopped to water the horses at a stream. Pulling Hetia down from her saddle the one who had spoken first took the gag off Hetia then untied her hands and offered her a drink of water. "We have to keep you in good condition," he said, "our boss wants to talk to you and he can't do that if you are hurt or injured. I can't say what he will do to you if you don't co-operate though so don't get any funny ideas about that. Now drink up then we will be on our way." Saying nothing Hetia accepted the drink and began to probe the minds of these two men. She discovered that they were just thugs who had been hired by the leader to keep the rest of the men in check. They were a nasty pair and she decided that it would be unwise to cross them, so Hetia decided that she would just say nothing at all until they reached their destination. They let her hands loose until she climbed back on her horse then tied them once again. Hetia settled in for the rest of the journey taking in her surroundings so that she could pass the directions on to Solcaan.

It took until halfway through the afternoon before they reached the camp where the men were sitting around talking to one another. In the centre of the group was a big ugly man who was obviously the leader and it was to this man that she was taken. "Well, well" he said to her, "are you the one who has been causing me all this trouble? Take her off her horse and you two go and get some grub, you have done well. By the looks of the tattoos and stuff in her hair this is one of those magicians, maybe even a witch, so she will be important to them. Come here lady and sit down. I don't want to hurt you, just want some information then after I have made your people understand how easy it is to get at you all you will be taken back out and set free. I won't mess with people like you." Hetia came over and sat down on the log near the fire in the centre of the camp. She accepted a dish of food that was offered but only ate some of the vegetables. It would not do her any good to become ill from not eating at all. "Good to see you have an appetite" the leader said. "My name is Dagrel and I am getting mighty annoyed at this stormy weather that seems to be following me about. Now lady, what have you to say about that." "Nothing" replied Hetia, "you must have upset the Gods." Dagrel laughed out loud. "Hear that men" he called out to his men, "We must have upset the Gods." There was a burst of laughter amongst the men and Dagrel turned back to her. "So you say lady, however, I think your friends might like to stop what they have been doing or we might hang on to you a bit longer. There is no way I am going to harm you because I don't want to end up like old Starreck did, but I don't know about these men, they don't always do what I tell them you know and it's been a while since they had a woman. You be good and I will see that you are protected. Now, you just sit there and eat up while we send your friends a message." Roughly taking a bracelet from Hetia's arm he turned and approached one of the men. Giving him the bracelet and telling him what to say he sent the man off to a farmhouse they had passed along the way. "Now lady," he said to Hetia, "we will just wait and see what value your people have on you. Right you lot," he said to is men, "you leave this one alone. No one is to touch her unless you have my orders, right?" The men all nodded agreement and went back to what they were doing. Hetia knew she was safe for the moment because they needed her but she had no doubt that if Dagrel went off she might not trust some of the men. They had not replaced the gag but her hands were still tied. There was a belief that magicians could use their hands in secret ways to create their magic. They were wrong in Hetia's case, she mostly used her mind and her connection to the Earth itself.

It was dark when the messenger returned to camp reporting that he had done as he was told. The people would take the message to the magicians so all they had to do now was wait. Hetia was given a blanket to lie down on near the fire but with her hands and ankles tied to prevent her escape. Lying quietly she looked up into the night sky. There were no clouds that night and as the moon came up into the sky Hetia noted her position with the moon and a large star she often used to find her way in the dark. Making note of her position she eventually closed her eyes and pretended to be asleep. In this way Dagrel and his men didn't know that she was 'talking' to Solcaan. It wouldn't take long before Erik would know where she was and, hopefully, she would be rescued.

The next day, after an uncomfortable night's sleep, Hetia was woken by one of the men nudging her with his foot. He had a plate of food and a cup of water in his hands and he offered it to her. "I don't want any trouble with you magic people," he said very quietly, "we have spoken between ourselves and none of us want any part of this because some of us were with Starreck and we know who you are. Don't worry though, we won't tell him. You were alright with Starreck and we remember that. However, there's Dagrel to deal with and he calls the shots now so we have to go along with him. It's not worth our lives if we say no to him, so take this please lady and just do as he says. He's a mean one that, nothing like our old leader at all. This one is just plain nasty and I wouldn't trust him with me mother." Hetia took the food and water and tried to eat with her hands tied. "I can undo your hands while you eat," the man added, "but please don't try any funny stuff or we have to tie you up again." Hetia noticed after a while that the men stayed far away from her and later in the morning Dagrel's two henchmen gathered up most of the men and ordered them to their horses. She realised that they weren't talking about what they were doing in front of her and she knew that was so she didn't hear them. She watched carefully and saw that they didn't take any food or their bedrolls with them. This meant they weren't going far, so settling back against a tree she waited. It wasn't long before Dagrel came over. "The boys and I are going out for a little ride lady," he said with a sneer, "you just sit there nicely and no harm will come to you. I've left a couple of the men to keep an eye on you. If you have to go into the bushes for a pee they will go with you and you will be on the end of a rope so don't get any fancy ideas. We'll be back before you know it." He turned and joined the men at the horses and they all took off. Luckily the one who had brought her food that morning was one of those left to guard her so she relaxed and began to meditate on what was happening.

Just before noon the riders arrived back in camp. "Well you are in luck" Dagrel said to Hetia, "we have had a message that the magicians are willing to talk to us. Seems like they think a lot of you which makes me think we can use you to make us a bit of profit. I've sent them word that we will hand you over if they pay us and we have demanded quite a tidy amount for your safe return. Mind you, I might even decide to keep you a bit longer. It might be interesting to have ourselves a witch. You're not bad looking either so it might be interesting to see what it's like to have myself a special woman." Stroking the side of her face he laughed evilly and turned away but he wasn't aware of the silent words that were forming in Hetia's mind. Threatening her personally was one mistake Dagrel had made that she could do something about. It was an old "spell" that had been used since time began by those who had taken vows of chastity. The words began to form in her mind then when she had built them up to power Hetia opened her mouth and silently mouthed the words to Dagrel's back that would bring his manhood undone forever. Of course he was totally unaware that his life was changing from that moment on and he wouldn't find out for some time yet. She had been taught that she must never use her powers to hurt another being but this wouldn't hurt him, only make him frustrated. "Oh Dagrel" she thought, "you will have a lot of trouble keeping the ladies happy from now on, especially those who are not willing. There will be no power in that little appendage of yours. And so it be done." She smiled as she thought of Dagrel's disgrace, being such a man as he it would be important for him to be able to have any woman he wanted at any time. Those days had just come to an end and there would be women over the land who would be just a little safer.

The rest of that day was quiet as Dagrel waited to get an answer to his demands on the magicians. Little did he know that this delay was being used by Solcaan to organise Erik and the two young magicians on a rescue mission. By that evening Dagrel was becoming restless. "We should have heard from them by now," he said to his henchmen, "you would think they would be in a hurry to get her back. After she has eaten make sure she is well tied up, tie her leg to a tree just in case she tries to get away in the dark and post a couple of guards over her. I don't want to spend any more days camped here." As the night wore on it was very obvious that the men didn't want to be anywhere near Hetia. The guards sat well back in case she reached out and touched them. They knew that witches were able to hurt you by just a touch and they were taking no chances. Eventually the camp fell asleep all except the guards and Hetia, who seemed to be asleep. She was waiting because she had been sent a message from Solcaan that help was on it's way.

Meanwhile back in Flessia the two young magicians had arrived at Hetia's cottage and made their way around the back to Erik's hut. "Are you Erik?" one asked, Erik nodded. "We have come to tell you that Hetia has been captured by the Horde of Doom and is being held in a forest about half a day's ride from here. They seem to want to hold her to ransom so that the magicians stop interfering with their raiding and killing, but they obviously don't know that Hetia can use mind talk to contact Solcaan. He sent us to help you to get her back. We can both ride well and we can fight if we have to, although we have taken a vow not to kill any human or animal. So, we know where to go but you can tell us what to do." Erik was taken aback. He leaned back against his doorway for a moment letting this news sink in. He had never thought about losing Hetia, his life now centred around her. After a moment he grabbed his coat and led the other two along to where he could get a horse. "We will ride straight away," he said, "you can guide me along and we will make plans along the way. Come on." They left Flessia straight away after letting the Spirit Leader know what was happening and rode like the wind in the direction the magicians said. After a while they came to the forest where Hetia was captured and entered it on foot. They tied their horses to some bushes well hidden from the main trail and sat down to make a plan. As they were talking one of the magicians received a message from Solcaan. "I know where they are" he said, "and we are getting some very strong help from the Tower. We are to wait until well into the night then there will be a sign that lets us know what to do." They all sat quietly for a few hours and readied themselves. As the forest carried sound, it was on silent feet with no talking that they made their way towards the camp of the Horde of Doom.

Lying near the fire as if she was asleep Hetia listened to the conversations around her. Feeling very tired she was about to still her mind before going to sleep when part of the conversation pulled her back to pay attention once more. "He shouldn't have done that, he's an idiot." one voice was saying, "The boss wanted any of these magic lot taken alive to use as hostage. That fool can't keep his pants on round women, now she's dead and where did it get him. The boss was furious when he found out and he hasn't settled down yet. I'll bet the Gods won't let this lie without taking revenge. I reckon he deserves what he got from the boss, although if I was in charge I'd have sacrificed the idiot to the Gods to try and appease them. Whipping was too easy on him in my opinion."

"Yeah, I agree" came another voice, "even though she had no marks on her according to him, I reckon she was one of those witches that came to work on Starreck in the mountains. I was on my way out of camp the day they arrived and I swear it was one of them. Bloody fool, what was he thinking?" "He wasn't thinking," the first replied, "well not with his head, that was his problem."

Feeling very angry and extremely sad, Hetia realised they were talking about her friend Mariat. Mustering all her self control she pretended to be asleep while planning what she could do to avenge her very dear friend. It may not be possible on this night but avenge her she would and the man concerned would pay dearly, eventually with his life, after suffering unspeakable agony. All her vows of peace and compassion seemed so unimportant to Hetia as she lay there with silent tears running down her cheeks into the soft dirt beneath her.

During the night Hetia noticed the energy changing around her. There seemed to be an eerie glow some distance away among the trees but nobody else had taken much notice, thinking it was the moon shining down. Hetia knew it was not the moon and, to herself, began a silent chant that was being matched in the magicians' tower far away to the north. Slowly the glow came nearer and nearer to the camp and intensified until it seemed that the whole camp was within a blue bubble. Hetia pretended to be asleep but was peering out from almost closed eyes. "Oh beautiful energy" she said silently to herself, "welcome. I invoke your power to clear the way for those who will come to my aid. Bring your protection to these good people who now approach the camp. Keep them safe from harm." Not so far off Hetia became aware of a presence that she was very familiar with, the man who now shared her life, and she knew her rescue was near at hand. Getting ready to rise in a hurry she waited, patiently, for the moment to flee. As the glow had neared the camp the guards who were placed around the edge began to fall asleep. One by one they sat silently on the ground, lay back and fell asleep. Those who were curled up in their blankets went into deeper sleep and all was quiet. Silently, carefully, Hetia rose and untied the rope on her ankle. Her footsteps would have fallen on deaf ears anyway but she was careful as she made her way silently to the edge of the clearing. There, waiting in the dark, were her rescuers. As she reached the trees Erik took her hand in his and drew Hetia away from the camp, back into the gloom of the forest to the two magicians waiting a short way off. Still silent, they all turned and moved back from where the men had come. All the time during this escape the mysterious glow around and in the camp had remained, keeping everyone there fast asleep. It would stay that way until just before the sky began to lighten with the early morning and by then Hetia, Erik and the two young magicians who had accompanied him had stopped running. They had arrived at the place where their horses were tied in a thicket unseen from the track and sat down for a moment to rest. Taking a water flask from his horse Erik offered it to Hetia and they spoke for the first time since her rescue. "Are you alright?" Erik asked. "Yes, thank you," replied Hetia, "I am tired but safe. I knew they wouldn't do me any physical harm because they think I am a witch and that worried even the leader, so I decided to wait quietly. It turns out that some of the men rode with you Erik and recognised me. They didn't tell their leader Dagrel who I was and I think they would have protected me from him if it became nasty." Erik looked at her with great concern. "Did you say

Dagrel?" he asked. Hetia nodded. "I didn't know he was the one who was leading the men" said Erik, "That was who turned me from a quiet young kid into a killer and began the worst years of my life. That means they are being led by the worst of human scum and we do need to rid the world of them as soon as we can." He turned his face from Hetia and she could tell he was visibly upset by the news. She decided the best thing to do was keep moving and not tell him yet about what she had overheard regarding Mariat. There would be time to tell him when they were safe, so she gently nudged Erik towards the horses. "Solcaan did very well," she said, "but I didn't expect my rescuer to be you, or these two young men. Thank you all. Now, we shall see about removing that energy and waking them all up. It would be very interesting to see their faces when they wake up and realise I am not there and I left them quite a surprise to find. I will tell you about that later. Dagrel had tied me to a tree by my ankle by the way, in case I tried to escape, and they thought that by tying my hands as well that I would be secure with the guards posted to keep watch. One of the 'tricks' I learnt as a young trainee was undoing knots with magic. It was a lot of fun when I was young but of course it isn't something that was useful- until now." This made Hetia show a small smile and Erik looked at her and knew how much he loved her. "So, shall we finish removing our little sleeping 'potion'?" Hetia said to the two young magicians. They stood together holding hands and recited the incantation that would see everyone awake in the camp. Rising as one, the four mounted the three horses, Hetia riding behind Erik, and set off at a gallop for home.

As the sun rose Dagrel woke from his sleep and looked around. His men were all rubbing their eyes and grumbling as they would normally do in the early morning. However, he noticed that the guards were also rising from the ground, rubbing their eyes and looking around them strangely. This made him look to the place where they had tied Hetia. She was gone. Roaring angrily Dagrel began to kick the men nearest to him then called the guards. "Where is our prisoner?" he shouted, "you were asleep instead of guarding her and she has gone. Look, the ropes are untied so she must have had help. Which of you helped her?" Ranting and raving he went through the camp kicking men and bed rolls, anything within reach. "You guards, come here to me." He screamed. The men came sheepishly towards him and Dagrel ordered his two henchmen to grab the two that were supposed to watch Hetia. "These two deserve to die" he said, "but we need them, so take them to the edge

211

of the clearing where that idiot who killed the other one is tied and give them a hiding. I want them to know that disobeying my orders comes at a price. Then they can stand night guard for a week. This was our only chance to find out what these lot are up to and you blew it." He stalked off and began to search around the edge of the camp for footprints. He thought he would be able to catch up with Hetia because he believed that she had escaped on foot because all the horses, including hers, were still tied up. "Hey boss," one of the men sent to deal with the guards called out, "you'd better come here and see this. It seemed that Witch wasn't as harmless as we thought." Dagrel strode over to the edge of the camp and there on the ground, tied up as he had been left the night before, was the man who had killed Mariat. He was spread eagled on his back and there were large red welts all over his body. He had been bitten by thousands of insects and ants and he was dead. Dead and cold. This had happened well into the night and no one had heard him. He had been unable to scream as his voice had been stilled. His mouth had been open to scream and had been filled with the big red ants that had the venom to kill, and they had. The look of terror on his face told of his last moments of agony. Dagrel swore and ordered his men to cover the body with dirt. "She must have heard you lot talking about what this one did," Dagrel said, "she must be a she-devil to kill a man like this. Right, when you get this sorted we will find her and this time we will not be so kind."

Rounding up four of his men Dagrel began the search. They would search all morning and not find any trace of Hetia. The footsteps of the rescuers and Wise Woman had been covered over during the early morning by fallen leaves, a gift from the trees, and no sign of Hetia existed. Later on that day the one who was responsible for looking after the horses noticed that the pony Hetia came on was missing. He had been untied neatly and the rope was hanging from the line it was attached to. The pony had disappeared and there were no footprints to follow. From that moment the men began to look over their shoulders in case there were spirits about and it was many nights before they slept soundly once again. Some even questioned why they were still with Dagrel and some would drift away over the near future never again to live this life on the road. Attacking and raiding normal people was one thing, messing with witches, magic and the Gods was a different matter altogether.

Meanwhile Hetia and her rescuers had arrived back in Flessia so bidding the magicians farewell Erik and Hetia returned to the cottage and the little hut out the back. Before she entered Erik placed his hand on her arm. "I thought I had lost you," he said quietly, "the idea that I would never see you again made me realise that I love you Hetia. I know that is something that will never come to anything between us but I just wanted you to know." He turned and walked round the back to his little hut. Hetia called him back. "Please, come inside Erik, I have something to tell you that you need to know." She took him inside and they sat down at the table. Hetia told Erik what she had heard during the night at the camp of the Horde but she did not tell him what she had done to the one who had killed Mariat. She would not tell anyone because it was against all her principles, and she would never forget because she was wide awake when the insects and ants attacked the man, holding his tongue with her magic while they did the work for her. Erik came around the table and laid an arm around Hetia's shoulders. "You poor thing," he said softly, "you know that if you need any help getting through this that I am there for you. I'll leave you for now but please, talk to me if you need to." He left her quietly alone and left the cottage, returning to his hut out the back. He understood that she would have made

the man suffer but would never ask her what she had
done.

Alone in her cottage Hetia checked that the door
was locked and crossed to a cupboard set in a dark corner.
From there she took a small wooden box. Inside the box
was a pale blue crystal wrapped in the skin of a newly born
animal that had died in her care, too small to make it in
this life.

The energy from the crystal was strong as she
unwrapped the small parcel, it had been many years in its
box protected from curious eyes. Hetia held it gently in
her hand. "Your powers may be needed once more" she
said gently to the stone, "I hope I do not have to use that
power but it is good to know you are here where I can find
you." The stone shone brightly in her hand and seemed to
flicker slightly at her touch. Silently she sat holding the
stone within her closed hand. The throbbing energy
reminded her of her strength. The strength no one knew
she had as it had come to her during one of her lone walks
in the mountains many years ago. She had not long
finished her training with the old woman and had ventured
alone high above the plains where she had spent two
weeks living on what she could find growing wild, drinking

from the mountain streams and sheltering in the caves at night. In the gorge beneath the mountains there were strange writings on the rocks in one of the caves she had shared with the bats one night. These symbols were alien to her and there were signs that there had been people living there for a short time many years before. Exploring, using the strong vision she had when she had been working with her inner knowledge, Hetia's bare foot stood on something hard and cold. Bending down she found the most exquisite pale blue stone that must have been cut by a craftsman as the sides were all equal and smooth. Turning it over in her hand she found it was like a small box. Holding it firmly she sent her awareness into the stone and was amazed at the pictures that had formed in her mind. Tall buildings, higher than the trees, seeming to be made of glass and metal, shimmering in bright sunlight. There were plants and trees she had never seen before. It was an alien world that had seemed so fanciful that Hetia thought it was just her imagination working. However, after a while she realised that it seemed to be the stone forming these pictures in her mind.

Slowly, over the next few days Hetia explored the stone's energy. It brought messages to her that she realised must have been connecting her to a much higher spirit, or a source of power she had never felt before. There seemed to be someone talking to her in a language that was foreign to her ears. In her mind she felt movement of people although she couldn't see their bodies or faces. At night she would wrap the stone in a cloth she had brought holding her travelling bread because she feared that during her sleep the images would penetrate her mind. This was strange 'magic' and Hetia was determined to discover more about it. Eventually, taking the stone home wrapped in the cloth, she had decided to see what it could do to bring healing and peace to those around her. However, it seemed to have different powers. One evening, alone in her home she took the stone carefully from its box and out loud asked the question – "What is it that you can do for me?" a simple question, full of possibilities, but one that needed answering. Then words formed in her mind as though someone was standing in the room with her. "I am from another place, another world to what you live in. I serve as a communicator between your world and mine. This artefact was left behind when my people visited your world to retrieve some of our criminals who had found their way through. It is very dangerous for your people to know of my world, we are not the same. Should anyone from your world find the way through they will die immediately and will leave the door open for our evil ones to come back through to you. You cannot destroy this artefact in this form so you must hide it from being used by others. If you wish to be in contact with me, then you, and only you, can do so." These words seemed to come from Hetia's imagination at first, she was very young and only beginning her work with Spirit, but she believed them so she wrapped the stone and placed it in the small box in the dark cupboard. There it had stayed until now.

Holding the stone gently Hetia walked to the centre of the room. Lowering herself onto the mat she placed the stone carefully in front of her. Reaching for the objects she used in meditation she settled down, shutting out the outside world as she turned her awareness within. At first she could not settle, there were too many words going around in her mind, however, after several minutes she began to feel the familiar gentleness that came over her when she lowered her mind from the waking state. Breathing gently she reached forward to pick up the pale blue stone. "I need to contact you" she whispered, "There is work going on here that I must put an end to and I believe you can help me". Waiting patiently Hetia began to think that her imagination had been at work the first time after all when nothing happened. "A little longer" she thought, and once again repeated "I need to contact you, there is evil work going on here that I must put an end to and you are the one I need to contact because I believe you can help". Within seconds she experienced a warmth, as though someone had put their arms around her and embraced her gently. "I am here my child," the voice in her head replied, "I have been watching your magicians in their Tower and I understand your concern. They will never cross through the curtain, you hold the only key and I am sure you will not let them have this. However, you must make certain it never finds its way to anyone else. I will think of a way for you to rid your land of this key once and for all. You must never let anyone else know of this. It is for you only to know. My world is going through a time of power and some evil people are trying to take over. These people must never be able to cross over into your world. We can protect the door on this side, you must do so on the other. I will find a way to rid you of this key."

There were no more words coming into Hetia's mind. She sat quietly for a while then thanked the speaker and the stone. Placing it carefully back into the box Hetia dropped the little box into her bag, drew it over her shoulder as she left the building. Locking the door behind her she walked around using her ward to protect it from intruders. She then went to the little building at the back where Erik was cleaning some tools he used in the garden. Looking up he smiled and touched her hand. "Good morning" he said, "You look like you are off somewhere again. Will you be away long and should I come with you? You never know, Dagrel might learn where you are and come after you." She smiled back at him, "No, not long, maybe a few days. I need to go somewhere quiet for a while. I will not go far but I need some time alone, and don't worry, Dagrel will not find me where I am going. I have closed the house but you may enter as I trust you. I will see you in a few days." She turned and walked away towards the hills where the people flee to when danger arose. She could find somewhere quiet there and ponder the situation she now found herself in. Erik knew where she liked to go, he would leave her in peace.

After a short climb Hetia arrived at the caves. She paused there for a while then decided to go further. The trail led her into a forest where the trees seemed to guide her steps. The air was cool and fresh so Hetia walked a little faster. There was a small cave that she remembered from childhood and she made for it, enjoying memories of climbing trees and hiding from her father in the caves. Father never found her there, so it became her private place. Reaching the cave she realised it had been many years since she was in this part of the forest. So long had it been that the cave was smaller than she remembered. Taking the bag from her shoulder, Hetia had to stoop to enter the cave, but it was cosy inside.

Slipping off her shoes the soft earth felt cool under her feet as she walked around, touching the stone walls gently with her finger tips. She remembered the way she would sit with her back firm against the wall and her toes pushing gently into the sandy earth. Reaching into a little niche in the cave wall Hetia allowed her fingers to probe to the back then, smiling, she withdrew a little skin pouch placed there when she was only ten summers. Unbinding the string that held it together she dropped the contents into her palm. There was an acorn, a feather and a little green shiny stone from the stream down below the mountain. These were a child's treasures so she returned them to the pouch and placed it back into the niche. There were wonderful memories here of innocent times. It appeared that only small animals had entered the cave since Hetia was last here many years ago. This was very good for what she needed to do.

Sitting on the earth she took the blue stone from her bag and held it gently. Turning her mind away from thoughts of everyday life to the stone she remembered the wonders it beheld. The nearness of the cave walls were protective as Hetia began to release her spirit to search for a way to hide the stone. As her spirit began to ascend she found her senses expanding. It was as though she could see the land beyond the cave, as though drifting across the sky, though low enough to behold trees, flowers, animals and people. As she gained some control over her wandering spirit she passed over her village and saw Erik working in her food garden. He looked very peaceful, she thought so further on she went, across the plains, passing the camp of the warriors who were building homes and planting their crops. Onward, until she came to the Tower of Magicians where she stopped, allowing her mind to drop gently into the building below.

There were four men sitting around a table. None of them were aware of her presence and the Elder Solcaan was not there. "The Key must be nearby" one said, "it is written in the old scriptures that the key to the door between the worlds was lost after the strange ones departed. We must combine our thoughts to find this key." "I agree" another replied, "but Solcaan will not agree to this, he has said we should try to pacify the Horde of Doom. What good will that do. They will only think us weak fools. I think we should concentrate on our original idea and send them to another world." The others nodded in agreement and they began to discuss the ways they could find the Key, until the door below opened and Solcaan returned. Knowing he would sense her presence Hetia withdrew her spirit, retreating back to her earthly body in the cave behind Flessia.

The journey in spirit had depleted Hetia of physical energy, as was often the case when she sent her spirit soaring high to "fly" with the great birds who took advantage of the cool air a long way up from the earth. Those were moments when she returned exhilarated, this was a different kind of exhaustion, as she came to realise what she held in her hand and the fact that the magicians had discovered there was such a key as this. Sitting quietly, allowing her body to build strength, Hetia heard the sound of Erik's voice calling her from the forest. It was unusual for him to follow her, he had never done so before apart from the time when a baby had decided to come into the world early and the mother needed help. She thought that he might be worried about her and it gave her a feeling of being protected by something more solid than Spirit, however she also realised that if he worried about her every time she went off on her own then she would have to talk to him about that. Rising from the floor, Hetia went to the mouth of her little cave and stepped out, calling to Erik that she was coming. She quickly returned to the cave where she wrapped the blue stone with the skin and replaced it into its box. Dropping the box into her bag she looked around to make sure she had not left anything behind and went to join Erik, almost bumping into him as she hurried down the trail. "I am so glad I found you here" Erik said quickly, "we have had word that the Horde of Doom is returning to the Plains. I would say that Dagrel became very angry when you had disappeared and decided on revenge. I was sent to find you and to ask you to come back to the village. Can you please come now?" They spoke little as they hurried back to the village, the urgency of the moment overtaking the problem that Hetia needed to solve with the magicians.

People were hurrying about, gathering children and possessions. The old people were being brought together and those who had vowed to help the warriors on the Plains were saddling horses and throwing food and water into their travel bags. They would leave together for safety as soon as all were prepared. Hetia went to her home and gathered herbs and lotions that would be needed if any injuries befell the villagers, sealed the house with her secret words and calling Erik, headed for the Elder's home. She found him waiting for her along with the Spirit Leader and other Elders. "Can I ask you to lead the old people and children up to the caves Erik?" the Elder asked, "We trust you to do this and I know that you will protect them with your life." Erik felt humbled at that moment, the trust that he had been trying to build was finally showing, he nodded his head and turned to gather up his charges along with their supplies and to herd them up in to the hills when Hetia asked him to wait a moment. Turning to Hetia the Elder said quietly, "It is not that we don't want Erik here with us, it is because we believe that he has earned our trust. We are trusting him with the lives of our most vulnerable people, this is his opportunity for him to become one of the community. I hope you understand our actions." Hetia smiled and nodded. "I would have advised you to do this. I believe also that Erik has earned this trust. Please give me a moment to talk to him then we can work out what are we going to do next?"

Away from the others Hetia placed her hand on Erik's arm. "I just want you to know, before you leave, that you have become very important to me." she said quietly, "You know I can never have a proper relationship with any man as I have taken vows of celibacy, but I need to tell you, in case the worst happens, that I care for you very much." Erik looked down into Hetia's solemn face and at that moment he felt the same for her, although he had come to realise this when she had been kidnapped. "I understand Hetia, I have grown very fond of you too and I am glad that you have told me how you feel. Perhaps in another life we will be together but please know that I am content to live near you and look after the practical things in life for you. I would also defend you to the death if it became necessary." He placed his hand over hers for a moment then touched her cheek gently before turning to take on the task he had been given.

Hetia, the Elders and the Spirit leader moved inside the head Elder's home. Sitting around the table they discussed what they could do. "We could move our able bodied men and women and the older children to the camp on the Plains" one of the Elders said, "Or we could stay here to defend our village and leave the Warriors to be the first defence. Hetia stood, pacing the room for a moment, then said "I agree with the second idea, we should stay and defend. I believe that I can connect with the magicians in the Tower from here, and with you Spirit

Leader, we could lend our strengths. That way, if the Horde of Doom were to pass the Warriors' camp we could shift the magic energy in many directions. Although I was not in the first group, I believe that I can very quickly learn the ways that were used." The Elders and the Spirit Leader nodded in agreement. "That's it then" said the leading Elder, "we shall set up some physical defence here and you will both work together with the magicians. Let us start."

They left the house and called the remaining villagers together. Explaining what they were going to do the Elder gave everyone a task. As they set about these tasks the Spirit Leader took Hetia aside. "I am concerned about the magicians in the Tower" he said softly, "I feel some kind of energy coming from there that I do not understand. Do you have this feeling also Hetia?" Hetia nodded, "Yes Leader," she replied, "I have been concerned also and I was meditating in the forest on this when Erik came for me. I was able to connect my mind across the miles to the magicians and I did not like what I heard. They may be moving out of the safety of their traditional knowledge, trying to find ways to go beyond that which should be allowed. I was thinking of ways to stop them when I was called. As our Spirit Leader I was going to come to you. So now, together, we can see what can be done." She did not mention the stone or the conversation she overheard in the Tower. As the Spirit Leader, this man was responsible for the Spiritual guidance of the people, he did not know of the magical things that could be achieved, although he was aware of their presence. Hetia walked with him for a while as they discussed many ways that could be used to defeat the Horde. Finally they decided to contact the Spirit Leaders in the other villages, by working together they could be ready for anything untoward that might arise. In the meantime they would have many preparations to make. Hetia would be needed for healing and the Spirit Leader would be needed to guide the people through a very traumatic time if the Horde of Doom broke through. This time, they would be ready.

The village was buzzing with frantic but organised activity. Under the guidance of the elderly the children were given the task of collecting up everyone's valuables to be taken into the fields and buried deep into the earth where they could be dug up after the danger had passed. Then the children and elders left the village with Erik for the safety of the caves. The cattle and other livestock were herded up into the hills where those too young to fight were given the task of tending the beasts. They travelled along an old overgrown track, the cows were lowing and snuffling and with a bit of persuasion the animals were cajoled and prodded into moving as fast as possible. Two boys followed behind the livestock pulling branches and small shrubs across the trail to hide the hoof prints and footsteps from any who might try to follow. In the hills there were valleys hidden from anyone who did not know the way, and these were ideal hiding places that could be fenced off to prevent the stock from straying. They took food and blankets, it could be a long time before they could return to the village. Hetia spoke to them before they left and explained how important their job was and that they would be called in by a messenger once the danger was passed. If the animals were found and slaughtered by the Horde there would be very little food left for the survivors. One of the boys, a lad of fifteen years, was delegated their leader. He had wanted to stay and fight with his father but was given this very important task. "When you get as far as you can," his father had said, "take fallen trees or anything else you can find and build a barrier that will stop the animals trying to get back to the village. You are very brave my son and I am so proud of you. We may not see each other again in this life but I know that if I do not survive you will take care of your mother and sisters." The boy lifted his young chin and pushed out his chest. He did feel proud that he could do his part in this fight against evil. Turning back to his task he began to call in his dogs and the other children and they set off for the hills.

Without the laughter and squeals of the small children the village now seemed very quiet. Only the able bodied adults remained behind and they settled in to build barriers around the village to give some protection from invasion. This was a chance to protect their own belongings, their homes and their lifestyles as they never had before. Men and women armed themselves as best they could, keeping their weapons on hand at all times. This time they would be ready to face the Horde of Doom.

The waiting was tedious. Every time something moved on the Horizon a warning cry would be heard. Eventually the Elder called a meeting of the people. "We cannot stop working every time someone sees dust from an animal or the wind" he explained, "I would like you to organise a lookout. Pick a team of those who are fast riders and have good eyesight and each one can spend some time at a viewing place. Please read the signs carefully. We cannot have panic and we cannot stop work every time there is a dust devil. I leave it to you to select those who will carry out this important task." He turned and walked away. After much discussion six people were chosen as lookouts. They would share the responsibility and would also have time to tend their own work in the village.

15 RETURN OF EVIL

It was three days later that a genuine warning came. The rider, a young woman, galloped into the village calling everyone's attention. "There is a rider coming" she warned, "He is coming very fast and straight towards the village. He is on his own so it cannot be the Horde of Doom." The Elder hurried forth with Hetia at his side. As they watched the rider coming closer they realised that it was one of their young warriors, a youth of sixteen who had left with the warriors who were guarding the Plains. He jumped from his horse in front of the Elder, catching his breath and handing his horse over to one of the men who had come along to see what was going on. "The Horde of Doom has been seen in the same gorge as before. The magicians have joined us and we are getting ready for a fight. I have been sent to let you know that we will try everything possible to stop them from leaving the gorge but you are to be alert that they may get past the magicians and come here. The Warriors and the Magicians will ride to the hills above the pass to begin their work and the rest of the camp is ready to fight. I am to wish you well and return as soon as I can." He stood for a moment in silence. The people began to speak softly among themselves, concern showing on their faces. "Thank you young man" replied the head Elder, "you are very brave to undertake this task and I commend you." Hetia stepped forward, "Will you take a message for me to Solcaan please?" the young man nodded, "Tell him that we will assist him from here. Ask him to contact me, he knows how, and we will do what we can to aid him in his task." The messenger did not ask how this would be done, he, like most of the people of the land, didn't want to meddle in the workings of magic in any form. He accepted a drink that was offered him and some fruit then climbed up upon his horse once more. Turning towards the Plains he wished everyone the strength they would need and headed back to the fight knowing he may never see his home again.

Hetia turned to the Elder and begged her leave. "I will be spending some time with our Spirit Leader and request that we be left alone to our task. I will keep you informed Elder." He nodded as she left and turned to organise his people.

On the way to the home of the Spirit Leader Hetia stopped by her cottage. As she entered she turned and said a few words of warding to ensure no-one would enter behind her. Closing the door she went to the box that held the tokens and other items that she used to strengthen her magic work. There were only a few items inside and these were very personal, including a jar of blue pigment that she used to deepen the colour of her tattoos. Taking this from the box Hetia went to her small mirror and took a few deep breaths. Closing her eyes for a few moments Hetia began chanting the words that she had used first at her initiation then on only a few occasions over the years when she had re-stained the symbols. Opening her eyes she dipped her index finger into the blue mixture and applied it carefully. This time she added another chant as she painted over the marks. The chant was one of power, incurring the strength of the Goddess to enable work to be done with the energies of the Earth, Water, Fire and Air. The chant was long and needed to be repeated three times in order for the power to be raised. When the marks were all strengthened Hetia opened the box once more and replaced the jar that held the pigment, then she took from the box an amulet with rune markings to invoke the Earth energy, she placed the amulet's cord over her head to rest upon her chest with the markings turned towards her skin so no other person would catch a glimpse of the sign. She added an eagle feather to her hair to respect the power of Air and a small phial of water she hung around her neck. The power of Fire would be invoked at the Spirit Leader's home. Checking that all was in order Hetia replaced the box in it's special place and left her home, locking the door behind her and sealing it from intruders. It was a short distance to the Spirit Leader's home so it only took her a few moments, however she wore a cloak with the hood up so that the villagers would not notice that she had strengthened her secret markings and was ready for magic work. Once inside with the Spirit Leader she begged leave to light a small fire in the grate, explaining that she needed to invoke the energy of Fire. He took notice of her markings and adornments and was aware of the fact that Hetia would only appear in front of him like this when very strong magic would be invoked. This would be a long day and they both knew that it could end badly. However, in her heart Hetia believed that they could overcome this Horde of Doom once and for all, she was just unsure exactly how it would be done.

Sitting quietly within the walls of the Spirit Leader's home the two trained in their own forms of magic and power closed their eyes and waited, breathing steadily and allowing their minds to be open to receive word from Solcaan. It wasn't long before Hetia felt the tentative touch as an attempt was made to contact her. Accepting the touch she began to concentrate. Solcaan and the other magicians had come up with a plan that could work with each doing their own part. The power that would be required from Hetia was her knowledge of the elements. Especially her knowledge of the Earth was extremely important. The plants and insects that lived within the earth could be called upon to assist in this task. She wasn't sure how this could be done so allowed herself to be guided by Solcaan. Slowly the knowledge came, what plants would the Horde of Doom rely upon for food on their journey? Her herb lore would be very important and she began to understand what was required of her so sent the thought back to Solcaan. Hetia told him of a leafy plant that was commonly eaten by travellers. It grew in many places and when added to the pots of stew that was common food amongst large bodies of travellers it would give them the sustenance that gave energy to the body. Very like the leafy greens that were grown in most food gardens. There was also another leafy plant that would cause pain in the gut and it would be necessary to spend many hours emptying the bowels. The two plants were very similar and grew in the same places, however, all those who were used to cooking plants that grew in the wild would know the difference. Hetia's task was to confuse the one who collected the food for the Horde of Doom. Smiling inside herself she understood her task completely. She began to search for the mind of the one who collected the food . It took only minutes. Not being used to the probing thoughts of one such as Hetia, the cook had no idea that she was exploring his mind. The next thing she needed to do was confuse his thoughts so that both plants looked exactly the same to him when he went to gather the leaves. She enjoyed this task, something she had never had the chance to do as it was bad manners to interfere with the thoughts of another. Gently, very gently, she began to plant the idea into the cook's mind that there was an abundance of this green "vegetable" in the gorge where they would set up camp. He would find so much of the plant that they would eat well for days and he would see no difference between the two similar plants. Leaving this thought in his mind she gently broke the connection. Now she would await the results of her work. Sending Solcaan one last message, Hetia opened her eyes and waited quietly for the Spirit Leader to do the same.

Twenty riders, their horses covered in white foam, thundered into the canyon. They were wild men with weapons strapped to their bodies, some wearing masks that only showed their eyes and mouth, others with leather helmets jammed over unruly hair. A few had fashioned leather armour to protect them from spears and arrows and all had bed rolls and saddle bags with their worldly goods packed in, for these men had no homes to go to, no village or town had their allegiance. They had not even sworn allegiance to their leader, they only followed him because he was stronger in mind and nastier then anyone of them. These were bad, evil men willing to do anything that would bring them rewards. On this day they were heading for a village where, it was said, precious stones had been unearthed and were being kept until the next gathering of the Plains folk where they would be sold and traded. The men of the Horde were all thinking of this treasure and they would take everything from these 'helpless' people and carry it to the coastal towns where they could sell it on to the traders who didn't care where the goods came from. Trying to out-ride each other and be the first to reach the Village so they could take the best for themselves was their priority. However, ahead of the rest was the leader, Dagrel. He was a big man, clad in leather with thick plates of double leather on the front and back of his upper body and a helmet of leather protecting his head from being stoned or killed by a blow. He had a deep, long scar running down his right cheek that pulled his features into a peculiar grimace. He had lost two front top teeth in a fight and had many other scars on his body from the hard life he lead. His horse was mean and bad tempered which suited him as no one would ever try to steal it from him. The company he kept was never to be trusted and he was always on the look out for trouble. Behind the Leader rode his two deputies. One was tall and lean dressed all in black with gold rings through his ears and a leather thong tied his long hair back behind his neck. He had ridden with the last Horde led by Starreck. The other one was built like a rock with broad chest and shoulders and tattoos on just about every part of his body. He had forgotten how to be a decent human being long ago and was absolutely ruthless with anyone who managed to get in his way. None of the men took him on and no-one questioned his authority. These two men made sure that no one passed Dagrel, for their job was to make sure no trouble was able to fester among the men. The last town they had gone through was two days' ride behind them. They had camped out of town and gone quietly in to stock up on supplies. It was in a tavern that the leader had heard a rumour about the precious stones. "Sapphires as big as a hen's egg" someone had whispered, "and emeralds. All just lying about. Apparently the people just pick them up. They have stashed them in a cave with their other valuables I am told, ready for trading later in the year." Being sceptical at first the Horde leader had decided to wait and see if anyone else mentioned it, just in case it was the rantings of a drunk. But it wasn't long before an old man, bent over and walking with a stick, sidled up and told him the same story. Not wanting anyone else to get the same idea they left the tavern and headed back to camp. At sun rise the next morning they had packed up camp and headed off.

Nobody noticed the old man standing on a hill overlooking their camp. As they left he smiled and turned away heading back to town. He would contact Solcaan and let him know another step had been taken to eradicate the Horde of Doom once and for all.

That night the Horde camped in a Gorge where there was shelter against the cliff face. Although they were all eager to find the Village or the hoard they realised they couldn't find their way in the dark. The old man at the Tavern had given them reason to believe that the stones were hidden in a cave in this gorge so they would sleep on it and start early the next morning. No-one was going to argue with Dagrel and his two deputies, they figured they could deal with him after they found what they had come for. During the night a few of the men mumbled to each other that they would do Dagrel and his two deputies in once they had found the hoard. As they sat just a little distance from the others they began to quietly plot what they would do.

Around midnight a mighty storm came thundering through the gorge, drenching all their gear and putting out the fire. They backed up against the cliff under a small outcrop to find shelter and spent the rest of the night in misery. In the morning, wet and cold, they mounted their horses and rode through the gorge until they could climb high and look out over the Plains.

The night before, on the Plains, close to the Gorge where the Horde of Doom had made camp, the Magicians had gathered. Under the leadership of Solcaan, sitting in a circle clasping hands and centring their minds, the magicians began their work with the elements. As before, the weather was brought in to aid their defence. As the energy was called in dark clouds began to form on the horizon, they swirled and deepened becoming very dark and gloomy. Lightning flashed and crackled through the clouds as the power built up and thunder boomed shaking the ground beneath. Within moments the clouds filled the sky, covering the moon and rolling and twisting until the sky looked as though the Gods were going to descend to Earth, then wild winds tore loudly through between the cliff faces on the mountains loosening stones and dirt, and finally torrential rain soaked every existing thing that was not under shelter. Nature could be terrible when aroused and the magicians did their utmost to pull in as much of this power as they could.

High on a cliff top overlooking the Plains the leader of the Horde sat his horse and pointed to the place where the Magicians were working. Turning to his left he spoke to the man who was his second in command. "That's where this bad weather comes from" he snarled, "I thought it wasn't natural for this time of year. We shall sort out those troublemakers once and for all. Fetch me the prisoner." One of the men turned his horse and rode to the camp, returning a short while later with another rider who was bound at the wrists and ankles and tied to the stirrups of his saddle. It was one of the young magicians, still only three years into his long training of twenty years, who had been captured that morning riding between the tower and his family home. As his family were unaware of his visit the young man had not been missed.

"Well now" growled Dagrel, "we'd better let your people know that we have one of their whelps. Suppose you tell me who is the leader and you won't get hurt. Come on lad, who's the boss?" Sitting upright and proud the young magician held his tongue. With a signal from the leader the man holding the captive's reins raised his gloved hand and slapped it hard across the young lad's head. "Answer, quick and clear" he snarled. Once more there was no answer, inviting another blow from the leather gloved hand. With blood appearing at the corner of his mouth the magician stared in defiance at the Horde of Doom's leader.

"Alright son," the leader said calmly, "we'll do this another way. Orek, take the amulet from his neck and bring it to me. We'll see if your boss knows you by this." Holding the amulet in his hand above his head, he took off his weapons in a way that he would be observed by the magicians watching him and rode towards them with his hands out wide. When he was close enough for them to hear he called out, "I have one of your whelps Magic Man, here is his amulet so you know I am not lying. " Throwing the amulet towards the magicians he continued, "If you don't stop the magic I will skewer the lad and leave him to die slowly amongst the ants and vultures. Stop what you are doing. Otherwise, look for his body." Turning his horse he rode back towards his men. "Now we should have some peace from those interfering old men" he mumbled as they rode back to camp. What the leader was unaware of was that the magicians could communicate with the lad. Solcaan reached into the boys mind, speaking words of calming. They would stop the work so the lad would live, however, others were working to help in different ways. All they needed was time. Understanding the ways of his Elder the boy began to relax, when his food was brought to him he accepted the bowl and settled in to wait.

Solcaan gathered his group together in the Grove beside the Tower. "We will need to think this one out" he said quietly, "there is one who can achieve what we cannot. I will need you all to remain calm and stay here while I talk to this person. The Horde of Doom will believe we are beaten and will likely begin their attacks again tomorrow. We must trust the warriors for a while, but hopefully, not for long. I will be back in a day or two." He turned and collected his bag and staff, mounted his horse, then set off for Flessia.

Reaching the village before evening, Solcaan found Hetia waiting for him at her door. "Greetings my friend," she said "I was expecting you. Please come inside." Leading the way Hetia sat by the fireplace, indicating the other seat to Solcaan. "We seem to have a problem that needs to be solved once and for all." Hetia stated "I am getting quite fed up with this Horde of Doom. I am very tempted to do something a bit drastic but it is against my principals. My worry is your young magician, if the Horde of Doom were to disappear then the lad may go too. I am about to reveal to you the secret of the key your magicians have been talking of. I have been keeping this for many years but it is time that we trusted in it's power. Once I reveal this to you and we have used it to rid us of the Horde of Doom then I must find a way of destroying the key." Hetia closed her eyes for a moment knowing that what she was about to say would change her relationship with Solcaan. "Many years ago I discovered a "gateway" between this world and another, so very different from ours. I am sure you understand that these places exist and I know that you have knowledge of the Rune markings in certain caves across the land. I have in my possession the key to travel between the worlds although I have never used the gateway myself. This secret has been with me for many,

many years and, until now, I have never spoken of it to anyone. I will not tell you what the key is as I intend it to be sent back to the other world, but this may be the answer to all our problems with the Horde of Doom. I will need to contact someone in the other world and I must do this alone." Solcaan had listened quietly to Hetia and sat thinking over what she had said. "I trust you Hetia" he said, "and I know you will do what is right for our people. You have my support and my silence my child." Accepting his promise of silence, Hetia spoke quietly, "I need to go to the hills for a few hours and I ask you to stay here. No one must follow. Please, help yourself to some supper and I will return before long." Leaving Solcaan to rest Hetia collected her bag with the blue stone inside and left the cottage.

The moon had risen so Hetia was able to find her way in the dark. As she began the gentle climb into the forest she began to form a plan in her mind that would see the end of the tyranny they had experienced in their lives for many years. As she neared the pathway that would take her up into the hills where her little cave was hidden from view she tried to centre her mind on the journey. The path began to change to a rocky little track that ran through the dense trees. The moon wasn't able to penetrate the thick vegetation so Hetia began to touch the trees gently to guide her way and to bring about a grounding of her energy. She was about to take drastic action against the evil ones, to rid the land of them once and for all. By sending them through to the other world they might not survive the journey, she had been told this, and as she had never killed a human being, and only killed an animal if it was badly injured or was incurably ill, the idea that she might be sending these men to their death was heavy on her mind. However, she decided to trust in her belief that the Goddess would take care of life and she would need to trust her unseen friend on the 'other side' of the portal. By the time she reached her little cave, well away from any trodden path, she had made up her mind. These men needed to leave this land and there was no other way out. Entering the cave she sat on the soft sand and took out the stone. Holding it gently in her palm she closed her eyes and began to concentrate. "I need your help my old friend" she said quietly, "I have a very big problem." Waiting a while she repeated her words. A feeling of warmth, as before, crept over Hetia's shoulders, like an invisible embrace. "I am here my child." The words appeared as if in her mind, "What troubles you so that you are in contact with me so soon?" "I am very worried for my people" Hetia replied, "this Horde of

Doom that terrorises my people is getting bolder. We have fought them with magic but they have one of our young magicians held captive. They are ruthless, they burn and rape and kill, nothing seems to stop them. I know it is wrong for me to talk of this to you but can we send them to your world to be dealt with by your laws? I understood from our conversations that you retrieved criminals from here. I assume that you have some way of dealing with them that we do not have here. You also said you guard the doorway between our worlds. If we send them through would they survive? Or can we send them somewhere else where they would become harmless? I have told only Solcaan, the Elder of the Community of Magicians, about the doorway, although he does not know how to use it or what the key is. There are suspicions among those in the Tower but Solcaan will dispel those suspicions." Once she had explained her idea to rid the world of the Horde of Doom once and for all Hetia began to have doubts. Was she sending her troubles to someone else? As she pondered this for a moment, the voice came back to her. "I think we can solve this one Hetia, but of your young apprentice I am not so sure. He might suffer the same fate as the others although we would take very good care of him at our side. I have an idea and you can let me know if you wish it to happen."

The plan was explained to Hetia who agreed to give it a try. Thanking her unseen friend Hetia replaced the stone in its wrappings and dropped it into her bag. Standing, she turned and walked back to the village to explain to Solcaan the plan that should rid the land of the Horde of Doom once and for all. The only problem was the young magician, however, Hetia would explain the idea she had discussed with her friend from the other side.

Sharing a late supper, Solcaan and Hetia were deep in quiet conversation until Solcaan lifted his head, "Yes Hetia, we will follow your idea. What will become of my apprentice?" "That is not difficult" replied Hetia, "there is a plant that clings to the cliffs in the Gorge where they are holding the lad prisoner, its' flower is small and yellow and gives off the smell of honey. If he takes a leaf and holds it in his mouth for ten seconds then spits it out he will pass out, his heart will appear to have stopped and he will not breathe more than a very gentle puff. This is so gentle that only a true healer would know he was not dead. After about four hours he will wake and only have a bad headache. I will need to contact him through spirit so he can gather a couple of the leaves when they let him go to relieve himself. No-one will ever know. However, he will be instructed not take the leaf into his mouth until we have the Horde of Doom in place because it works very quickly and he will only have one chance. They will think you have killed him by magic to stop them from doing it their way. Now, I must contact my friend again, but this time I shall do it in my back room, you must not know by what means."

The next morning Hetia rode away with Solcaan. They rode fast to the place where the others were waiting. "We have to lure the Horde of Doom to the cave of the ancient markings" Solcaan explained, "please do not ask any information from me, just trust me and follow my lead. We need to plant a thought into their heads that some people have hidden their precious belongings in that cave. When they see the markings they will think they are protection symbols. It is not a very large cave but without their horses they will all fit inside. Once they are in we will seal the entrance with a rock fall. There is a way to save our young apprentice so he will not be with them and Hetia will take care of that. Our job is to lure every one of the Horde of Doom, especially the leader, into that cave. We will place pictures of gold and silver and anything else of value we can conjure up, into their minds. I will work on the leader. This is where we will lead them." He proceeded with his instruction drawing a small map in the dirt to show the location of the cave, until everyone was clear of their task. Meanwhile Hetia sat aside to inform the young lad of what he was to do. "This is Hetia of Flessia" she sent silently to the young apprentice's mind, "Can you hear me? Just think your reply and give me your Master's pet name for you so I know it is you to whom I speak." She waited a moment then sent the message again. This time there was a reply, faint at first then she felt the fear in his thoughts as he gave her the name she required. "Good" Hetia answered, "Now this is very important and you must do exactly as I say so your life will be spared. Do not be afraid, but we must make very sure you do not enter a cave we are sending the Horde of Doom into." Explaining the plan Hetia finished by assuring the young man that he would be safe back with his Master very soon. By the time of the midday meal they were all ready and began the work to rid them all once and for all of the menace of the Horde of Doom. The other magicians seemed to be of the opinion that the Horde of Doom were to be buried alive in the cave, though no-one questioned Solcaan on this.

16 TRANSPORTATION

The day was quite warm, only a light breeze seemed to drift through the Gorge as the men of the Horde spent some time cleaning their weapons and checking their gear, for they were to head out before the day drew too hot. It was more than a week since they rode into the Gorge but they had spent a very uncomfortable time since arriving. Most of the men were suffering from a blight to the bowels, one after the other running off to find a bush or rock to squat behind. Even Dagrel, who normally didn't get sick, was suffering from this blight. The cook was being blamed for poisoning them and despite his argument that there was nothing wrong with the food the distrust was beginning to form in all their minds. During the night the idea of a hidden treasure had entered their dreams. Early the next morning the leader had called his men together. "There is a cave," he said, "where I believe the people around here have hidden their valuables so we won't find them. With some 'persuasion' this young lad we have here has confirmed this, although he doesn't know exactly where it is. It can't be too far though because these people would have to have stashed it in a hurry. These are the only cliffs around here that could have a cave in them. So, we are going to have a look." One or two of the men spoke up and said they had heard of this too but could not remember who had told them. They didn't tell each other that they were also going to try and get rid of Dagrel, but all had the same idea. "Alright" Dagrel said, "get yourselves ready to ride." He turned to the young magician. "Oi youngster, stretch your legs for a bit because I am going to tie you to that tree over there while we are gone because we might need you again. But make sure you don't go too far, and no funny magic business, I'm watching you."

The young lad walked a short distance from the men and turning his face to the cliff he pretended to relieve himself. What they didn't see was the small leaf he plucked from a little plant growing from the rock face. Slipping it into his mouth he returned to the others. Within minutes he fell to the ground as if dead. Dagrel was called and he bent over the boy, placing his hand on the chest to see if he was alive. "He's not breathing," he explained, "those damned magicians have killed the boy somehow with magic because he was very fit and wouldn't have just keeled over. That changes the game, we would have needed him again if we didn't find the valuables but now I'll have to think up something else. Well, we can't help it now. Put him up against the cliff face out of the sight of the vultures and throw some brush over him and maybe they will come and get him once we have gone." Angrily he then hustled the men on to their horses and they rode off towards the direction of the cave he had "remembered" during the night before.

Scrabbling along the cliff face, pushing aside bushes and rocks, it was an hour before they found the cave entrance hidden by a clump of gorse bushes. None of the men thought about how they had found the cave but they had seemed to be suddenly standing in front of it. The entrance was quite narrow, the horses wouldn't be able to enter, so they were tethered to the bushes outside. No-one wanted to stay to mind them, just in case he missed out on some treasure, so they all pushed their way through the cave entrance where they found themselves in a passageway leading to a large cavern. The men in front lit lanterns they had brought to see their way after leaving the daylight behind them. As they went further in they noticed that the walls were covered in some unusual writing. Thinking these were symbols to protect the treasure from marauders such as themselves the men made jokes of the writing. "Here look" one of them scoffed, "this one looks like you boss, and he has others around him. Maybe they thought that drawing pictures of men would scare us off.

And these look like numbers. If I could read maybe it would give a clue." The others gathered about and Dagrel came to see what they were talking about. "Don't worry about that" he grumbled, it is all rubbish, these people wouldn't know any magic stuff, it's probably just someone scribbling something." Of course they couldn't know that these were numbers that would help a traveller move from one place to another. Those who had placed the numbers on the wall had passed through here decades before.

Once they were all inside the deeper cavern Dagrel ordered them to start looking about. "I don't think they would just leave their valuables out in the open," he said, "so begin to search in crevices and holes, look for places that have been dug over or disturbed, don't leave anything to chance and don't think you can keep anything from me, if I find you have then you're as dead as that boy out there." They all began to search every nook and cranny looking for signs that someone had been there. "Hey boss" called one of the men, "I think you must have been dreaming, there's nothing here but rats bones and dirt. There is no sign that anybody has been there except for those marks on the wall and they could have been there for years." Dagrel turned on him and grabbed him by the front of his shirt. "You think you're so clever, did it not occur to you that if the magicians are clever enough to stir up wind and rain that they couldn't hide a few trinkets? Keep looking while I see if I can figure out this writing." Not wanting to upset their leader the men went back to their hunt. Dagrel was the only one of the men who could read but he couldn't make any sense of the writing. At first he thought the numbers might have been measurements so he began to pace out in different directions from the entrance. Groping around with his hands only gave up dust and stones so he returned to the writing. Could it be that it was a language from some other land.

Dagrel knew of other lands, he had plenty of contact with strangers when he lived in the coastal towns. The pictures looked slightly familiar but he still couldn't work it out. He was deep in thought when a small rumble was heard near the cave entrance, followed by a loud crash, then rocks fell at the doorway of the cave blocking their way out and thick dust filled the cavern. When the dust settled the men began to panic, pushing and shoving each other to dig at the fallen rocks. No amount of shouting from Dagrel would stop them. Panic was driving them. Digging with their bare hands they made little headway against the rock-fall. One of the older men had thought to bring along a small spade so with desperate effort he began to dig at the top of the rock fall. "Those damned Magicians must be behind this," grumbled the leader, "it's only rocks and dirt so if you dig long enough we will get out. Just keep going." Then suddenly they all stopped, turned their heads and stared, for standing in the centre of the cave was a small group of strange warriors. There had been a whooshing sound as the soldiers arrived, and an eerie light that disappeared once all were in the cave.

These were not the warriors of the Plains, nor were they like anything the men had seen before. Their armour was thick padding the colour of the trees and bushes, their helmets were round and close fitting made of metal. In their hands they held weapons with long round pipes attached to a handle where they were held with one finger on a small stick within a round circle. They were tall, all of them taller than the Horde of Doom's leader, who was considered tall amongst the people of the Land. In the middle of the warriors was a man who was obviously the leader. He stepped forward standing in front of Dagrel who he recognised as the Horde's leader from Hetia's description. Looking Dagrel in the eye he announced "You are all my prisoners and if you think that all of you can beat my small troop then think again. Sergeant, fire a shot into the ground in front of this man." The Sergeant fired one shot, missing Dagrel's boot by a finger width and a very loud noise filled the air. "That bullet can enter your heart and kill you instantly. If you doubt that then please feel free to try your luck." "He tells the truth" one of the Horde of Doom whispered to his leader, "I have heard the stories, they are warriors from another world and those weapons can kill from a long distance. I was only a small child when I fell through the doorway from that world to this with my father so I have never remembered much about it, but now I see these warriors I recall my father talking about the Cities of Steel and how their warriors roamed the land looking for outlaws. He died when I was still a little boy so I never knew any more about it and anyway I thought they were just the stories a father tells his children. I can't see how we can escape and I think I would like to return to my world in one piece to see where I came from." The men of the Horde of Doom were so taken aback by the very presence of the warriors that not one moved but Dagrel, not wanting to give in reached for the sword he had strapped to his back and snarled "I am not afraid of you, there's twice as many of us and we can take you easily." He rushed forward, followed by one or two of his followers. They only took a few steps when a large 'crack' rang out, blood appeared on Dagrel's forehead, his eyes stared ahead and then went blank as he fell heavily to the ground. The others stopped dead in their tracks in shock as they realised that they had met a foe with weapons that they could not fight. "Alright, alright" one of the two henchmen cried, "we will obey." and they all backed up towards the blocked entrance of the cave.

"Right," the leading soldier said, "now I want you to move closer together so that you all stand in a tight group. That's the way, now stay very still and you won't get hurt. You are going to a place where you will no longer be able to wreak havoc on innocent people. I am going to put you to work rebuilding villages that have been flattened by a huge earthquake on an island in our world. There will be no-one for you to terrorise and for your work you will get properly fed and a place to sleep, nothing else. None of you deserve any better and I'll bet none of you have done an honest day's work in your life, so this can be a new start for you. If you try to leave the work site you will be put in a jail cell and remain there for the rest of your life. If you behave then eventually your life will get a little better, but you will not be coming back here. Do you understand?" The men, who were feeling trapped and very uncertain of their future looked at each other and began to nod. There was obviously no way out of the cave and they could not argue with the weapons pointed in their direction. "Ok" the soldier said, "Sergeant, give the signal." The Sergeant took from his pocket a small square box and pressing a button he spoke quietly into it. At that moment the air began to change and shimmer then a bright light flashed throughout the cavern. Within a blink of an eye the cavern was empty, not a soul was left, only dust that settled once there were no feet to disturb it and the body of Dagrel, left behind in case someone came into the cave in the future and wondered about the disappearance of the Horde. All was quiet.

On the other side of the gateway, in a far, far away place, a group of very confused men stood surrounded by the armed soldiers. As they were all stunned by what had just occurred they were easily herded as one along a pathway through a gate. This gate was immense, it was standing between two towers that reached several stories high and either side was a very imposing fence with sharp razor wire running around the top creating an impenetrable barrier for anyone trying to enter or leave. Still numb from their experience, not understanding what was happening to them, the men were herded further into a building where they were searched and handed uniforms to wear made of drab material. They were handed a thick jacket for the cold days and told to keep their own boots. These uniforms would distinguish them from all other people and show them to be prisoners. They were then taken into a holding area where there names were recorded and from then on they were prisoners of the modern world so far distant from where they had come. They would be separated and taken to various work groups. Their lives were now in the hands of the people who would take them each day to their work. They would never, ever return to their own land again.

17 RELIEF

Hetia travelled with the Magicians as they went to search for the young apprentice. She had ridden most of the way with them until she stopped at a fork in the trail. She bid Solcaan farewell then took a different direction. Reaching the place where the horses were still tied up, she dismounted and walked to the blocked entrance of the cave taking out the blue stone. "I give you our thanks my friend," she said aloud, "as you promised I will not ask where you have taken the evil ones, I trust that you will be humane. I am placing the stone on the place you instructed. Once more, thank you with all my heart." She placed the stone upon a large boulder beside the blocked entrance and, untying the horses to take them with her, she walked back to her own horse. As she faced away from the cave she heard a rush of air and turning, saw before her the one who had helped them rid the Land of the Horde of Doom. He smiled at Hetia as he picked up the blue stone. "Don't worry my child," he said softly, "they live and they will be made to work to compensate for what they have done to your people. We do not put people to death, but we do make them pay for their crimes. We have a place upon an island and they will be made to work there until 20 years have passed, unless they die beforehand, then they will be free but upon our world, which is much harsher than this one. If they die in my lifetime I will send their bodies back to the cave behind those fallen rocks so that anyone digging there in the future will think they were buried alive and that will explain their disappearance. The leader of the men made a fatal mistake and he was shot and killed. His body is still there in the cave.

You have done well as have your magicians. Please know that you can go to your little cave in the hills at any time and if you think hard enough I will hear you. You and I do not need the communication device. Before I go I should tell you that my name is Captain Brendan Hill. I have a family in my world with a daughter that longs to travel. One day I might send her here to you to train in the natural ways because that knowledge has become extinct in our society. I would let you know in plenty of time if that is to occur. However, it seems such a shame that you will never see the wonders of my world. I have thought long on this and have decided that I should give you the opportunity to come back with me to visit. I would take very good care of you and return you back here within a few days then take the communicator back with me. What do you say?" Hetia was taken aback with this suggestion and for a moment felt quite excited at the idea. "No, I don't think it would be a good idea." she replied, "I have all that I need in this life apart from peace, and now we are rid of the evil ones then I should have that also. If I come with you I might see and hear things that will question the knowledge I have and cause feelings that will take away the life as I know it. Thank you all the same."

Captain Hill looked at her eyes and saw a deep and ancient wisdom there and knew he shouldn't push her on the issue. "Alright" he said, "I thought that's what you would say so I brought along some pictures that we call photos of my city. Would you like to see them?" Hetia was curious and held out her hand to take the photos. She gasped as she took in the tall glass covered buildings and the masses of people and vehicles on the streets. The second picture was of a beach with boats on the water, but no buildings in sight. "We stopped building near the sea centuries ago when the seas rose and flooded everything." said the Captain, "We still go to the sea for pleasure though, we swim in the sea and sail our pleasure boats that you see there. For many decades the sea was too polluted with rubbish to catch fish to eat but we have cleaned it up and now we can also fish. I know you have a small city near the sea as I have seen it myself, but as your people only have small boats it is best that it stays that way with just short journeys to catch fish. My world is on this same planet Hetia, just very far across the wide ocean that begins it's journey at the edge of your land. Our government, our leaders, have made it against our laws for our people to travel too far from our shores for we know that no good can come from introducing our advanced ways into the simple lives of people such as yours and others who live on other islands. We have isolated ourselves to keep others safe. In our childhood we are taught that the world must never go through another climate catastrophe that devastated most of this planet many centuries ago and we take a vow in our teen years not to try and travel across the seas. I am one of the peace keepers who make sure no one breaks that promise. So my Hetia this is goodbye, not necessarily forever, you know I will come if you need me and I will see if my daughter would like to come and study with you in a few years time when she becomes a woman. Farewell my Hetia, live long and strong." After taking Hetia in a gentle embrace, as suddenly as he arrived, the visitor had departed and Hetia stood there silently, thinking of what she had just learned. She would never see his world and was content that it be so. The blue stone had gone with him, she would not have to worry about it ever getting into the wrong hands. Hetia was at peace as she gathered up the reins of her horse and headed back towards the camp of warriors on the Plains of Parlat, the horses she had freed followed behind. They would be distributed amongst the warriors for their bravery.

That evening there was celebration as the people realised that they would now be able to rebuild their homes, restock their herds and know their children would be safe to grow into adulthood without the constant threat of the Horde of Doom. Across the land people were building bonfires and dancing to the beat of many drums. It would be days before everyone settled down to a normal and peaceful life.

Hetia returned to Flessia, to her cottage with the little hut out the back. She looked around the Village with the piles of rubble and timber, for the people were getting ready to rebuild their lives. Looking to the Earth Hetia sent a quiet prayer "Thank you Mother Goddess, we seem to have survived another crisis you and I. Now I had better visit my friend out the back and see how he is getting on." She turned and opened the front door. All was as it should have been so she walked around the side of the house to greet Erik and hear how he was getting along. He had returned the people safely after word came of the defeat of the Horde. The people had begun to respect Erik and were including him in their social life. Hetia admitted that she enjoyed their chats and the simple life they led together, he had become quite a pleasant person to have around.

Life went back to normal and within a day one of the women gave birth, the first child to be born in the safety of the new era. That night there was a noisy and very happy celebration as the new child was introduced to the Village. A bonfire was lit and the people gave offerings to the Goddess for their safe delivery from evil. Now there would be peace in the land.

A few months later during the night the rain began to fall. It had been a long time since even a sprinkle had been felt. This was rain, steady, ground soaking rain. The sound of water on the roof was such a pleasure that Hetia was half tempted to stay in her bed that morning and just listen to the rhythm of the raindrops on the roof. Reluctantly she rose and threw her cloak around her shoulders then opened the door to allow the smell of wet earth to permeate her nostrils. "Oh thank you Earth Mother" she cried, "this is just what the people now need." There had been peace in the land for such a short while now, however it had been hard to recover from the burnt crops and stolen livestock so when the rains didn't come as usual in the Spring the first crops had been meagre. There was enough to eat but not enough to store away for the next winter. The stream where the fish could be caught had dried to a trickle and the people of the land were almost ready to give up. After years of violence at the hands of the marauders followed by little rain, helplessness was setting in. And now it was raining.

The doors of the village houses were being flung open. There were children running outside into the rain, splashing in puddles, turning their little faces up to catch the rain on their tongues. The people were standing in doorways with smiles on their faces and the rain kept on falling. Within a couple of days the grass would show across the land and the newly planted crops would spring to life.

Hetia walked along the path through the village with her arms outstretched and her face turned to the sky. "Give thanks to the Goddess" she cried out to the people, "come and join me and we will thank her for this rain". The people began to follow as Hetia walked, all smiling and happy for the first time in many months. They gathered up their children and went to the field behind the village where rituals and celebrations were held. "Gather round" called Hetia, "hold hands and lift your faces to the rain." As they did her bidding two young women came forward, one with a pitcher of milk and the other with a pot of honey. As they poured their bounty onto the Earth the people called out "Thank you Mother for this wonderful rain". Then they danced. They danced with all their energy, young, old and in between. They danced and laughed and began to heal. However Hetia had a sad task to deal with and she left the people to their celebrations and returned home to tell Erik what she had to do. He was waiting in front of the house as he had been watching the celebrations from a distance. Knowing he was to blame for many of the deaths among the people he had thought it best to stay away. Seeing Hetia's face looking so sad he came forward. "What's the matter Hetia?" he said gently, "You look so sad, I thought you would be so full of joy this morning." "I have to go and look for Mariat's body" she answered sadly, "I had a strange message from her cat. I know that sounds odd but he wants me to find her and bring her home. I will take the trail she would have taken from here to her house and see if there is anything there." "Then I will come with you" said Erik, "if you do find something there you shouldn't be alone. You have gone through enough." She looked at this man who had become such a part of her life and sighed. "Yes you are right. I would appreciate your company." So gathering some food for the journey they both set off along the trail. It was with such sadness that they eventually found what was left of her body lying amongst rocks just on the far side of the forest. The Earth had gently consumed her flesh leaving only the bones and the remnants of her clothing. There seemed to be no sign that animals had touched her flesh as if they had respected her body as sacred. Hetia gathered up the remains of her friend and, with Erik's help, wrapped them in her cloak to take and bury Mariat within the garden she had loved so much. Others may know she had passed on to the next life but only Hetia and the Horde of Doom would know the fate of the man who sent her there.

Meanwhile, sodden with the rain and laughing with joy, the people of Flessia danced in a huge circle, round one way then the other, then they broke off and danced in the rain with their loved ones, ridding their minds and bodies of the horrors of the past. The same thing was happening all over the Plains of Parlat as the people felt free of danger for the first time in so many years.

The rain settled in and kept going for three days. Not heavy damaging rain but gentle consistent rain. The Earth began to be covered in green and the stream ran once more. In the fields the new shoots of barley showed their faces above the earth and the land began to recover.

The story of the disappearance of the Horde of Doom would take many turns over the years around the camp fires but no one would know the truth apart from Hetia and Solcaan. It was widely believed that the Horde were killed in the rock slide that sealed the entrance of the cave. Too many dark stories of ghosts and evil spirits centred around the cave, so the secret would be safe for many years. Eventually it was believed that the few skeletons found within the cave of the Rune writings were the only trapped Horde of Doom, and that the others had somehow escaped and fled the land.

The Tower of the Magicians became a place of learning for young people who wished to study the natural magic of the world, taking an oath that they would never use their magic for evil. To break that oath would strip them of their powers. Solcaan lived a very long and contented life within this tower. He would die at the age of 108 peacefully in his bed. There were many great minds who passed through the academy and eventually other subjects were introduced such as science and mathematics and was named The Solcaan Institute in honour of their old beloved leader.

18 A NEW THREAT

Sometimes it is necessary to move on and start all over again. To cleanse away the recent past and take a deep breath to begin a new direction. This was the decision Hetia had come to and as she locked the front door her determination built up to something quite solid. Turning her back on the cottage she had spent the past 20 years of life in she took that first step forward. Feeling the sun on her face and a backpack slung over her shoulders she headed East towards the coast and the morning sun.

There were a few people about in the Village of Flessia at this early hour and those who saw the tall, slender woman striding along the road waved in greeting, they would not know that it would be some time before they saw their Wise Woman again. She didn't stop as she left the village, because she knew that it would be too hard in her heart to turn away and keep going East. "Leave now" her Spirit Guide had told her, "You have to leave or all your life's work will be wasted." These words had come after several days in contemplation, alone in the cave she had used since she was a small child. It was hidden from view up in the hills behind the village and only a few people knew where it was. Over the past months Hetia's powers had begun to wane. The energy she called upon to bring strength to her people were being drained by an unknown force and she could feel little power when she needed it. The power had been strong in her for many years, through the dangerous times of the Horde until their final defeat at the hands of the magicians, shamen and Wise Women. In the years following when the folk were rebuilding their lives, Hetia had been strong. But this was something new. Her power was being drained and the cause of it all was towards the East, the sea, so that was now her destination. One step at a time, day after day, she would find the strength she needed to fulfil her journey. To what end she had no idea, but her trust in her Spirit Guide was strong and in no doubt at all.

At the end of the first long, tiring day's walk Hetia had arrived at the small cottage of a very old and dear friend. She was about to knock on the door when his head popped around the corner. "Oh hello my dear" he said smiling, "what a lovely surprise. Please, wait until I gather up this wood I came out for." He disappeared for a moment then returned with an armful of firewood and led Hetia indoors. The cottage was cosy and full of the aroma of a rich stew bubbling away on the fire. Hetia had always felt at home in this place and Garan was like a father to her. She had known him since coming to tend his dying wife many years before and he was one of very few people she could talk to about her loss of power. Once she had explained why she was on this journey Garan placed his old gnarled hand over hers and asked, "What of Erik? Have you told him of this?" "No" replied Hetia, "There are many things I share with him but I am afraid that this is not one of them. When he came into my life it was in my best interest to make sure he had no power over me. He was an enemy of the people who did eventually change his ways but deep down I never really gave him any opportunity to know too much about me. He still lives in the hut behind my cottage and we are close but I do not let him know of the true nature of the power I can access. I told him I will be away for a while and that is all. Perhaps one day I will drop my guard with him but not yet."

Garan sat back in his chair and looked into Hetia's eyes. "You love him though don't you my dear?" Taken by surprise Hetia actually blushed. She thought to herself that she was acting stupid, blushing over such a thing like a young girl but she replied, "Perhaps I do, and this could be because I have never allowed myself to feel that kind of love. It was discouraged from the beginning of my training when I was just a girl and I have always believed that to give in to such feelings would be very wrong. I have had many male friends in my life but have always maintained a distance from them. This has been easier because of the way Erik came into my life, he still has not made up for all the killing and violence he committed when he led the Horde. However, while I am away from him I suppose I will give some thought to that. I did meet him once when I was just a girl, he was very young too and very handsome but I have always kept that to myself."

The two friends talked for a short while longer then Garan showed Hetia to a bed set in the wall that he kept for guests. She slept well that night, the long walk had worn her out and she felt safe in Garan's cottage. It was bright and early when she waved goodbye and headed East.

As the days past Hetia began to feel weak, her legs ached at the end of each day and even though she was able to find safe, warm places to spend the night she began to be fearful of shadows and dark places. This was something she had never felt before and it worried her. Eventually she found that after the day was only half way through she had to rest for some time before moving on. Her whole body ached now and she had developed a light fever. "Oh no," she thought, "This can't be just a dose of the flu, not now. I don't get sick, I have never had the flu and this is not the time to start." It was with trepidation that she kept going but by the end of the day she was totally worn out and when she found an abandoned hut she curled up inside with her cloak wrapped around her body and decided that sleep would be her best medicine. Rummaging around in her bag she made a small meal from her dried fruit and bread and settled down on a pile of old straw to sleep.

Hetia's eyes flew open. She was awakened by a strange energy all about the hut that was humming loudly. It was a powerful energy and was getting stronger. Sitting bolt upright with her back against the wall Hetia took a moment to get her bearings then crept towards the open door. Outside all was quiet except for this strange humming sound. She tentatively reached out through the door with one hand and felt what seemed like a soft wall. Pulling her hand back Hetia took a small step but her foot could not penetrate the wall. Using her mind she tried to probe this energy, slowly at first then with more strength she pushed her thoughts outward. What she found was a void, nothing, as if there was nothing outside the hut at all. Feeling quite apprehensive Hetia went across to a window on the opposite wall and tried again. This time she could see out past the energy, the trees behind the hut were close to the outer wall and it appeared that they were preventing the strange force from coming close. Hetia picked up her bag and climbed up on the window ledge. There had been shutters over the window once but over the years they had fallen out and were lying on the ground. Stepping lightly down Hetia stopped and listened. The sky was just turning grey, about an hour before sunrise, so she could see what was ahead of her. The energy field was there, just a bit further out, so summoning all her strength Hetia began to chant. She used an ancient incantation of protection and felt the power building within. Soon she could try to escape, the protection barrier should be enough. After a minute or so she moved forward and then she was through. Before anything had a chance to stop her Hetia made off down the road, only stopping for a moment to look back towards the hut where the energy field was still surrounding it. "Strange," she thought, "it seems I am believed to be still in there." Turning back towards the East Hetia hurried along. All the aches and pains had gone and she even felt a lot stronger than she had been in many days. Whatever had been affecting her was still back there around the hut, so she determined to put as much distance between her and that evil energy.

It was well past midday before Hetia came to a halt. She was on the edge of a large town, too large to have been attacked by the Horde so it was also where many of her people had fled. There were streets and buildings that were close together and much larger than those Hetia was used to. Many people were walking about so it wasn't long before someone noticed her. She took a deep breath, dusted off some of the dirt of travel and walked into town. People turned to look at the tall woman striding down the road. Her strange tattoos and magic tokens decorating her hair and body were not often seen in town. As she walked straight backed and proud the people moved out of her way. These were town folk, not the simple people of the country, and they knew that this woman was one of magic. Most avoided eye contact as they had heard strange stories of being overpowered by such as this. Hetia stopped for a moment and looked about her. It suited her to be avoided, she didn't wish to become involved in idle chat but when an old woman came up to her and reached out with a bony hand Hetia turned and smiled. "Can I be of help my dear?" the old one said, "These folk aren't used to seeing such as yourself but I came from a village that was attacked by the Horde and I think I know you. It's Hetia isn't it?" Hetia took the hand of the old woman, "Yes, I am Hetia," she replied, "I am heading to the coast, the East, and need somewhere safe to rest for a while." The old woman took Hetia's arm and led her away, "Come with me my dear, my home is just up the road and you are welcome to stay as long as you need." They walked together for a short distance and once inside Hetia relaxed. The home was cosy and reminded her of home. There were bunches of drying herbs hanging from a rack in front of the fireplace and jars and boxes along the walls that Hetia recognised. "Are you a healer?" she asked "Yes I am" replied the old one, "Although here in the town people tend to go to the place called a Clinic where the herbalists and other formal healers practice. There are quite a few different kinds of healers there and they also have places where women can go to have their babes. It's all very new to me but I suppose it is the way of the town folk so I just accept that this is the way of things." She turned to look at Hetia and smiled. The Wise Woman of Flessia had drifted off into a deep sleep, the first proper rest she had taken in many days. So taking a blanket from her own bed the old woman placed it over Hetia. She would sleep for hours, safe for a while in the protection of her own kind.

Several days later Hetia stood high above the city of Ban that nestled into the Bay of the Whales. Many years before the trouble with the Horde Hetia had travelled to the City with her mentor and teacher to buy supplies of healing oils that could not be found elsewhere. They had not stayed very long as the hundreds of people and strange smells made them feel uncomfortable. They had spent the time in the home of the Priestesses of The Earth Goddess, a beautiful old building surrounded by a walled garden. Hetia decided to make her way there for she knew it would be a safe place to stay while she was in the City. As she neared the outer part of the city she began, once again, to feel the aches in her limbs, then her whole body began to feel heavy, she also had the beginnings of a fever again. The strange energy had once again caught up with Hetia. By the time she reached the house of the priestesses Hetia was so near to exhaustion she had trouble lifting her feet to walk, her arms hung limply by her side and it was all she could do not to collapse on the ground. At the gate she rang the bell to announce her arrival, then with her back to the wall she slid to sit upon the ground. Moments later a young woman in the long dark green robes of a priestess opened the gate. "Its alright, I have you," she said to Hetia, "come on, let's get you inside." Two other women came hurrying to the gate and between them they half carried Hetia to the house where they were met by a tall grey haired woman who was obviously in charge. She had tattoos on her face and arms to denote that she was a leader of the priestesses and quickly took charge of the situation. "Bring her inside," she told the others, we must act quickly as she seems quite ready to faint." As Hetia lay back on the bed they had brought her to the head priestess looked at her and exclaimed, "Goodness me, it's Hetia isn't it? What on Earth are you doing so far from home?" "Yes it is me Mother," Hetia replied, "I am so relieved that you are still here, I don't know what I would have done if you weren't." She then told the Priestess of her journey and what had been happening to her. While the story was being told the other women had prepared food and drink, and feeling refreshed Hetia joined them at the long table set outside in the garden. When they had finished the Priestess asked Hetia to join her in the small temple garden, a peaceful place surrounded by a high hedge. In the centre of the garden an altar had been fashioned from stone and a pool of clear water surrounded by round, smooth stones lay nearby. It was obviously of great significance as there were offerings and ribbons around and in the water. This garden was a holy place, Hetia could feel the peace and tranquillity there and she understood why she had been led. "We will ask for guidance from the Earth Mother," the Priestess Karlina said as she took Hetia's hand, "I believe that there is an answer to this problem here in the city and I am sure we will be shown the way to deal with it." The two women stood together at the altar and as one they began a chant of protection, the same one Hetia had used on her journey. Once the energy was in place Priestess Karlina invoked her Spirit Guide and asked for guidance. As they stood, side by side, they both began to feel a cool breeze gently lifting wisps of their hair and moving the leaves in the garden. There was no way a normal breeze could enter this enclosed garden so they both knew it was a visit from Spirit. "I feel your presence" said Karlina, "we seek your guidance. Some force is attacking our sister Hetia and we wish to know what it is and how we can deal with it. Can you help?" Suddenly there appeared before them a shimmering light and a picture began to form within. It appeared to be a room with a table and chairs. Seated at the table was a dark figure with a hooded cloak wrapped around it. The hood was up and over the face but Hetia recognised a ring on his finger that was only worn by the Magicians from the Plains of Parlat. Also seated at the table were two rough looking men, one was grossly overweight and the other was strong and fit looking. They were both looking at the magician with menace and Hetia had no doubt that they were planning to do something evil. The hooded figure raised his head to speak and Hetia gasped. It was the face of a Magician who had left the others before the final capture of the Horde, explaining that he was going on a journey to discover the magic practised in another land. As Hetia watched the scene in front of her one of the other two men fiercely grabbed the magician by the arm and snarled, "Why can't you find her? You had her this morning and now you say you have lost her. What kind of magician are you? Now try again and this time no messing about. We've got her in the City and you will make sure she comes into our trap." Looking very frightened the magician nodded his head, "I'll do my best, but you have to leave me alone to do it. Please, I'll do as you say." "You'd better" the fat one said, "when Dagrel and the others disappeared it left us to deal with this Witch and I made him a promise to do just that. She will suffer for what she did to Starreck and pay for making Dagrel disappear into thin air. Now if you want your Mother and Sister to live, although we could have some fun with your sister, you will get that woman here and soon. Find her." The two men left the room and the magician was left with his head in his hands. "Oh what have I done" he moaned to himself, "what have I done. I have betrayed my people and especially Hetia, I wish I was dead then they wouldn't have any reason to hurt my family." Slowly he reached for the large clear crystal on the table in front of him and began his incantation once more to find the Wise Woman.

Priestess Karlina waved her hand and the image disappeared. She turned to Hetia and said, "Well, now we know what you are up against, it seems we have some work to do." The two women turned and went into the house. Within the comfortable room of the priestesses they sat down to work out how to rescue the magician and his family then deal with the two thugs.

Over the next few hours the women of the Temple of The Earth Goddess began to form a plan that could rescue the magician and his family. Remembering the plant that was used by the young apprentice magician who had been captured by the Horde, Hetia explained it's properties to the others. "It seems as though they are dead, however once the effects wear off the person recovers and it appears as if they had just been asleep. If we can somehow find this magician and get the herb to him he could appear dead and they would have to abandon their current plan and hopefully let his family go.

However, there is also the risk that when they thought him dead they might dispose of his body in a way that he would be lost forever. I could make contact with him but that would also allow them to know where I am in the City. While I am within your walls they cannot find me. There must be some other way." Karlina placed a hand over Hetia's and said quietly, "You might not be able to contact him but I can. We don't know his name but I am sure I can manage to find a way to him. Once we know where he is we can work out how to free him and his family. Now, the best thing we can do is rest, so please sleep and we can begin in the morning." Feeling very exhausted, Hetia was glad to lie down in the safety of the Priestesses' dwelling and it didn't take long for her to fall into a deep sleep. During the night she dreamed. The dream was peaceful and to her surprise she remembered it in the morning. She dreamed of a beautiful place with many trees and grass that spread across the land. Unlike her home that was very dry and arid in many places. Within the dream she found Erik. He was living alone but nearby where she seemed to be, just like they were in reality. He glanced over to where she must have been and smiled then went back to his work tending the garden. Hetia felt very calm in his presence and noticed that she had feelings that were more than that, the feelings were almost erotic and she found herself enjoying the moment. During the dream there were children running around that looked like Erik, and it was in wonder at who their mother would be when she awoke with the sun shining through the open window in the room where she slept. The dream stayed with her for some time and only faded when she was called to break her fast with the others in the garden.

Karlina came out from the house and sat down beside Hetia. "I have been working during the night on contacting your magician. Although I am not able to find out his name and contact him directly, I do have some idea where he is. I consulted the image that forms in the Pool of Seeing, you saw it in the Temple Garden. The magician is within a building in the part of the City where many of the criminals reside. All I could see was a red building, made of old brick. There appeared to be wooden shutters on the windows and it had two floors. However, there is a market nearby and I have a good idea where it is. We often go there to give alms to the poor so it is very familiar. Perhaps we can use this knowledge to get to him. Now, we shall eat and I will tell you of an idea that I have." The women finished their morning meal and Hetia walked with Karlina into the Temple Garden once again. "You must stay here Hetia," Karlina said, "once you leave they can find you once again and I am sure that will be the last we will see of you. I don't know how they are doing it but they are able to block out my scrying and that takes more magic than your magician could have. There is someone else behind this, someone very powerful, and I would think he has revenge on his mind for more than sending a bunch of criminals to their next life. You must have upset someone in your past." "I can't think who" said Hetia quietly, "I didn't really use my powers until this evil Horde came our way. I shall spend some time meditating on who that may be. However, you obviously have some idea on how to rescue this man and his family so please, what have you in mind?" Karlina began to tell Hetia of her plan and when she had finished left her in the garden and returned to her priestesses. "Come on ladies," she announced, "we are going to rescue some people. I want you to change into the garb of the Sisters of The Street, we are going begging."

Dressed in robes that had seen better days and with only sandals on their feet three women made their way out of the gates and walked towards the poor quarter. They saw much poverty there, children begging in rags and old people huddled in doorways. As they went they handed out small loaves of bread they had brought for the purpose

and bestowed blessings on those they met. By the time
they reached the street with the market they had built up
quite strong credibility of their roles. Karlina looked up
and down the street and noted a red brick building nearby.
This had to be the one, it resembled the one she had seen
in the pool. Making their way slowly along, blessing those
who sat on the footpath and giving small items of food to
the children, Karlina motioned her women to sit down on
a doorstep where she could watch the house. It was quite
a while before someone emerged from the door. He was
the fit looking man she had seen with the magician and as
he stepped out he looked furtively up and down the street.
Karlina dropped her head and covered it with the hood of
her cloak. She peeked out and watched as the man strode
away up the street. "One less to worry about" she said to
her companions, "Now we shall wait a bit longer to make
sure no-one else comes out." As they sat quietly, eyes half
shut and appearing to be weary, they were surprised by a
voice nearby. "Can I offer you some comfort ladies?"
Karlina looked up and there before her was an old
woman. "I noticed that you were giving out food to the
children but you don't look that well fed yourselves. You
are Sisters Of The Street aren't you? Please come inside
and rest, I will make you some soup and I have fresh
bread. Please, come inside." They turned and realised that

they were sitting on the step of the woman so as one they rose and went inside. "Now what are you really up to?" The old woman said with a crooked smile, "You are no more Sisters of the Street than I am a helpless old woman. I am Strylia, High Priestess of the Temple of The Dead and Dying and I am also interested in that house you are watching. So, come on now, what is going on here?" Karlina felt that this woman could be trusted. She knew of the Temple and it's work in sending people quietly on their way when they were dying. If Strylia was interested in the same house then it was important that they work together. Over a bowl of delicious soup Karlina told her story. When she had finished, Strylia took a breath and said, "Then we must work together. A woman came to me recently to say that her sister had disappeared and she thought she must be dead. We found out through Spirit that the sister had in fact been taken, along with her daughter and son, by some evil ones. I have used power to find this house and I believe it is where at least one of them is being kept captive. Because I did not want to compromise any of my priests or priestesses I decided to have a look for myself. This house belongs to our order, we use it to comfort the dying in this area who cannot come to us. At the moment there is no-one else here apart from my attendant and myself so we are quite free to discuss anything. Knowing you are also here is a great relief because I think this is going to take some Power. From what you say, we are dealing with someone who is strong in the Magic Arts and we will have to be very careful not to let down our guard."

While the women were discussing the situation a door opened a little across the street in the brick house. Slowly the large fat man who had been with the magician emerged and looked about. Seeing a hooded figure striding down the street he waited quietly. The figure came up to the door and entered, followed by the fat man closing the door behind him. Strylia suddenly sat up, "There is someone new in the house," she said, "I have placed a warning energy at the front of the house and someone has entered who hasn't been there before. We must try to find out who it is. Please come with me to the back room, I have set up a scrying bowl there and it might help." The women followed Strylia through to the back and sat around a table containing the bowl of water. "I shall have to be very careful," Strylia said, "if that is someone with magic arts in with the magician then I do not want him to know I am watching." Slowly she called in the energies that she used for her work and asked the question, "Tell me please, who is at present in the red brick house across the street?" After a short while a picture began to form in the bowl. It showed a family, two adults and three children. Silently Strylia asked to extend the seeing to take in other rooms within the building. Eventually she could see a door, closed and sealed. The seal was a magic one and was placed there to prevent anyone from physically entering, it didn't, however, stop Strylia from pushing gently with her mind and going through the door. There, sitting at the table as before, was the magician with his crystal. They could not hear the words spoken but as they watched the new man threw back his hood. He had very black eyes and a darkness that seemed pure evil. Around his neck was a talisman that Karlina recognised as being from an order of priests that practised the dark arts. He looked at the magician sitting trembling at the table and flicked his fingers. All of a sudden the magician sat bolt upright, he picked up his crystal and his mouth began to work as he seemed to be chanting. Karlina could make out the words, it seemed he was using the same words he had used the day before when he was looking for Hetia. After a while the evil priest picked up the crystal and threw it savagely against a wall. He then raised his hand and hit the magician across the face so hard he fell off his chair and appeared to be shouting, although he had his back to Strylia so she could not make out what he was saying. Then shaking his head in frustration the evil one left the room. Moments later one of the lesser priestesses watching from the window of Strylia's home announced that he had left the building, walked down the street and around a corner. Moments later the fat man also left. Strylia waved her hand over the water and the image disappeared. "It seems like we might have a chance now," she said, "I am going to go over there and see what I can find out. You had better stay here, they can trace you back to Hetia whereas I am unknown. I will use a guise to enter the house and see what is happening there." Agreeing to this, Karlina and the others went to watch from the front window.

Strylia crossed over the road and knocked on the door. One of the children they had seen answered the door and called back to her mother. "There is an old lady here" she called, "she wants to come in and bless us. Can I let her in?" Then a woman came to the door and motioned for Strylia to come in. "Please mother, come in. Would you like a drink of water? I have seen you in the street lately and I know you. It would be lovely to be blessed as we haven't had much luck lately." Strylia entered and followed the woman inside with the bent appearance of an old lady. "You have a very big house for one family." she mentioned, "I suppose you rent out the rooms upstairs." "No" replied the women, "our landlord keeps the rooms upstairs for when he is in the City. We aren't allowed to go up there and besides the door is always locked. Mind you, I think there is someone there at the moment because I have heard noises when the landlord is out. But I don't want to interfere, he is not a very nice man." "Is that the fat man I have seen coming and going?" Strylia asked. "No, he just looks after the place, the landlord is that man with the hood that just left." the woman replied, "we are quite frightened of him and live quietly down here. There aren't many houses to rent as cheaply as we get this place so we are just going to mind our own business." Strylia accepted the glass of water the child had given her and asked if she could sit for a while. "Yes of course you can," the woman replied. "I have to go down to the market but please, sit and relax. My husband is at work and the other children are at the park so Mary and I shall leave you for a while. Won't be long." At that she gathered up her shopping basket and the two left for the market. Waiting a moment, Strylia then hurried up the stairs to the locked room. Reaching tentatively for the door she felt a tingling so withdrew her hand. "Hah, no you don't" she said quietly and said a few words of power before trying the handle once more. This time she opened the door and there on the floor was the magician, holding his face with blood trickling down his fingers. "Are you alright?" Strylia asked quietly. "Who on earth are you" the magician cried, "how did you get past the door?" "Never mind that" replied Strylia, "I have come to get you out. Do you know where your mother and sister are being held?" "No" he said as he stood up, "but I don't think they are far away because they seem to be able to come and go between us quite easily." "What is your mother's name?" Strylia asked, "Fantia" he replied, "Then give me a moment and I shall try to contact her. If she is close by we will make contact fairly quickly. Strylia closed her eyes for a moment then broke into a smile. "The Goddess is with us my friend" she said, "they are in this building. Come on, we shall have to be very quick." Turning and leaving the room with the magician in tow, Strylia flew down the stairs and kept going to the basement. The door to the basement also had an energy upon it and this was quickly removed. There sitting on a bed by the wall were the two women looking very dirty and afraid. "Don't worry mother," the magician said, "come on, we are leaving." Without questions the women rose and as quickly as possible the group left the building, crossed the road and entered the house of the Priestess. Once they were inside Strylia called an incantation and sealed the house from prying eyes. If anyone tried to find them they would only find an ordinary old lady living with her companion. "Now please, go through to the sitting room where you will find some other women. Wait for me there." Once they were gone Strylia concentrated for a few moments and made mind contact with the woman and her daughter who had gone to the market. "You will not remember me" she sent, "I did not come to your door and when you get home the door was open and you will think that you have had burglars." Leaving it at that she straightened up and went to join the others.

Karlina explained who she was and why they had rescued the magician and his family then they all sat round and made a plan. They would have to be very careful when they moved out from this place, the evil one was a very powerful priest and it would not take him long to find Hetia if they were careless.

Later that day one of the priestesses called Karlina to the window. "Look, there is the fat one about to enter the house. It looks like the family that live there have told him they have had burglars and he is none to happy. I have been watching their faces and I do believe that they have no knowledge of Strylia. Oh look, the fat one is now coming out again and he looks very angry." As they watched the scene it became obvious that he had discovered that the magician and his family had fled. Before long the other man arrived and the two of them were looking very scared. It seemed that they were more worried about the evil priest because the two of them made off up the road in great haste and disappeared down an alleyway. "I don't think those two will show their faces around here again." said Karlina, "Perhaps this is the best time to move one. Come on everyone, we are going to leave. We will take the women with us disguised as we are. They will be safe there." and turning to the magician she gave him a mental picture of where he was to go. "You will be taken in as a priest of the Earth Mother and I would think it best if you stay there. They will protect you and no one will be able to detect you. I think you should remain there for a very long time. I will look after your mother and sister and after a while they will be able to contact you, but for now it is best if you put them out of your mind and that will make them even more safe." He nodded his agreement and left the building in the guise of an ordinary man. He would use the back streets and move swiftly to his destination. Meanwhile, in the garb of the Sisters of the Street, the small group of women left, two at a time, and made their way quietly back to the Temple of

the Earth Goddess. The relief the women felt on arrival
was obvious as they gathered in the house of the
priestesses. Hetia greeted Karlina in the fashion of their
kind, then leading the two confused and worn out women
inside they were given the gowns of the priestesses and
taken to a room they could share. "The poor things
haven't said a word since we rescued them," said Karlina
to Hetia, "I don't know what was done to them but I am
sure it will take time for them to regain some semblance of
normality. I will guide them as best I can and perhaps the
daughter might become a priestess in time, but I think the
mother will retreat into her own mind and live her life out
here. We will look after them. Meanwhile my friend, we
have some work to do. It seems that you have an enemy
and we will need to find out more while you are safe here
in our home.

Late that evening Karlina was walking in the
Temple Garden where she came across Hetia sitting by
herself. "I thought I would find you here" she said, "the
others are all asleep now and I felt like clearing my
thoughts under the stars." Sitting down next to Hetia the
Priestess looked up to the heavens. "Have you ever
wondered whether we would have finally reached another
galaxy if the world had kept advancing? I have read of a

programme many centuries ago that's sole purpose was to find another planet with intelligent life forms. In a way it's probably best that it all faded out. Life must have been so complicated then. Anyway, we will not solve your problems with talk of the stars, so Hetia, have you any ideas as to how to overcome this evil priest? "I think I shall have to confront him." Hetia replied. "From what I gather he has a personal grudge against me when I had only a small part to play in ridding us of the Horde. Perhaps it is time to sort out once and for all just what kind of person his 'friend' Dagrel really was. I have thought long and hard about that and I have to admit that what I face here is not the two men who held the magician captive but the priest who seemed to be the main force. I wonder if it would be possible to find him through Spirit and discover more about him. I have found that sometimes there is more to a grudge than what appears on the surface. Can you help me to find him Karlina?" "Yes, I believe we can find him the same way we discovered your magician" replied the priestess, "I can protect us here in the Temple Garden so that it will be only a one way seeing, he should not be able to see us at all, although he will hear us. Shall we try?" Hetia nodded and so the two women stood, and as before, Karlina invoked her Spirit Guide and explained what they were trying to do.

Within minutes the shimmering energy appeared as before and revealed to them a picture of the priest. He was sitting in a room with several others of his sect and as Karlina concentrated her thoughts they, as one, looked up and around. "What is that" one said angrily, "I think we are being probed by some arcane energy." The group stood and looked around the room, seeing nothing there. One who seemed to be the leader, spoke. "Perhaps it was just a breeze coming in through the open door. We need to get on with our work and not be distracted. It has come to my attention that one of you has been using his powers to coerce a practitioner of the lesser magic into going against his order. You all know this is forbidden. There are those who believe that all we practise is evil when we do much work that others do not dare to try. I have been attempting to teach outsiders that our practises are necessary as are those of healing, moving out of this life to the next and teaching, but if the lesser folk see us as evil then we will never convince them. Now, I could find out the hard way or you can tell me now, who is it?" The group sat very still, waiting to see if any of their number would be brave enough to admit that they had broken the rules. Suddenly one stood up and Karlina recognised him as the man in the hood that had terrorised the magician. "I admit to this My Lord" he said. "I had a friend called

Dagrel who looked after me when I was just a boy, and I have discovered that a woman who I believed to be a witch, made him disappear from this life. I admit that I used my arts to make the magician find this woman so that I could deal with her, and I am sorry that I used someone who only uses his arts for good. I did coerce him, and I believe this was wrong even though I was trying to avenge a friend and protector. However, if you wish me to make amends to you then I will but I have sworn revenge on the woman called Hetia and I will have that revenge." He sat down sullenly once more and the leader looked squarely at him and said, "You have broken the rules and you know what you must do. What you have done and what you intended is not our way and you cannot say sorry like a spoilt child who has been caught red handed with his hand in the jar of sweets. You must face this woman and sort it out in a civilised way. If you harm her then you will have to deal with me and I will take away all your rights and privileges. You will be sent to the Island of Priests to live the rest of your life in contemplation. Now, come with me and we will see what can by done to find this woman and settle your differences." Rising he left the room with the recalcitrant priest in tow.

Hetia drew in a deep breath and, after Karlina dismissed the image before them, the two sat down on the nearby bench. "Well this is a turn for the better," Karlina said, "it seems we have given their sect a bad reputation. However, it remains to be seen as to what will occur so tomorrow I shall contact their Head Priest and see what shall be done." Hetia had been quite shocked by the confrontation and quietly returned to the house where she went straight to bed after bidding Karlina good night. It was some time before she finally dropped off for a restless sleep for she didn't believe for one minute that this priest would do as he was bidden.

In the early hours of the morning a hooded figure made his way towards the gates of the Temple of the Earth Goddess. His face was one of terrible anger and the few people he had passed had quickly moved out of his way. After leaving his head priest he had spent some time alone in his room brooding over the punishment he would be given if he did not make amends with the witch. "She will pay Dagrel," he said quietly, "if it takes me forever, she will pay. I don't know where she sent you but I know you are still alive somewhere. If I can I will find you one day and bring you back. She will pay." He had waited until everyone had retired for the night and silently left through a back entrance. The anger had built up as he strode purposefully towards the last place the Magician had traced her to. He was unsure what he would do but his anger was building with every step he took.

The gates of the Temple were very high and were deliberately made to prevent anyone from climbing over the top. Around the perimeter of the grounds grew a strong hedge and in the centre of the hedge was a fence. Within the property Karlina had set wardings throughout so that if anyone had attempted to enter without permission she would know. So it was at these impregnable gates that the evil one came to a complete stop. He knew he would not be able to enter but he could wait. Knowing that Hetia was here was enough for now, so he retreated down the road a short way where there was a small park and found a place where he could watch the gates. Sooner or later she would leave and he just had to wait.

Early the next morning Hetia rose and made her way into the Temple Garden. She found it was so peaceful there it gave her a chance to think about her situation. All she wanted to do was to return home and get on with her life. However, this had to be dealt with first so she needed to meditate on a possible confrontation with the evil priest. She felt that he would not quietly arrive at the door offering to talk about his anger and then go away. He had made it quite clear that he intended to revenge Dagrel, that seemed to be the core of his existence and no apologies or talk would allay that anger. She would have to be stronger than him and be ready to defend herself. At this time she thought about her past contact with Captain Hill, she could really use his help now but it was impossible as he had taken the stone with him. Then she thought about what he had said to her and decided to try anyway. If she could only talk to him it would help so closing her eyes and going into her meditative state Hetia began to concentrate on the face of the Captain. "I think I need your help Captain Hill," she said quietly and waited. Before long she felt the familiar warmth within her mind and smiled. He had heard her after all. Waiting for whatever happened next Hetia felt calm. She didn't know what she would ask of the Captain, but she did need to talk to him. After a moment there was a gentle buzz in the air and the Captain appeared before her. "Hello my daughter," he said with a smile, "what is so serious that you need my help once again?" Hetia walked forward and placed her hand on his arm. "I am being sought by one with evil intention." she said. "He was a friend of Dagrel and seems to be bent on finding me and doing me harm. I do not have the power to deal with this priest as he is of an order that practice very strong magic. He lured me here to the City by draining my energy but making sure that I came East where he was waiting." She related the rest of the story to the Captain and by the time she had finished felt that her very soul was under attack by this priest. "What would you like to do about it Hetia?" asked Captain Hill, "I could just transport him away but I don't thing that would solve the problem. He sounds like the sort of person who would make it his life's work to find a way back and seek revenge. We must think a bit more about what to do. Let's sit down here and talk. As you know, even though it seems that I must be from some other 'planet', we are actually on the same Earth. Should I transport this evil one away from here there is nothing to say that over some time he will not find a way to use his powers from a distance and still be able to harm you. We do have workers in magic but they are confined to using their power to help us with the elements. They hold ceremonies to celebrate the seasons and other gentle ways so I am not concerned that this one would corrupt them into helping him. However we must try to deal with him here, in the city, at this moment rather than having him always on your mind. I do have an idea and I would like you to ask the Head Priestess here to come and discuss it with us." Hetia agreed and went inside to find Karlina. When she explained what was happening Karlina, very curious, was eager to come and meet Captain Hill.

Once the introductions had been made and Karlina accepted this man from another place within the garden that was sacred to her women, she sat down with the other two and they listened to the Captain's idea. "Can you get in touch with the Head Priest of this order that the evil one belongs to?" he said, "Yes, of course" replied Karlina. "I will send one of my women to him at once. I am sure he will be happy to meet once he realises what his priest has been doing. Please, come along to the house and we will provide you with refreshments while we await his answer." They made their way back where one of the older women agreed to carry the message. She would leave by a back gate so that she would not be noticed and, dressed in plain street clothes she went swiftly on her way.

It wasn't long before the priestess returned and with her was the Head Priest. He bowed to Karlina who greeted him as her equal. "We must talk." she said, "One of your priests has been seeking revenge on a friend of ours, a wise woman from the Plains of Parlat. He seems to have a grudge over the removal of someone who was the leader of a horde of bandits that terrorised the Plains for some years. The man was dealt with, as was his gang, and it was not only the Wise Woman who did this but it was a combined effort of all the folk of the Plains. She is now in my protection and will stay here until this priest is dealt with. We are not in the habit of killing people and I assume you are not either. I have heard of the good work you do. So I have had a suggestion of how we can deal with this priest put to me and I would like your co-operation." During this time the Head Priest had sat respectfully listening to the story told to him. He nodded his head and said, "I do know of who you speak. He told me he would talk to the woman and sort it out. However, I have been informed that he has found himself a place down the road from here where he can watch for her to leave your protection. He has already gone against my wishes. I do agree with what you have said, he needs to be stopped. Please, can you leave this with me? I shall be in touch with you once it has been done." Karlina agreed to this and led the Priest to the front gate where they made their parting gestures as was fitting to their ranks and two lesser priests waited to escort him away. Making off down the road they suddenly stopped and turned to their right. Seated beside a large tree was the evil priest and he jumped up in surprise when he realised who was standing before him. "You will come with us, now." Stated the Head Priest, "You have broken your vows and you will be punished. Take him." he instructed the other two. Between the two priests the evil one had no choice but to go along. During the meeting between the two sect leaders Hetia had been waiting in the garden talking with Captain Hill. "I am pleased that you contacted me again Hetia," he said, "it is always good to talk with you. Our countries are so very different and it also gives me the chance to get away from the perils of the modern world. It would give me great pleasure to continue our relationship over the coming years, so please feel free to call me whether you have a problem to solve or not. However, I must return as there is much work to be done. Your group of criminals have settled in to their new life and most of them are working hard. That Dagrel was a tough one though, it was probably best that he died in the cave. I think the others realised that the best thing they could do was go along with their fate. So my Hetia look after yourself." Before activating his transporter Captain Hill embraced Hetia then stepped back. Once he had left she made her way back to the house.

Later that day a messenger came for Karlina who called Hetia to her. "It seems that your Captain Hill had the perfect solution to deal with the evil priest. I have been invited to take tea with the Head Priest and he would like you to come along. He has assured me of your safety and I believe he is sincere. Please, gather your cloak and we will go with this messenger. I would also like to let you know that I will never reveal Captain Hill to anyone else. He is to be our secret." The two left with the messenger and two attending priestesses and made their way through the city to the Temple of The Dark Arts. It wasn't at all what Hetia expected, it was a very large stone building set within grounds that were beautifully maintained. As they entered they were greeted with respect by the priest on the front door and taken into a comfortable room with deep leather chairs. The women seemed to be taken by surprise at the comfort until the elder Head Priest entered and smiled. "Yes, we like our comforts too," he remarked, "just because we look after the 'darker' side of things doesn't make us rigid and boring. Please sit and we shall have refreshments. We have dealt with the one who was attacking you Hetia. Yes, I know your name because he told me. He will undergo a ritual tonight that will strip him of any magical powers then he will be sent to the Island of Priests where he will live out his days in contemplation and service. He will not be able to leave the island, it is out in the ocean and there are no boats kept on the island. He will live in a meagre hut with one meal a day provided from the stores that are sent there once a month. There is one priest there who will make sure he does not try to leave, and believe me he will not leave. We deal with our own in this way. He will no longer be a priest, he will be a servant, and as such he will do whatever needs to be done for the rest of his days. It will not be a comfortable life." The women looked at each other and a silent message passed between them. Karlina turned and thanked the Priest. "We trust you to deal with your own" she said, "I am sure you will make sure he does not cause any more trouble. We must take our leave now so that Hetia can prepare for her long journey home. Thank you and please, come and visit me some time. It would be nice to discuss our different beliefs over a pot of tea." The priest smiled and rose, leading the women to the front door himself. They took their time walking back, it was the first time Hetia had really looked at the City and she had made her mind up by the time they arrived back that she didn't want to stay any longer than necessary.

Early the next morning Hetia was preparing to leave when a messenger arrived at the front gate. It was a lesser priest who had been sent the day before to bring them along. As Karlina met him at the gate she was given a note and as she read the words she turned to Hetia. "You don't have to worry about your evil priest any more," she said, "it seems their boat sank about half way to the island and he drowned. The boatman managed to swim to shore but it turned out the priest couldn't swim. His body has been found and will be cremated today." Knowing that any death cannot be celebrated Hetia just stood quietly, then to Karlina she said, "I read in ancient texts about a belief in a thing called Karma. Perhaps this is what they meant." Hugging Karlina she turned and made her way down the road heading West. Her step was light as she went and over the next few days she felt free for the first time in many years, before the Horde rampaged over the land. She looked forward to getting home and regaining the quiet life she had always enjoyed.

Erik was waiting for Hetia when she returned. His face showed relief when he saw her coming down the road. "I was worried for you" he said, "I had no idea where you were and it felt like you were in danger. I am so glad you are home safely." He turned and walked with her back to the cottage. "Strange," she thought to herself, "I missed this man." Silently they walked together. Peaceful in each other's company.

19 PEACE REIGNS

Hetia stood in the centre of her garden as the early mist rose towards the sky, her basket and knife in hand. She raised her face to greet the sun and spoke the words she had used so many times before. "Oh Great Father Sun, thank you for your warmth and strength" Looking down she incanted, "Earth Mother, Mother Goddess, thank you for the plants that grow in my garden. Please guide my hands as I choose the herbs that will be used today. I need to ease the heart pain in our Elder Charlea." As she looked around the garden her attention was drawn to a little used corner. A great old willow tree had been there since before Hetia was born and although she had never used any of it for healing she did spend many hours on the bench beneath its boughs. "Aha", she exclaimed lightly, "what is it that you can do for my old friend?" The tree began to gently sway in the morning breeze and as Hetia stood beside it she was drawn to put her hand on the bark. Its' rough, gnarled surface felt strong to her touch, so placing her basket on the ground she held her sharp knife close to the tree. "I need to take some of your bark to help an old man's pain." she said softly to the tree, "May I please carefully and with respect take a small amount?"

She felt the tree move gently once more in the breeze and accepted this as agreement. Very carefully, she slid the knife under a piece of bark and levered it off. Taking care she placed it in her basket and turned back to the tree. "Thank you, I shall try to use this wisely."

Turning, Hetia continued through the garden to collect more supplies for her day and to hang up to dry for future use. There were many flowers growing between the rows of herbs and vegetables so as she passed the bright coloured foxglove Hetia picked a stalk, remembering this would also help her aging Elder, but much care was needed as it could be deadly if taken in the wrong amount.

The house was warm when Hetia entered, so hanging her thick cloak on a peg by the door she placed her basket on the work bench. Selecting the willow bark she turned it over in her hand, feeling the texture and waiting for the knowledge she knew it would impart. "Ah my beauty" she crooned, "you are wise. I know what I must do." Placing the bark in her stone bowl, she placed a heavy pot on the hook over the fire and returned to grind the bark down. Once she was satisfied with her work she placed the bark in the pot with cool water from the barrel outside the door and left it to heat slowly. Her training told her that bark needed to simmer slowly, so she returned to the work bench. Hetia knew she had to be careful with the Foxglove, too much could kill the old man, too little would not be any help at all. This was a familiar remedy to her so she proceeded with the usual care.

A walk to the Elder's cottage later in the day would be a pleasure. They would spend a few hours in deep conversation about many things. The old man was a store of information for Hetia and he enjoyed her visits very much. One more task was required before she ventured forth so collecting her market basket Hetia went to her food store. There were jars and small boxes stacked on the shelves containing preserved food and herbs harvested from her garden, plus many from those folk she had helped over time. Reaching up to a high shelf she felt around until she found what she was after and took a small stone jar with a big cork stuck in it down and placed it in her basket. This jar contained some delicious olives in oil brought from a far off land by a wandering bard. He had come to Hetia with a damaged hand and although she gave her healing for free the Bard had given her two jars of the unusual fruit. It had taken Hetia weeks to finish off one jar, eating only one olive at a time to savour the taste. This jar was going to the Elder as a treat. Next she took a jar of jam made from the blackberries that Erik picked for her in the field behind his hut then she reached to the back of the shelf and found a bag filled with nuts bought at a market months ago. She placed half of these in a smaller bag and added them to her basket. Finally she collected a few small cakes she had made the day before and some fresh vegetables and set off for Elder Charlea's cottage. It was a pleasant day for walking so using the time Hetia decided to gather wild herbs along the way.

There were so many herbs to be found that her mind drifted back to a conversation she had years before with a traveller. He told of a time, a few hundred years ago, before the great climate calamity, when most people had forgotten the natural ways of healing. Artificial medicines and cures were used instead, however these proved to be only useful in the short term and folk became ill after they stopped their use. There was a land, many moons' travel over the vast seas, where they still lived in the ways of that time. He told her of folk who took medicines for every ailment, small or large, and no-one there was able to heal themselves any more. Much of their food was artificial and although they lived long it was only because of the medication. Hetia had decided to keep that information to herself, she did not think it wise to let her people know.

They were contented and healthy and would remain that way with natural food and healthy living. Just like her cave in the hills and other places where magic symbols lined the walls, they were her secrets and would go to the grave with her.

With a spring in her step Hetia took in the view from the road as it began to climb gently towards the top of a hill. There was a wonderful view from the top. She could see Charlea's cottage in the distance and the few cottages along the way. Stopping for a moment she closed her eyes and listened. Feeling a gentle breeze she tuned in to the sounds of the Earth. A buzzing nearby told her there wild flowers in bloom being visited by very busy bees, she recognised the deep drone of the large fluffy yellow and black bumble bee. Reaching out with her hearing she heard the song of a local Thrush and far in the distance Ravens were calling to each other. The sound of wood being chopped and the voices of people mingled with that of nature gave her a feeling of contentment. Refreshed and grounded Hetia made her way over and down the hill, collecting flowers and leaves as she went. It was a good day to be alive.

Charlea was waiting at his cottage door when Hetia arrived, his face was a picture of happiness, the old grey eyes smiling and his almost toothless grin showing his pleasure at her visit. "Welcome my beautiful friend" he said "it is always a pleasure to see you. Come sit in the garden, I have much to tell you." Arm in arm they made their way to a big shady oak tree and sat on the bench beneath. "I have some treats for you my old friend." said Hetia, "My pantry has given up some of its' treasures. Perhaps I could go into your cottage and make us some tea?" "What an excellent idea" Charlea replied, "In fact the water should have boiled by now and the pot is ready. I shall let you take care of it, my old legs are a bit wobbly today." When Hetia returned with the tea she found Charlea nosing about in her basket, with the packet of cakes firmly in his hand and grin like a little boy on his face. "Ha, you found them" laughed Hetia, "well open the packet and we shall indulge ourselves. Now, what is this news you have?" "Well," began Charlea, "I had another visitor a few weeks ago, a wandering bard. He entertained me and a few friends with his tales and songs, so I asked if he would like to stay for a few days, which he did. He told me he had wandered this land near and far and that he had spent some time on a ship sailing the big seas up and down the coast. Although he had been to sea before he found himself on the water for many weeks as the ship was that of a trader. One port of call was a very hot place with tall trees that swayed in the wind called Palm trees. He had some dried fruit called Dates and left some with me. I saved one for you Hetia. However, he also met up with an old acquaintance of yours called, oh what was her name? Oh yes, Roselind or Rosie. Now, wasn't she the lass who came here many years ago with you?" Hetia nodded, keen to hear the rest of his tale. "Well" he continued, "Rosie and her father have been travelling for many years and she recounted some of her tales to the Bard. One of these stories was of a country, many moon's travel from here, where people make power from the sun and wind in order to make things work. Light comes into a building at the press of a button and there are carts that move without horses or donkeys to pull them. Do you think these things could be true Hetia? It would be amazing to know of this before I leave this life. What do you make of it?"

Hetia thought for a moment, this was too much like what she already knew. "Well that sounds incredible indeed" she said carefully "If indeed Rosie did see these things I would say there is some truth in it. I have heard stories of people who live so very differently to us but had thought it only tales to entertain, like the stories of fairies and goblins. I don't say is isn't so, only that it could be just tales. However, what I was told makes me think there are people who kept an ancient knowledge from the times hundreds of years ago before the climate catastrophe. They may have been sheltered from the disastrous seas and barrenness that followed, the likes of which we hear of in the ancient stories. It is possible of course, and would be wonderful to know more about, but I think that sometimes it is best to be ignorant and to live a happy and healthy life as we do today. Perhaps some of our young people will travel and find these things, but I am happy to stay as I am." Charlea thought for a moment, "I think you are right Hetia" he said quietly, "perhaps we shall keep this knowledge between ourselves for now."

They sat quietly for a while, then spent some time discussing the local goings on, each trying to lighten the earlier conversation until neither could hold it any longer. The rest of the morning was spent discussing this new knowledge and the possibilities it could mean to the civilisation of their land. However, at the end of Hetia's visit it was agreed to keep the knowledge to themselves. Hetia left after lunch, leaving Charlea with the herbs and food that she had brought and made her way home, her mind buzzing with their conversation. Could there really be people who lived so very differently? She knew of the city where Captain Hill was from and the amazing glass buildings. Her common sense allowed that there must be all kinds of people out there and if there were huge cities there must be ways of providing light to those cities. She remembered a conversation she had once with a young Rosalind when they were travelling together. It was a long journey, Rosalind was coming back with Hetia to Flessia to learn herb lore of this land. As they rode at an easy pace to give the horses a break, Rosalind had asked if Hetia knew anything of the ancient times. "I have heard" said Rosalind, "that there was a time hundreds of years ago when there were big settlements called 'cities' with very tall buildings and hundreds of people living in them. There was machinery and many other things that are no longer in use. Some of the farmers had found things that could not be explained. Have you any knowledge of this Hetia?"

Hetia had been taken aback with the thought that Rosalind would know of this, and had made light of it by saying that such stories are probably tales and fables. But she had always known that there was an earlier civilisation who had inhabited the world, in fact she knew that there was an advanced civilisation still in existence. The 'magic' she used to rid the land of the Horde Of Doom wasn't magic at all, it was with help of that other, outside world that finally removed them as they were transported to the other side of the earth and into another modern civilisation.

Maybe, one day, Hetia would travel there herself, however, at this time of her life she had no intention of doing so. She was happy and contented, living in peace with Erik in the hut behind her cottage and the people she cared for. She arrived at her front door and with a smile on her face, entered her cosy cottage and put the kettle on the fire.

20 THE FUTURE

Many years later an old woman sat huddled against the warm front wall in the early morning sun, her ancient body wrapped in a warm blanket and her feet encased in soft sheepskin boots. There wasn't much flesh left on her bones now, her skin wrinkled and sun dried, hiding the crackling joints. The precious fur lined boots that had been made for her years past by the old man who had lived in the hut behind her house for so many, many years were keeping her old feet warm. She couldn't remember exactly how long he had lived there, although her memory was just as good as it had ever been. Time passed slowly now and she had been so young when she had first laid her eyes on him and, she thought, so proud that she could not let her feelings show to him or anyone else. She often thought of him since he had passed on to the world beyond this a few years past. People said she had never loved a man but did she love this one? Yes some would think of their later relationship as one of love, although that emotion was rarely openly spoken of. He was handsome, oh yes, he was so very handsome, with his dark flashing eyes and tall, straight body even as his hair turned to grey in his elder years. The first time she had cast her eyes on him he had sent a shiver through her young body and many times in the following years she would catch a glimpse of his face, take a deep breath and feel the heat rising in her. She smiled as she thought of the later years, years of companionship but no more. There could never have been more than companionship, she knew that now. But to dream of more was a waste of her dreaming, and dreaming is precious to a healer such as herself. She was content with her memories.

Life was much better for Hetia lately than it had been for most of her life. The people would bring her tasty treats and make sure she was comfortable as she aged. There were few threats to the land now apart from the elements, and she had survived her fair share of storms and winds. Oh, life had begun well enough. She'd had a good childhood with the other village children. She would run through the fields in spring and summer, as free as a deer with her long spindly legs racing as fast as she could, climbing trees, jumping over fallen logs and hiding from her father in the woods as he called for her to come and do her share of the work. Yes childhood had been good. There was a tiny cave she had found when she had seen five summers, and if she curled up in a dark corner behind the stone that hid the entrance her father could not see her. She imagined she was a little mouse crouching there.

The hardest part was trying to suppress the giggles with her hand clamped tightly across her mouth when her father was near the cave calling to her. If she had been caught in her cave then all the secrets she dreamed of would be gone in a puff. This was her secret place and even her beloved father could not encroach on the thrill of being totally alone yet knowing she could call out for him if she was afraid. There was a ledge at the back of the cave and she kept her special things there. Best of all was a purple stone she had found in the stream bed that sparkled in the sun, a feather that had fallen from an eagle as he flew over her head and the discarded bird's nest she had found in the forest. No one else knew of this cave, it was her magic place where she could close her eyes and imagine that she could travel in the sky, far across the land or up amongst the stars. Thinking of the cave now, Hetia felt the warmth of that special place as a distant memory, so many years had passed since she was able to venture up into the hills on her own as the path was too steep for her old legs. She had never taken anyone else to her little cave, that was her precious memory and she had not wanted to share it with anyone except her Spirit Guide who she had learned to contact whilst sitting with her back to the wall of the cave as a thirteen year old. Hetia had experienced much more than most women in her land over those many years in this life on the Earth. The knowledge she had gained through years of training with other healers and the friends she had made throughout her life, were all as important to her as the time she had spent alone in the forests searching for spiritual knowledge.

That was all in the past. Now, all the old woman really wanted to do was sit in the sun in the early mornings, warming her bones to take away the aches and being surrounded by those she cared for. By her reckoning she must have seen well over 90 summers. Taking into account the lives that she had seen come and go there was only one other left in the village now from her childhood. Perhaps, she thought, in the next life she would meet the handsome man once more. In the next life they might be able to be more than companions. This brought a slight smile to her old wrinkled face. However, the only one who knew her fate in the next life was the Goddess and Hetia had no intention of hurrying that experience along. Meanwhile it was time to move from her stool and the wonderfully warm sun to see what she could do to help the young woman who was learning the ways of the healer. Ancient knowledge, passed down through centuries from one healer to the next, knowledge that it had been a privilege to use during this life and now to pass on to another before she left her aging body to wander in the land of Spirit. It had been an interesting life – so far. As she rose and moved into the house her mind began to wander back, back to a time when life wasn't as quiet and peaceful as it was now in this land she loved. However, pushing those thoughts away she looked out at the garden - "No" she said to herself, "I will not spoil a beautiful day with those kind of thoughts."

EPILOGUE

NEW GENERATIONS

The small girl sat on a mound of dirt left behind by her father as he formed the earthworks around their home. The home had become part of the fortress the people had built over the years, as walls and buildings were joined together. Bricks formed from mud and straw were easy to build with out on the Plains of Palat, there was plenty of clay and the rains that fell in the Spring were good for brick making.

The people of the Plains numbered around 200 now as the children who survived their first two or three years grew into healthy, strong young adults. Many years before this their grandparents had begun the settlement when left to guard the other villages from the Horde of Doom. The children were told stories of heroism and magic, of the power of the mighty storm that had chased the evil Horde of Doom away and the eventual death of the evil men in the cave that collapsed leaving their ghosts and spirits to haunt the place. Many a night was spent in front of a fire as the children asked for the stories again and again. Some of their parents were not even born when the tale began and the old woman, who still lived on her own in the village of Flessia, brought the leader to justice before beating his men. The tale had grown, as tales do, to tell of Hetia putting a magic spell on Starreck, who then became Erik, to bring him back to face the people for the many villagers he and his men had killed, and of how she kept him in a hut behind her house until he died many years later, a quiet and peaceful old man. Some said that Hetia loved the man dearly, but could not show him that love because of the wicked things he had done to her people, and that she never married anyone else because she loved him. He became devoted to her, and his Goddess, and although they didn't speak very much to each other, when he died she mourned him for many months. That was ten years ago. Now, Hetia lived quietly in her home, surrounded by her herbs and potions and still looked after the health of her people. But now a younger woman delivered the babies and rode to the outer homesteads when it was needed.

The little girl on the mound of dirt turned to her father, watching his work with keen eyes. Her eyes could look straight through you, deep with meaning and curiosity. Lately, following her fourth birthday, she had found that if she tried really hard she could read her father's thoughts. Sometimes he said bad words in his mind if he hurt himself or dropped something. It was fun to be able to listen to him when he didn't know about it. Her mother's mind was a bit harder to read because she was a very quiet person who just did things. She had tried it on her grandmother and felt a funny sort of sting, as if her grandmother had smacked her. Spotting her grandmother walking towards them, Gorani jumped up and ran to her, throwing her arms around the tall, elegant woman. "Granny Satty" she called happily, "I have been watching my papa working with the bricks", "You have been doing more than watching him work" Satiane replied with a smile, "you have been listening to his mind too haven't you?", "Uh, yes Granny Satty," the little one admitted, casting her eyes to the ground, "I didn't know that you knew about that". "Oh yes, I know" replied Satiane, "you have been trying to read mine as well haven't you little one? Well, I think it is time we spoke to your father about that. Come on, it might be time to begin your lessons."

Satiane took Gorani by the hand and they walked to the girl's father. "Truron," Satiane called, "We need to speak of Gorani's future, it appears that your beautiful daughter has inherited my gift of clairvoyance. I have caught her reading my thoughts and she tells me that she reads yours, *and* that she has learnt a few naughty words from you. It is time we taught her how to control this ability and the other gifts that come with it. I would like to have her with me each day if that is alright with you".

Truron put down the spade he was using and turned to face the little girl. "Well my daughter," he said, "I wasn't sure that you would have this gift, however, as you do then you are to spend some time with Granny Satty each day and learn how to control it. You will do as you are told and learn your lessons well. So each morning after you have done your work that your mother requires you to do you will go to Granny Satty until the evening meal. Go and tell your mother of this and I will see you later." He turned to Satiane with a smile, "Well, it seems to have jumped a generation mother, but I am not surprised. I have seen her look into my eyes as if she sees straight through me and it is better that you teach her than have the gift run wild. Thank you." He hugged his mother then turned to finish his task. He thought of the tales his parents had told him of how the wise women, the Shaman and the Spirit leaders had fought off the Horde of Doom and felt comfort in the fact that should they have to face such danger again the fortress they were building and the new generation of Spirit people would be able to once more, face such an enemy. As he began the next batch of mud bricks he looked up to watch the men raise the next wind turbine.

THE PLAINS OF PARLAT

GEOGRAPHY

The Plains of Parlat exist between the mountain ranges of the west and the coastline in the east of the island once known as Kingsland. Many centuries before the Great Climate Catastrophe that affected every corner of the planet, part of the area was covered in forest, with streams trickling over rocks and a river full of fish running through its centre. The forests of the Plains were originally full of wild life with many smaller creatures living among the undergrowth and larger animals that could be hunted for food. Trees had grown to be hundreds of years old in the forest and it was able to sustain itself whilst supplying the people of the land with timber. The area called the Plains of Parlat was quite flat and very good for growing crops because of the wide expanse of almost treeless land that took days to walk from the mountains to the gentler sloping hills of the forest. However this was also the result of heavy land clearing in the 20th Century at a time when the Earth was warming up at a rapid pace so it became a cause for much controversy between farmers and the conservationists. In the end a compromise was reached that allowed reasonable

333

clearing but this was in the 21st century after much of the land had already been cleared.

The mountains were ancient. There was evidence that they had been extremely high, but they had worn down in time to be less imposing apart from a strange pointed mountain that seemed to have been pushed up during a very ancient volcanic era. A road led down into the Plains from the mountain ranges and, although it had worn away over the centuries, it was originally paved and was still a good hard surface – although not many people went that way anymore. On the other side of the plains the road led to the coast, but that wasn't used much anymore either and there were few people who had travelled that road in the last few hundred years.

HISTORY

People had lived on the Plains since before recorded time. However the original inhabitants had been nomadic and had left little trace of their occupation. During the time of discovery, over 3,000 years in the past, people had settled there and developed simple farming communities that enjoyed the freedom of being away from the cities on the coast. The farming communities had grown into towns and there had been quite a lot of industry based around agriculture for several hundred years. The houses were always quite modest and most of the farms were small and run by families, except for one or two communities that had grown from combining several smaller farms. All in all the Plains of Parlat had always been a place for a simple life. The towns would hold weekly markets and had for hundreds of years, the remnants of these markets were still held seasonally four times each year. The children all attended school back in time, most of them locally, although some had gone away to the big cities on the coast for University education or to learn a trade. However, over the years people taught their children what they could at home because there were no teachers coming out from the cities any more. Besides, the children would take over the work of their parents eventually so people lost interest in educating the young past simple reading, writing and numeracy.

One of the villages was Fleshurst, later to be called Flessia, a nice little village with the usual bits and pieces. There was a post office, a police station and of course a school. Most of the people shopped in the bigger town down towards the coast but they bought their smaller goods at the local store and their fruit and vegetables at the market. The local butcher did well as did the baker, but otherwise most used the big supermarkets in the town about an hours' drive away where they did their banking and other business. That of course was when they had powered vehicles. People liked living in this village because it was very friendly. There had been two churches once but as folk began to move away from organised religion the churches were sold and became private dwellings. All in all it was a nice village, much like all the other villages on the Plains

DIRECTIONS

To get to Fleshurst you would leave the main highway from the coast at the edge of the Plains and take the detour that had been called the Tourist Route. This road was just a bit smaller than the highway but big enough for two way traffic. Of course that was in the days when there were vehicles that were powered by motors that ran on petrol or diesel and could go quite fast for long distances. Later on, when the fuel ran out and there were no more vehicles being manufactured these cars, trucks and buses were converted to run on solar electricity but eventually began to fall apart and they couldn't be fixed any more because spare parts were no longer being manufactured and the second hand ones became harder and harder to find. Besides, they had to get to the coastal cities to find parts and that could take days. People found that it was so much easier to ride a horse or pull a cart or wagon. The horse feed could be grown locally so there was no need to leave the Plains and the wagons were made of wood when the scrap metal rusted away so the local carpenter made a good trade fixing and making these vehicles.

Travelling along the roads on the Plains became a bit more difficult when there was no-one to fix them. Potholes turned into large holes, the bitumen began to break up and the vegetation grew over the surface. You could still see where the roads were so people used them and eventually ruts appeared where the wagon wheels and the horses went but of course the local folk could fix these kind of things, after all, most of them were farmers. The people who used to look after the roads were the Government agencies, as were those who looked after the water supply and the sewerage systems. However, as it became so much more difficult to get about they just didn't bother coming that far from the main cities on the coast, so of course nothing was mended properly, only made to work for a little while longer. Things just fell apart.

COMMUNICATIONS

Next to go was the communications. Once there had been quite an amazing communications network with internet, telephones and television, but of course when the power was no longer being produced it put an end to all of that. Even the mail service died out through lack of transport. So people just got on with what they could do locally and no one really minded. If you needed to send a message to someone in another town or village you hired a rider to take it or you made the journey yourself.

WEATHER

Before the Climate Catastrophe the temperature began to be unbearable. First of all it just meant staying indoors or in shade during the middle of the day but then when the power was no longer available there was no cooling and heating in the buildings so many people in the cities just died. Old people, little babies and invalids just began to die from the heat or cold. It was far too hot for anyone but the healthy folk and older children, who could always find some way to cool down and eventually the people who had survived began to adapt to the hotter weather.

THE GREAT CLIMATE CATASTROPHY

It came to pass that The Earth could no longer tolerate what people had done to her, so She just wound up the heat. Over a year or two this melted the small amount of ice left on the north and south poles and the seas rose up to swallow huge cities and towns along the coastlines over a fairly short period of time. Some small islands over the planet disappeared under water never to be seen again. People on the larger islands and continents fled inland and tried to take over the smaller towns, but of course without power and water these city folk just didn't survive. Unlike the country folk who had been doing so for some time.

It took almost two hundred years once the sea stopped rising for everything to change completely. What was left of Kingsland was a dry, arid land with very few rivers and streams. Where forests had stood since ancient times became a huge dry and dusty plain with scrubby bushes here and there. The people knew that this was how the centre of the island had been for thousands of years but it was as though the whole country was drying up. Up in the hills it was still green where the air was a little cooler. The trees had created enough shade to keep the soil moist and if it did rain at all that's where it would fall. The people didn't move into the hills though, some of them were worried about forest fires because there had been plenty of those when the temperature rose. But they did use the forests in the hills to let their livestock run and they would escape there during the day, if they could, at the hottest time of the year. Once this had been a rainforest but that had disappeared many centuries ago.

The mountains on the edge of the Plains of Parlat had been covered with thick dense bush, but now they were just red, dry and treeless with steep canyons dropping down to barren dry earth and rocks below where once a mighty river had flowed, and lakes the size of inland seas had held enough water to keep the land green and supply the people with water. There was a little water flowing through the canyon now but it was just a stream not a river. The river and lakes had left behind many holes and caves in the canyon walls and these became home to many folk who could not live out in the heat where the depth of some of the caves kept them cool. There was even talk that mysterious things happened in those caves because strange writing had been found, but of course these could have been stories told to children.

NEW INFRASTUCTURE

Over the centuries the villages that had stood for millennia had shrunk when so many old folk and babies had died as the temperature had risen, but the village of Fleshurst had remained, as had a few others, and with time the babies began to survive to grow into adults once more and the populations grew slowly. Somewhere along the line the name had changed to Flessia but apart from that the houses were still very basic. There was a lot of rock in the area, so many had built their houses from the ancient stone because the stone made the houses cooler than timber houses, making the roofs from whatever they could find. The rain had appeared after a while, although not the heavy rains that used to come through the Plains, and the temperature had begun to fall a little. The farmers were able to grow crops once more and the new generation learned how to produce many vegetables and fruit that had once grown in the area. Slowly but surely the villages began to take a different shape, looking a lot like the ancient buildings and villages from times before the world became industrialised and technology took over. Old skills had been learned from trial and error and some books that had survived the centuries gave the people some ideas. People didn't need big houses any more as they didn't have all the trimmings of the old 'modern' world. Besides, most spent their hours outdoors when the sun went down a bit in the afternoons when they would get together with neighbours and friends and talk about life.

RELIGION

Religion began to disappear when people came to realise that no God they had been praying to was making any difference to their lifestyles or the rising temperature, so they had begun to pray to the Earth Mother to help them grow crops and for the weather to be more reasonable. It was much easier to be able to just go outside and ask the Earth to let the seeds germinate than it was to go along to a church building and spend time on your knees. Oh yes, the Old Religion raised it's gentle head once again and people began to believe. The wind, rain and the sun could also be spoken to and asked for mercy. That was much more simple for these farmers and tradespeople. And so a new Old Religion grew from just a few believers to be the religion of choice for the whole country. Spirit Leaders and Shamans began to emerge once again and it seemed that was so much better for the beliefs of the people because with the cooling of the Earth many thought their prayers to the Spirits of Earth, Water and Sky had been answered.

HEALTH

Hospitals had closed down so very long ago because there was no power or technology to run them so one by one the doctors had returned to the country and began to pass their information on to apprentices. However, the herbalists and what was called Naturopaths became the choice of the people and Midwives once again delivered the babies. The ancient practice of each village having a Healer or Wise Woman began to resurface very soon after the fuel ran out because there was no transport to the hospitals and main towns. These were a new version of the old village healers and they began by learning about herbs and healing from each other, they were taught how to deliver babies by the town midwives and after about three decades there came the next wave of healers being trained by the first group. The Wise Women chose to be celibate in order to put their total energy into their work and slowly the use of magic and shamanism became part of their training. They were considered very powerful indeed and people gave them every respect.

THE OUTSIDE WORLD

Over the centuries since the great Climate Catastrophe, with communications and travel being so limited, the Plains gradually lost contact with most of the outside world. Although there was travel to the coastal town, and some had taken this journey in their lifetime, the people had become used to their simple ways and left well enough alone. However, much of the outside world had not reverted to medieval times and had found new ways to rebuild their infrastructure and way of life. Because there was no longer air travel and the only ships that sailed the seas relied on wind power countries in the southern hemisphere were once more isolated from the rest of world. However, there were cities in the cooler parts of the country and their technology had taken a different turn.

Once more, humans adapted to their situation and slowly moved on to another generation.

......

ABOUT THE AUTHOR

After retiring to her little bit of paradise in an Eco Village west of Bundaberg in Queensland, Australia Heather finally found her muse by imagining what life would be like in a future on the Earth so different from the present following global warming. After many years of jotting down ideas, writing articles for newspapers and many other ways of expressing the written word she gave a life to Hetia and her people.

www.ingramcontent.com/pod-product-compliance
Lightning Source LLC
Chambersburg PA
CBHW071918130726
47909CB00014B/2063